And that left one

"Come out from there," Bolan told the sole survivor. "Make it quick."

The Scotsman wriggled from his hidey-hole but did not stand.

"I'm looking for the Irishman," Bolan said. "I don't suppose you'd have a clue on where to find him?"

"No."

"It might be worth your life."

The trembling soldier thought about it. "There's a flat I heard about on Broadley Street, in Lisson Grove. Somebody special hiding out, was all they told us."

Bolan glanced around the small, blood-spattered room. "I'll catch you next time."

"No next time for me, mate. The first train out for Tayside, and I'm gone."

The Executioner backed off toward the office door. "You know," he said, "that's not a bad idea."

DON PENDLETON'S
MACK BOLAN®

BLOOD STRIKE

A GOLD EAGLE BOOK FROM
WORLDWIDE®

TORONTO • NEW YORK • LONDON
AMSTERDAM • PARIS • SYDNEY • HAMBURG
STOCKHOLM • ATHENS • TOKYO • MILAN
MADRID • WARSAW • BUDAPEST • AUCKLAND

To the four ATF agents who gave their lives and the fourteen who were wounded in performance of their duty at Waco, Texas, on February 28, 1993. God keep.

First edition December 1994

ISBN 0-373-61439-X

Special thanks and acknowledgment to
Mike Newton for his contribution to this work.

BLOOD STRIKE

Cruel is the strife of brothers.

—Aristotle

A successful revolution establishes a new
community. A missed revolution makes
irrelevant the community that persists. And
a compromised revolution tends to shatter
the community that was, without an adequate
substitute.

—Paul Goodman

The Belfast "revolution" has been compromised
from the beginning. Now, it's boiling over into
my backyard. That makes it intervention time.

—Mack Bolan

He could stand a bit of stiffness for the short duration of the trip. It was, in fact, a great relief to be finally on his way.

He had been waiting eighteen months to take this ride, from the surprise by federal raiders in his "safehouse," through a series of arraignments, hearings and appeals. Political asylum was the angle of attack chosen by his attorneys. They presented William Connolly as a soldier and a prisoner of war, billing his revolution by the hour for their ultimately futile services. A week earlier, the United States Supreme Court had ruled against Connolly's team. Case closed.

His extradition back to London was arranged in record time. The pickup team had not come out to fetch him, but it would be waiting for him at La Guardia. A special British Airways flight would take him "home," or so they called it, with a man from MI-6 to deal with all the paperwork, and muscle from the SAS to make it stick.

With any luck at all, they would be disappointed this time.

Luck of the Irish, sure.

He had the details from his chief defense attorney, O'Toole. A solid son of Erin was O'Toole, and afraid to get a touch of dirt beneath his fingernails good cause. The rest were high-priced errand boys, would always count on Rad O'Toole to bring the or take a message out, if Connolly had any- say.

lking was behind him now. He had no use for the predawn hours of a Friday morning. ime to act.

Mineola, Long Island

The escort team arrived for William Connolly at 5:30 a.m. He was waiting for them, having finished breakfast thirty minutes earlier. The standard jailhouse fare of runny scrambled eggs, limp bacon and toast sat inside his stomach like a lump of clay, but he was counting on the energy.

For later.

They sent five men to fetch him. The two Suffolk County jailers wore khaki uniforms. One carried keys, the other chains that jangled as he walked. Behind the uniforms were three men Connolly recognized.

The point was Joseph Alderson, a so-called special agent for the FBI. He was in his late thirties, with his pale hair thinning out on top, his overcoat unbuttoned and a blue suit underneath. It had been Alderson who led the strike team in Mount Vernon, showing Connolly the muzzle of a 12-gauge shotgun, giving him a choice: show empty hands or kiss his ass goodbye. He had been first at the arrest, and he was leading at the finish now.

Or so he thought.

Behind the G-man came a mismatched pair of U.S. marshals who had shadowed Connolly since his arrest. The older of the pair was Wilder, no first name, tall and broad, his rugged features chiseled out of ebony. His cap of wiry hair was shot with salt and pepper, advertising age. He rarely spoke, and when he did it was to issue orders with a voice like river gravel.

Wilder's partner was a slender white man in his early thirties, Richard Seefeld. He was cultivating a mustache these days, but having trouble with it on the left side of his lip, as if the hair were thinner there. The young man compensated with a kind of smirk or sneer that curled his lip. A pair of wire-rimmed glasses magnified his shifty eyes.

"It's time to go," the turnkey told him, opening the cell. "Stand up and raise your hands."

Connolly did as he was told, his face impassive as the second uniform secured a chain around his waist, padlocked in front, then brought his arms down to the cuffs that dangled from his belly chain. A set of shackles finished the ensemble, leaving Connolly at liberty to walk with baby steps and scratch his crotch if need arose.

"Let's go," Alderson said. "Our Billy's got a plane to catch."

"Sure, and I wouldn't want to miss my flight."

"That's what I figured," the agent replied.

Outside the cell, he found himself surrounded, uniforms in front, with Alderson beside him on the left, the U.S. marshals walking almost on his heels. They lost his Suffolk County jailers at the elevators, where three more federal suits were on station, armed with automatic weapons. Connolly recognized one of the men from his last court appearance; the others were strangers, but cut from the same bolt of cloth.

They always looked the same, Connolly thought. In New York, London, Belfast. Institutional haircuts and suits off the rack. Minds and faces closed against

emotion. If they ever felt an ounce of passion in their souls, they hid it well.

He understood these men, and understanding made it easier to spill their blood.

The crowded elevator took them to a subterranean garage. Two unmarked cars were waiting, with a van between them, like the meat in a fat sandwich. Five more suits stood around the vehicles, with hardware on display. Three idling engines filled the basement with a sharp aroma of exhaust fumes.

"Here I thought they were deporting me," Connolly commented, "not giving me the bloody gas chamber."

Beside him, Alderson looked sour. "You caught break there, Billy boy. No executions where you're ing. What a shame."

"I can't be held responsible for weakness in emies."

"Just get a move on, will you?" That ca Wilder, bringing up the rear.

"Of course."

He shuffled toward the van, ham ti shackles, taking twice as long to cross t feet as he would otherwise have done. alert, as if expecting an attack i County Jail garage. Benighted idio

As Connolly approached the va dogs breaking up, dispersing to sitions: three men in the poin behind. Young Seefeld would up front, while Alderson nolly in back. The metal against his buttocks, th shifted restlessly and th

Mineola, Long Island

The escort team arrived for William Connolly at 5:30 a.m. He was waiting for them, having finished breakfast thirty minutes earlier. The standard jailhouse fare of runny scrambled eggs, limp bacon and toast sat inside his stomach like a lump of clay, but he was counting on the energy.

For later.

They sent five men to fetch him. The two Suffolk County jailers wore khaki uniforms. One carried keys, the other chains that jangled as he walked. Behind the uniforms were three men Connolly recognized.

The point was Joseph Alderson, a so-called special agent for the FBI. He was in his late thirties, with his pale hair thinning out on top, his overcoat unbuttoned and a blue suit underneath. It had been Alderson who led the strike team in Mount Vernon, showing Connolly the muzzle of a 12-gauge shotgun, giving him a choice: show empty hands or kiss his ass goodbye. He had been first at the arrest, and he was leading at the finish now.

Or so he thought.

Behind the G-man came a mismatched pair of U.S. marshals who had shadowed Connolly since his arrest. The older of the pair was Wilder, no first name, tall and broad, his rugged features chiseled out of ebony. His cap of wiry hair was shot with salt and pepper, advertising age. He rarely spoke, and when he did it was to issue orders with a voice like river gravel.

Wilder's partner was a slender white man in his early thirties, Richard Seefeld. He was cultivating a mustache these days, but having trouble with it on the left side of his lip, as if the hair were thinner there. The young man compensated with a kind of smirk or sneer that curled his lip. A pair of wire-rimmed glasses magnified his shifty eyes.

"It's time to go," the turnkey told him, opening the cell. "Stand up and raise your hands."

Connolly did as he was told, his face impassive as the second uniform secured a chain around his waist, padlocked in front, then brought his arms down to the cuffs that dangled from his belly chain. A set of shackles finished the ensemble, leaving Connolly at liberty to walk with baby steps and scratch his crotch if need arose.

"Let's go," Alderson said. "Our Billy's got a plane to catch."

"Sure, and I wouldn't want to miss my flight."

"That's what I figured," the agent replied.

Outside the cell, he found himself surrounded, uniforms in front, with Alderson beside him on the left, the U.S. marshals walking almost on his heels. They lost his Suffolk County jailers at the elevators, where three more federal suits were on station, armed with automatic weapons. Connolly recognized one of the men from his last court appearance; the others were strangers, but cut from the same bolt of cloth.

They always looked the same, Connolly thought. In New York, London, Belfast. Institutional haircuts and suits off the rack. Minds and faces closed against emotion. If they ever felt an ounce of passion in their souls, they hid it well.

He understood these men, and understanding made it easier to spill their blood.

The crowded elevator took them to a subterranean garage. Two unmarked cars were waiting, with a van between them, like the meat in a fat sandwich. Five more suits stood around the vehicles, with hardware on display. Three idling engines filled the basement with a sharp aroma of exhaust fumes.

"Here I thought they were deporting me," Connolly commented, "not giving me the bloody gas chamber."

Beside him, Alderson looked sour. "You caught a break there, Billy boy. No executions where you're going. What a shame."

"I can't be held responsible for weakness in my enemies."

"Just get a move on, will you?" That came from Wilder, bringing up the rear.

"Of course."

He shuffled toward the van, hampered by the shackles, taking twice as long to cross the span of fifty feet as he would otherwise have done. His escorts were alert, as if expecting an attack inside the Suffolk County Jail garage. Benighted idiots.

As Connolly approached the van, he saw his watchdogs breaking up, dispersing to their preassigned positions: three men in the point car and another three behind. Young Seefeld would ride shotgun in the van, up front, while Alderson and Wilder sat with Connolly in back. The metal bench was cold and hard against his buttocks, through the denim jeans. He shifted restlessly and then gave up on comfort.

He could stand a bit of stiffness for the short duration of the trip. It was, in fact, a great relief to be finally on his way.

He had been waiting eighteen months to take this ride, from the surprise by federal raiders in his "safehouse," through a series of arraignments, hearings and appeals. Political asylum was the angle of attack chosen by his attorneys. They presented William Connolly as a soldier and a prisoner of war, billing his revolution by the hour for their ultimately futile services. A week earlier, the United States Supreme Court had ruled against Connolly's team. Case closed.

His extradition back to London was arranged in record time. The pickup team had not come out to fetch him, but it would be waiting for him at La Guardia. A special British Airways flight would take him "home," or so they called it, with a man from MI-6 to deal with all the paperwork, and muscle from the SAS to make it stick.

With any luck at all, they would be disappointed this time.

Luck of the Irish, sure.

He had the details from his chief defense attorney, Rad O'Toole. A solid son of Erin was O'Toole, and not afraid to get a touch of dirt beneath his fingernails in a good cause. The rest were high-priced errand boys, but he would always count on Rad O'Toole to bring the word...or take a message out, if Connolly had anything to say.

The talking was behind him now. He had no use for lawyers in the predawn hours of a Friday morning.

It was time to act.

Fresh Meadows, Queens

JOHN BREEN WAS TIRED of waiting for the other shoe to drop. He had been looking forward to this moment for a month of bloody Sundays, covering the bases, leaving nothing to chance. If he did not succeed this morning, there would be no second opportunity.

His men were ready; Breen was confident of that. There were five hands in addition to himself, and two cars waiting with a clear view of Interstate 495, the Long Island Expressway. Rolling west, the federal caravan would be exposed for some two hundred yards before it reached Breen's vantage point, another hundred yards beyond the stand if things got dicey.

But he meant to do it right, the first time. Any fumbling off the mark endangered Connolly, and if the bloody pigs had time to do for William, all Breen's effort was in vain.

No worries.

He was counting on the four LAW rockets, for a start. There had been seven launchers in the batch he purchased, stolen from a National Guard armory in Connecticut and sold from a black-market warehouse on Staten Island, but three had gone for practice, firing at old junk cars in the New Jersey Pine Barrens. There was one each for the appointed gunners, and to hell with second chances if they couldn't get it right the first time.

Dragging on a cigarette and studying the highway, Breen decided they would do. There was, in fact, no bloody choice.

LAW rockets for their stopping power, Uzis and Berettas for the mopping up, and he had spent eleven thousand dollars of the movement's hard-earned money just on hardware, planning for this moment.

It was all or nothing. Do or die.

Breen had been waiting when the call came through from Mineola, Fergus spelling out the details from his spotting post hard by the Suffolk County Jail. Cellular phones were a bloody miracle, and no mistake. A few days earlier, on television, Breen had watched a program that explained how cordless phones were linked with tumors of the brain, some talk about magnetic fields and such. It made him smile to think about that now, as if the SAS would let him live that long.

He checked his watch again and pitched his cigarette away. He made it twelve miles from Mineola, with the short jog north on Interstate 295 to reach the Long Island Expressway. Six miles beyond their vantage point lay La Guardia Airport and the waiting charter flight, but Connolly would never be delivered to his British captors. Breen had made his mind up on that score. He had spent five years fighting for the Sword of Erin, serving Billy Connolly, and thirteen years before that with the Provos. Breen had never failed on an assignment yet, and he was not about to break his record now. If he could not lift Connolly, his orders were to die in the attempt. There was no middle ground.

The trick was hitting fast and hard enough that Billy's captors would be dead or dazed before they knew exactly what was happening. No time for itchy trigger fingers in the van to ruin everything. It all came down to timing and efficiency. No waste, no want.

The cordless phone chirped in his hand, and Breen lifted it to his ear. "Yes, Fergus?"

"Crossing Francis Lewis Boulevard right now," his spotter said. "I'm running sixty meters back."

"That's grand, lad."

Breen smiled as he dropped the cordless phone inside his car. "Stand ready, boys," he said. "Be on your marks."

It took only a moment for his men to lift their weapons out of Army-surplus duffel bags, mere seconds to prepare the three LAW rockets, pulling safety pins to let the lightweight tubes expand. It was an age of marvelous technology, Breen thought, which gave a freedom fighter throwaway bazookas light enough to aim one-handed in a pinch.

"Look sharp and hold your targets steady," Breen instructed, as he chose an Uzi for himself and cocked it. "If you have a chance to waste them in the two cars, front and back, so much the better. Danny, you be careful with the van, just like we talked about."

"I hear you, John."

Gray dawn was breaking, switching off the roadside mercury vapor lamps. He saw the point car now, a carbon-copy fifty meters behind it, with the prison van between. It was a lucky thing, Breen thought, that Billy's captors had not called a helicopter out to prowl along the route. They would have had a damned hard time disposing of a watchdog in the sky. Breen's sources had been just a trifle short of antiaircraft guns.

Breen's gunners took position automatically, the three with rocket launchers crouching well apart and sighting down the fat tubes of their weapons, Breen and two more standing clear of the impending backflash.

"Take your time and do it right," he muttered.

One away, with a rattling whoosh, as the rocket took flight on a bright tongue of flame. The point car's driver might have seen it coming, but he had no time to save himself. The armor-piercing rocket bored in dead on target, peeled the Chrysler's hood back like a strip of tinfoil and exploded in a rolling ball of fire. Momentum kept the car moving another thirty yards, bright flames erupting from the windows, trailing oily smoke.

By then, two more flaming birds were sizzling downrange. The tail car's driver tried to brake and veer away, but it was hopeless. Breen could see the unmarked four-door skidding when a rocket struck amidships, exploded and stopped it cold. A lake of blazing gasoline spread beneath the shattered vehicle, enveloping a passenger who staggered from the wreckage. He jigged and capered briefly, shrieking as he fried, and finally toppled forward on his face.

Breen focused his attention on the van that held Billy Connolly caged in back. Experience told Breen that prison vehicles were stoutly built, their passenger compartments separated from the driver's cab by thick steel plate for reasons of security. If Billy somehow broke his chains and overwhelmed his guards, the bloody pigs still had him locked up safe and sound, unless he had the necessary outside help.

It happened that the final rocket missed its mark by nearly a meter, but it was close enough. Instead of ripping through the square van's grille, it struck the right-hand window post and detonated with a fiery thunderclap. The vehicle drifted toward Breen, rearing as it tried to climb the steep embankment, losing traction in the soft, loose earth. Another moment, and the van tipped over sideways, sliding back down toward the highway where its escorts burned.

"Step lively, lads." Breen had a firm grip on his Uzi as he led the way downhill. "We're running out of time."

ALTHOUGH HE WAS EXPECTING it, the first explosion barely registered with William Connolly. The armored prison van was insulated, a fair soundproofing method in addition to security. Denied his wristwatch, the prisoner had been counting seconds to track their progress, but he had no means of knowing when and where his rescuers would strike.

The driver of his own vehicle broke the news, a startled outburst on the intercom connecting Connolly's two watchdogs to the men up front.

"Sweet Jesus! A bazooka!"

Seefeld shouted "Watch it! Watch—" before a stunning impact rocked the prison van, and Connolly was toppled to the floor. Joe Alderson, the U.S. marshal, came down on top of him, the muzzle of an automatic pistol jabbing Connolly between his shoulder blades, harsh curses grating in his ears. Alderson was on his feet for nearly five seconds, one arm braced against the nearest wall, but then he lost it, toppling in a heap.

The van was swerving to the right, decelerating, filling up with smoke. Alderson rolled clear of Connolly and struggled to all fours, losing ground as the van bounced over some unseen obstacle and began to climb a slope of forty-odd degrees. The Irishman and his disoriented keepers tumbled toward the tall twin doors in back.

Another moment, and the driver lost it. The van rolled over on its left side, and Connolly was pitched head-first toward Wilder, knocking heads with force

enough to stun the marshal. Connolly's ears were
ringing, a dull pain throbbed behind his eyes, and his
throat burned with smoke, but he still had the presence of mind to drag Wilder toward him, shifting position until he could grope for the man's gun.

The van came to rest with a jolt, driver's-side down,
smoke roiling up from the shattered engine compartment and the driver's cab. Connolly swallowed his fear
of roasting alive and kept his mind on business, using
both hands to release the safety on Wilder's 10 mm
Smith & Wesson automatic, drawing back the slide to
put a live round in the chamber.

Alderson was stirring close beside him, lurching to
his feet. The G-man blinked, recognized his danger and
stooped to retrieve the weapon he had lost. He had
perhaps a second left to live, but there was certain
death in Connolly's eyes, and Alderson bet everything
on one last-ditch effort.

He lost.

The automatic's report was deafening inside the van,
sharp needles pricking Connolly's eardrums, but he
squeezed the trigger twice more for luck, not trusting
his aim with hands cuffed at his waist. Alderson's body
jerked with the impact of each bullet, blood spouting
from chest wounds as he went over backward in a
boneless sprawl.

One down. Connolly swiveled on his knees, leaning
toward Wilder, pressing the Smith & Wesson flush
against the man's sweat-slick forehead.

No missing at this range.

The blast sprayed Connolly with crimson, but he was
not repulsed by blood. Alone, he would have tried the
cuffs himself—and maybe blown his nuts off in the
process—but he knew that help was on the way.

If only Breen would arrive in time to keep him from the hungry flames.

Was it his imagination, or could he feel the heat now, spreading backward toward the gas tank? He'd give it one more minute, he decided, going back to counting seconds.

He was on forty-seven when a hard fist struck the double doors and someone shouted, "Watch yourself, there, Billy! Men at work!"

The Irishman scrambled toward the front of the van and propped Alderson in front of him as a submachine gun hammered the outer locking mechanism. Seconds later the doors were open, and Breen leaned in to help him out.

"Are we all right there, Billy?"

"Safe as houses," Connolly informed his number two, all smiles.

"You'd best be stepping out then, so we can get your jewelry off before the cavalry arrives."

"You've done a grand job, Johnny. Grand."

Breen flashed an easy grin. "You ain't seen nothing yet, me lad."

CHAPTER ONE

Saint Francis Lake, Quebec

Mack Bolan smelled the forest well before he saw it, rising like a silent wall in front of him. He had been paddling the rubber boat for nearly forty minutes, covering three-quarters of a mile without resort to lights or compass. He was close now, and with any luck at all, the final hundred yards of his approach would be as uneventful as the rest.

He shipped his paddle for a moment, watching, listening. A light was visible well inland, screened by undergrowth and trees. He made it about fifty yards inshore and put it out of mind. The house was not his first concern.

Unless he missed his guess, there would be spotters on the shoreline, just as there were lookouts on the road. He had selected an approach by water in the hope that his opponents would expect assault by land, or even air, before they paid attention to the lake. If there were any weak points in the first line of defense, the warrior reckoned he would find them here.

Which did not mean that he was counting on an easy time.

His quarry were professionals and well-armed, the final head count still uncertain. He was flying blind in some respects, but it could not be helped. The risk entailed by sitting back and waiting for a more complete report had been too great. If he could end it here and now, so much the better.

The rural safehouse was a rustic cottage on seventeen acres of prime forest land, fronting the southeastern shore of Saint Francis Lake. Give or take, it was twenty-five miles as the crow flew from the target to Quebec's nearest border with Maine. An easy drive, if you were welcomed and expected; if you weren't, it was the kind of trip where you could catch your death.

Which brought Mack Bolan to the lake at 2:30 a.m. There was no moon, but Bolan still felt painfully exposed, a dark speck moving on the water, creeping toward shore. If there were sentries waiting on the shore who took their task seriously, he could still have problems going in.

Accordingly he had allowed himself some combat stretch, fixing his sights on a piece of shoreline well north of the house. It made for longer, harder paddling, but that was fair enough. A simple trade-off: more exertion in exchange for better prospects of survival.

Bolan laid on the paddle once more, bending low in the dinghy to reduce his profile. The effort would be wasted if they had a spotter on the shore with night-vision equipment, but Bolan was already close enough to draw fire in that event, and there was no sign of alarm from landward.

He was cautious, not splashing with the paddle, taking long, deep strokes that powered him toward shore. His ears picked up the sound of water lapping over sand and stones. If they cut loose on Bolan now, retreat would be a hopeless case. Behind him, to the east, his launching point from Frontenac Provincial Park was hopelessly beyond his reach.

There was no avenue but straight ahead.

Eight minutes later, he was trundling the rubber boat ashore, water swirling ankle-deep as he moved in a fighting crouch, dragging the raft behind him. Thirty feet inland, he secured the dinghy in a stand of firs with overhanging branches trailing almost to the ground. He spent another moment there in silence, barely breathing, listening for sounds that would suggest he had been spotted.

So far, so good.

The Executioner was clad in midnight black that fit him like a second skin. His face and hands were darkened with combat cosmetics, with nothing but the whites of Bolan's eyes exposed to any errant gleam of starlight. The weapon he lifted from his dinghy was an M-16 A-1 assault rifle, its graceful outline made bulky by an M-203 40 mm grenade launcher mounted beneath the foregrip. Bolan's selective fire Beretta 93-R pistol hung beneath his left arm in a fast-draw shoulder rig; a .44 Magnum Desert Eagle autoloader rode his right hip on military webbing. Ammunition pouches for the pistols ringed his waist, while bandoleers of grenade cartridges and magazines for the assault rifle crossed his chest.

He was prepared for whatever waited ahead in the darkness.

All things considered, it was meant to be a relatively simple mission. Hit-and-git across the border, reaching out to touch someone and make it stick. The target was an Irish terrorist, one William Connolly, who had escaped from custody in New York state eight days earler. Ten federal officers had died when Connolly's supporters from the Sword of Erin blitzed the transport caravan, while the gunners evaporated. Instead of driving out, they caught a charter flight from Flushing Airport, Queens, and touched down in the neighborhood of Auburn, Maine, while officers were fanning out across Long Island and Manhattan. Connolly was safe in Canada by noon on D-Day, slipping underground with contacts from a radical separatist group in Quebec. Though Bloc Québecois worked within the Canadian government for the legal separation of Quebec, Groupe de Liberté wanted quicker results and was not averse to the occasional terrorist act.

Which brought the Executioner to Canada, intent on tagging Connolly and friends before they had a chance to vanish or—worse yet—inaugurate a brand-new reign of terror. Hal Brognola had been interested enough to call his markers in with leaders of the Royal Canadian Mounted Police in Montreal, smoothing the way for Bolan's passage, providing a skeletal backup system if things went sour.

Time to move.

He left the shelter of the overhanging trees, moving parallel to the shoreline and twenty yards inland, keeping the sound of water on his right. He had a clear fix on his target, even though the cottage was invisible from where he stood. It was roughly two hundred yards away, and he would take whatever time he needed to traverse that distance silently.

A sentry gave himself up with the flare of a match, there and gone, immediately followed by a strong whiff of tobacco. Bolan homed in on the flash and the aroma, stalking with his rifle slung across his back, a Ka-bar fighting knife gripped tightly in his fist. Like all of Bolan's gear, the Ka-bar eight-inch blade was anodized in black to keep a flash of polished steel from giving him away.

He came up on the sentry's blind side, moving soundlessly on the balls of his feet, planting each step with precision to avoid loose stones and fallen twigs. He heard the sentry move before he saw his profile etched in shadow, with the lake behind him, leaning back against a tree.

It was the kind of negligence that got you killed in combat.

The sentry never heard him coming, concentrating on his cigarette, a Chinese knockoff of the classic AK-47 rifle propped against the tree beside him. When he placed it there, the sentry doubtless thought the weapon would be readily available at need. In fact, as he was soon to learn, six inches from rifle to hand made all the difference in the world.

Once Bolan satisfied himself the sentry was alone, he closed the gap in two long strides, his left hand snaking out to cup the gunner's mouth and give his head a violent twist. At the same instant, the warrior kicked hard behind the sentry's knee, buckling the outside leg, while his right hand brought the combat knife looping in on target. Warm blood squirted over Bolan's wrist. The sentry struggled momentarily, then went limp.

He eased the body to the ground and wiped his knife on the dead man's shirt. One down, and Bolan drifted back to his original position, tracking toward the cottage.

Another thirty yards, and sentry number two stepped into Bolan's view. This gunner was alert, his rifle braced against one hip, its muzzle pointed at the sky. He shifted restlessly while the warrior watched, now facing the lake, then fading back to wait and listen to the night sounds of the forest.

There was too much risk in closing to arm's length with this one, Bolan realized. He left the Ka-bar in its sheath and eased the sleek Beretta 93-R from its shoulder holster, easing back the hammer with his thumb. The 93-R was equipped with a custom-made silencer and subsonic loads that reduced its voice to a whisper, virtually inaudible beyond a range of fifty feet.

The spotting range was less than half that distance as he held the pistol steady in a firm two-handed grip. He waited for the gunner to complete a turn and face him squarely, shadows blotting out most of his solemn face.

Bolan stroked the 93-R's trigger twice in rapid fire, clean head shots, and the sentry toppled over backward with a muffled grunt. His heels drummed briefly on a bed of pine needles before his corpse went limp.

The warrior stepped across the body and continued toward the cottage, his senses alert for other watchers in the woods. Ten minutes later, he was crouching at the tree line, with the front of the two-story structure nearly thirty yards away, light showing through a pair of ground-floor windows. On the porch, a gunner in a sheepskin jacket occupied a wooden rocking chair, his feet propped on the rail, a submachine gun in his lap.

Bolan spent a quarter hour circling the house in shadow, checking out the various approaches, scanning for additional lookouts. None was in evidence, and the cottage's only door appeared to be in front, though Bolan recognized that fleeing targets could escape from any of a dozen windows in a pinch. No single man could hope to cover all potential exits from the house, but he would have to do his best.

And that meant acting swiftly, with the full advantage of surprise.

He brought the rifle to his shoulder, sighted on the door and stroked the trigger of the M-203 launcher. With a muffled popping sound, the 40 mm high-explosive round impacted dead on target. Smoky thunder rocked the sleeping house, tall windows shattering in front, the heavy wooden door reduced to shredded kindling on the fly.

A mighty shock wave dumped the lookout from his rocker to the deck, his submachine gun skittering across the boards and out of reach. He scrambled after it, blood streaming from a gash along his hairline, but the Executioner was ready for him, waiting with the M-16 A-1. A 3-round burst from thirty yards stitched holes across the sentry's chest and pitched him over on his back.

With that, Bolan was up and moving, pounding toward the cottage, reloading the M-203 grenade launcher on the run. From this point on, he knew, the sounds of battle would attract whatever sentries still remained at large. His first priority was those inside the building, where William Connolly and his companions had reportedly been spotted by an RCMP informant within the past two days.

He hit the porch running, ignoring the fallen sentry as he cleared the smoking threshold in a combat crouch, his rifle sweeping left and right for targets. Bolan found one coming down the stairs, a young man dressed in undershorts and a T-shirt, with a shotgun in his hands. He blinked at Bolan in amazement, shouted something in French that might have been a curse and tried to swing his gun around.

He never made it.

Bolan's M-16 A-1 rapped out a short staccato burst, the 5.56 mm tumblers ripping through his target's chest and spinning him. The young man folded, tumbling headfirst down the stairs, his finger still clenched around the shotgun's trigger. An aimless blast of buckshot struck the ceiling, raining plaster dust upon him as he fell.

The warrior veered to his left with long strides, hit the kitchen door with a flying kick and found the room empty. Retracing his steps, he kept the stairs covered, hearing angry, frightened voices on the second floor, but his next challenge came closer at hand.

Across the living room, a door banged open, giving him a glimpse of a rumpled bed behind the shirtless man who filled the doorway, brandishing an automatic pistol. Bolan met his human target with a rising burst that punched him through an awkward pirouette and dumped him back across the threshold, twitching where he lay.

A shadow moved behind the dead man, and a submachine gun opened up, spraying bullets high and wide. Bolan triggered the M-203 as he went to ground, unleashing another high-explosive round at less than thirty feet. The blast was louder here, up close and personal, with shrapnel whining over the warrior's head. A strangled cry of pain was cut off in midsyllable, eclipsed by man-made thunder and the sound of crackling flames.

Reloading as he rose, Bolan detected a flicker of movement in his peripheral vision. Two men were crouching on the second-floor landing, taking in the scene below. Both carried guns and seemed prepared to use them, but surprise and sleep piled crucial seconds onto their reaction time. One hesitated with his AK-47, edging back a step as if to flee, his young companion trembling as he raised an Ingram submachine gun in both hands.

Firing from the hip as he approached the stairs, Bolan's first short burst ripped through the gunner with the Ingram SMG and dropped him on his face. His weapon bounced between two uprights of the banister and dropped to the couch below.

The second gunner swung the AK-47 into target acquisition, squeezing off a ragged burst. The armor-piercing rounds chewed plaster, missing Bolan by a foot or more as he began to mount the stairs. Another second now, and the warrior's man would have the range.

Return fire from the M-16 A-1 cut a zigzag pattern between his target's knees and breastbone, rocking him back on his heels. The Kalashnikov kept spitting as he fell, his dead finger locked inside the trigger guard. The dead man fired off half a magazine before the Kalashnikov kicked free of his finger.

Reaching the landing, Bolan turned down a hallway with doors on either side. The closest two rooms were empty, and the warrior reckoned he had already met their occupants on the stairs. His finger was on the trigger of his M-16 as he approached the next room on his left, stepped back and gave the door a solid kick. The room was dark and silent. He found the light switch and flicked it on. The room was unoccupied.

And that left three.

Another unoccupied room was on his left. Bolan pulled back from the open doorway, facing the rooms directly opposite. Two doors, two chances, and he knew his time was running out. Surviving lookouts from the forest would be closing on the cottage by now, drawn by sounds of battle. He could hear the numbers falling in his mind, knew well enough the risk of letting hostile gunners flank him on his blind side.

He took a short step forward, raised one leg and was about to kick the door when a frantic fumbling sound to his right distracted him. The last door flew open, and Bolan was confronted with a short man in his early thirties, clad in white dress shirt and red pajama bottoms. The mismatched outfit was of less concern to the warrior than the Browning automatic in the stranger's fist.

The M-16 was stuttering before his adversary had a good clear look at Bolan, 5.56 mm manglers punching him backward, lifting him completely off his feet. Stepping across the bedroom threshold, the Executioner caught sight of a man with his back turned, halfway out the second-story window.

A short burst from Bolan's rifle propelled his target through the glass and window sash, toward outer darkness. Dead before he fell, the would-be runner made no sound until he struck the turf and landed in a heap.

And that was all. A quick scan of the bypassed room assured the warrior there was no one hiding out or waiting to receive him there. No stragglers, and he knew that William Connolly was not among the soldiers he had dropped so far.

Were any of the dead men Irish? It was possible, but Bolan saw the odds were running long against him now. His first, best bet at bagging Connolly had been lost.

Bad luck . . . or something else?

He hesitated near the landing, listening to voices drifting up the stairs. There were two men—no, make it three—all speaking French.

It would be dicey, going down those stairs with three guns hammering away. It took about a second and a half for Bolan to consider options and select Plan B.

He cleared the M-203's chamber, primed it with a fat incendiary round and closed the breech, his finger on the trigger as he sidestepped toward the corner that would put him on display. Precision work was not an issue with the thermite canister; a ballpark touchdown would be close enough and give him all the cover he would need.

So be it.

Bolan poked his piece around the corner, letting the incendiary fly, and ducked back as a pair of automatic rifles and a submachine gun started playing three-part harmony. Incoming bullets chewed the wall to tattered shreds where he was standing moments earlier, but Bolan wasted no time scoping out the damage from his wild shot toward the living room.

He crossed the hallway, ducked into the nearest empty bedroom and crossed directly to the window. It was latched, but Bolan opened it, raised the sash, ducked through and scanned the ground below. It was a twelve-foot drop to grass and loam—no problem in his present circumstances.

Bolan made the drop and came up running, circling back toward the porch. He had unfinished business here and never made a point of leaving hostile guns at his back.

The fire had taken hold inside the cottage's living room, spreading rapidly to walls and furnishings. The white-hot thermite coals would eat their way through steel and concrete given any kind of chance, and this was simple wood. The structure would be a write-off in a few more minutes.

Two gunners made it out, both gagging on the smoke, one slapping frantically at hot spots where his leather jacket had begun to smolder. Bolan let them clear the doorway, lining up his shot with firelight to illuminate the scene. It was no trick at all to target them from a range of forty feet and take them out with short precision bursts.

Two up, two down.

That made an even dozen for the night, and none of them was William Connolly. The warrior breathed a ragged curse and started sorting out his options. He had missed his prey and tipped his hand to native opposition, all at once.

It was a disappointing outcome, all around.

He wondered whether it was worth the time and risk to paddle back across the lake. A chance discovery behind the burning house—matching Jeeps in black and navy blue—made up Bolan's mind for him. The black one had a key in the ignition.

Fate, or pure dumb luck?

Whatever, Bolan knew it never paid to look a gift horse in the mouth.

The dinghy was expendable, with no trace of his identity on board or anywhere connected to the small inflatable. A Jeep would serve him nicely at the moment.

Bolan propped his rifle up between the seats, stripped his webbing and dumped it in the shotgun seat. The vehicle responded to his touch, and in seconds he was rolling. He knew from previous reconnaissance exactly where the unpaved access road was taking him, and he was ready when the rutted dirt gave way to asphalt, running north and south. He cranked the steering wheel hard right and stood on the accelerator, southbound.

His sweep had not been wasted, but he had come up short—and failed entirely when it came to tagging Connolly or any other member from the Sword of Erin. That meant starting from scratch, but this time with Groupe de Liberté aware that they were being stalked.

Bad news.

Before the Executioner could swing it, he would have to get more information. That, in turn, would mean more personal exposure, and another contact with Brognola's source.

He settled back and focused his attention on the highway, rolling toward another wake-up call.

CHAPTER TWO

Sherbrooke, Quebec

Bolan approached Sherbrooke from the east, following Highway 108 from Cookshire through a stretch of rolling farmland. It was still an hour short of dawn, the first pale trace of gray on the horizon showing in the rearview mirror.

Darkness suited him just now. It seemed to fit precisely with his mood, the purpose of his visit. There was something in his errand, Bolan thought, that would not flourish in the light of day.

The English-language all-news channel out of Montreal had so far broadcast nothing on his opening engagement with the radicals at Saint Francis Lake. He wondered if the racket and ensuing fire had managed to escape detection somehow, or if the authorities were holding back until they had a solid handle on the incident. Whatever happened, if there were survivors of the strike whom he had somehow overlooked, the Executioner was fairly confident that they would not be talking to the press.

Survivors *would* be talking to their comrades, though, and even with a clean sweep at the target site, he knew that the rest of his adversaries would be warned of danger to themselves within the next few hours. Every moment wasted now would give them more time to prepare, diminishing his chances of success.

He drove past the Victoria Hotel and circled the block, alert to any possible stakeout. A phone call to Brognola's contact had provided him with this address, but Bolan had not lived this long by taking anything on faith.

Betrayal was a daily fact of life, and he had learned to watch his back in military service, long before he ever qualified to vote.

Bolan parked the Jeep in the hotel parking lot. He would not entrust the ignition key to a valet who might be bought and paid for by his enemies. If that was paranoia, he could live with it.

A sleepy doorman glanced at him nonchalantly. The Executioner had swapped his blacksuit for a three-piece pinstripe, leaving all his hardware but the indispensable Beretta in the vehicle. With two spare magazines, he had sixty rounds to play with.

The lobby was deserted at this hour. A solitary clerk sat behind the counter, concentrating on his magazine and cup of coffee. Bolan felt the clerk's eyes tracking him as he moved toward the elevator, but he gave no sign of recognition. Let him wonder, if he had the energy. Hotel clerks in Quebec, as in the world at large, were generally satisfied to mind their own business in the absence of disruptive incidents.

Whatever else he had in mind, an incident at the Victoria Hotel was definitely not part of Bolan's plans.

He had the elevator to himself and rode it up to seven, stepping out into a silent corridor. Bolan passed half a dozen doors before he came to number 725. He knocked and waited, and was about to try again when muffled footsteps sounded from inside.

The man who answered was a rangy six foot two, with sandy hair and freckles. He had the classic farm boy look until you checked the eyes, which were gray chips of granite that had seen it all. The lines around his mouth gave him the image of a man who seldom smiled. He wore a wrinkled dress shirt with the sleeves rolled up. A Browning double-action automatic rode on his hip.

"Belasko?"

Bolan nodded, stepped inside, and waited for the door to close behind him.

"Rick Grant, RCMP."

The warrior shook his hand. "Lieutenant Grant."

"Let's make it Rick, shall we?"

"Mike," Bolan replied, sticking with the cover Hal Brognola had employed in his communications with the Mounties.

"Have a seat."

The room had two plain wooden chairs, and Bolan took one for himself. Grant sat facing him and crossed his legs, fired up a cigarette and left his lighter on the vanity beside his elbow.

"Problems at the lake, you said."

"The man I hoped to see apparently checked out before I got there."

"You took care of business with the others?"

"The ones who stuck around."

"How many?"

"Twelve, for sure."

Grant nodded, dragging on his cigarette. "Too bad about the Irishman."

"I'm hoping he hasn't traveled far."

"You think his friends are hiding him?"

"They've played along so far."

"True enough." Gray eyes watched Bolan through a drifting haze of smoke. "You'll need more information, I expect."

"I will."

Grant seemed to hesitate, and Bolan understood his caution. In the past two decades, RCMP officers had been accused of disregarding civil rights and legal safeguards in several well-publicized cases. Back in the "old days," when members of the American Black Panther Party had opened shop north of the border, Mounties met them with illegal wiretaps and harassment, once setting fire to Panther headquarters on the eve of an impending sitdown with Canadian leftists. Similar tactics had allegedly been used against targets ranging from outlaw motorcycle gangs and white supremacist groups to organized crime, with particular attention paid to left-of-center radicals. As with the FBI and CIA in the United States, new legislation and an outraged public called for changes in procedure, but the never-ending war went on behind the scenes.

In fact, the Mounties still took care of business when the opportunity arose. While they had never met in person, it was Rick Grant who had directed Bolan to the safehouse on Saint Francis Lake.

"I can't have any comebacks on this," Grant said. "Understand?"

"I do."

No comebacks.

It had been the rule of thumb for Bolan's war from the beginning. Hal Brognola's whole operation at Stony Man Farm was predicated on absolute secrecy, allowing measures to be taken that were not debated endlessly by some congressional committee or approved by half a dozen special interest groups.

There was a global war in progress, and in a shooting war the front-line soldier could not be concerned with making every move "politically correct."

"We need to talk about Groupe de Liberté," Grant said.

"It couldn't hurt."

A group known as the Front du Libération du Québec had been founded in 1963, ironically by George Schoeters, an immigrant from Belgium. Young French Canadians, frustrated by a constitutional system that moved with glacial speed, had flocked to his banner of independence by any means available. Over the next decade, those means included bombings, robberies and kidnapping for ransom. The nadir of the movement came with the abduction and assassination of Pierre Laporte, Quebec's minister of labor and immigration, which led Prime Minister Pierre Trudeau to invoke the Canadian War Measures Act, imposing a state of near martial law in Quebec.

Bolan had locked horns with the Québecois once before, when terrorists in Montreal sought to forge an alliance with the Canadian Mafia. Time had moved on since then, with Bolan's staged "death" and public declarations of the FLQ's demise.

Like Bolan, though, the spirit of revolt in Quebec was still alive and well.

Of late, survivors of the original FLQ had founded a new organization called Groupe de Liberté, and recruited a new generation of would-be "freedom fighters," steering them in new directions to support the cause. This group had joined forces with mafioso elements in Montreal, and were as much concerned with crime as with political separation for Quebec. In place of highly public, even self-destructive acts like bombings and assassination, the Québecois radicals had turned to covert methods of promoting their design. Intelligence secured through Stony Man suggested that the "liberation warriors" of Quebec were moving drugs, black-market weapons, even stolen cars, collaborating with the underworld.

And they were branching out, exchanging favors with the Japanese Red Army, Spain's militant ETA movement and the Provisional IRA.

"You're current on the movement's economic base?" Grant asked.

"I try to keep in touch."

"Right. You know about the drugs, then, and their other sidelines."

"Yes."

"They're slick, these bastards. Now and then we catch them with their fingers dirty, but they're learning from their betters. Even when we spot their operations now, we often have a hard time making out a case for trial."

"I understand."

"We're not discussing rules of evidence, though, are we?"

"No, we're not."

"I didn't think so."

Grant reached underneath the vanity and produced a battered leather briefcase. He opened it, extracted several sheets of paper from a yellow legal pad and handed them to Bolan.

"Names, addresses, this and that," he said. "Officially I don't know what their value is to you, and I don't want to know. You didn't get the list from me. In fact, we never had this meeting."

Bolan smiled. "What meeting?"

"Right."

A slim manila envelope was next. Inside, the Executioner found a dozen photographs, some Polaroids, some glossy black-and-whites.

"I found these snapshots cluttering the files," Grant said. "Names on the back will help you spot the leaders."

"Thanks."

"For what?"

"You're right."

Grant lit another cigarette. "We're positive this lot has taken guns and money from Khaddafi. A couple of their flunkies visited Iraq a month or so before the big push in Kuwait. Out east, they tried to cut an arms deal with the South Moluccans, but it didn't gel. Not too discriminating, this lot."

"Any port in a storm," Bolan said.

"I suppose. We've picked up whispers on the Irish end, but nothing solid. Both groups hate the Brits, of course. What else is new?"

Bolan studied the list of names and street numbers, matching them against his memories of Montreal.

"We try to keep in touch on our patch, too," Grant said. "I've heard a bit about this Sword of Erin, but my information's sketchy, I'll admit. If you could fill me in..."

He left it there, unspoken. Not demanding anything, but letting Bolan know that it was payback time—at least in part.

"The Sword of Erin is a spin-off faction of the Provisional Irish Republican Army," Bolan said, "organized in 1987 from a rift within the PIRA leadership. On paper, members of the Sword believe in justice, liberty and civil rights for Irishmen without regard to creed or politics.''

"On paper." Rick Grant could not suppress a sneer.

"In fact, they make the Provos look like Boy Scouts," Bolan said. "The IRA won't shrink from bombing a department store at Christmastime, but at least they always have some rationale on tap. The owners of the store do business with the Orangemen up in Belfast—something they can hang their hats on when the heated editorials come down.''

"I follow that," Grant said. "The PR game.''

"The Sword of Erin doesn't bother putting on a happy face. They're committed to a course of all-out terrorism, and they actually prefer civilian targets. It's supposed to weaken the resolve of their opponents, somehow, though I haven't seen it working in the past six years."

"This lot sees what they want to see," Grant answered, sounding bitter.

"William Connolly's a charter member of the Sword," the Executioner went on. "He came in as the second in command for Arthur Flynn, in June of 1987. Three years back, when Flynn got dusted by the SAS in Yorkshire, Connolly moved up to fill his slot. The word I get, he's been involved directly in at least a dozen murders. Make it three, four times that number when you toss in killings by the rank and file. I'd hate to try and count the bombings, drive-by shootings and God knows what else he's been up to in the past three years."

"You had him in the States, though," Grant reminded him.

"We did. He slipped across the water on a phony passport, and the Bureau grabbed him in New York. If you believe the word from Interpol and Scotland Yard, he had his eye on money, trying for a piece of that 're- lief fund' raised by Noraid for the Provos every year."

"It's not the cheapest pastime, killing strangers by the dozen. Did he get his dole?"

"It's hard to say," the Executioner replied. "We know that he was in New York three days before a state police informant gave him up."

"That was two years ago?"

"Close. He fought extradition, filing for political asylum. Claimed to be a prisoner of war, the usual."

"I've heard that line before."

"He lost his last appeal two weeks ago. Connolly was on his way to catch a British Airways flight when someone jumped the convoy, lifted him and smoked his escorts."

"Ten, I read it was."

"Right. We didn't have a clue on where he'd gone until your people turned him in Quebec. We appreci- ated your help, right down the line."

"It's a two-way street," Grant said. "Fact is, you're doing us a favor with the GL. We've had a hell of a time laying hands on them for anything of sub- stance."

"That might change."

"I'm counting on it. I ought to warn you, though. You should expect resistance from them all the way. They've been collecting arms for thirty years, in one guise or another, and we know they're not afraid to pull the trigger."

"And you don't need any foreign corpses on your turf, much less a scandal in the headlines."

Grant was working on a frown. "It isn't that, ex- actly."

Maybe not, but it was close enough, and Bolan knew how the lieutenant felt. A sudden gang war could be written off from time to time, if all the casualties were clearly villains. Someone would complain about the state of public safety, but the screaming editorials were generally reserved for incidents that claimed civilian lives. When innocents began to fall, the heat was close behind, and it would only be exacerbated by the death of a reputed foreign agent—unidentified or otherwise—in Montreal.

"I'm good at what I do."

"I took that much on faith," Grant replied. "Still, there is such a thing as luck. It cuts both ways."

"How many people know that we're cooperating?" Bolan asked.

"On my side? Myself and my commander, maybe his immediate superior. I'd bet my pension that it stops with three."

"No problem," Bolan said. "If you can trust the other two, there's no one on your end to burn my cover down, no matter how it breaks."

Grant stared at Bolan, wondering if he should take offense at the remark on his superiors' behalf, deciding there was no insult intended.

"Right," he said at last.

"I'm curious. You could just as easily have taken Connolly yourself."

"Ah, well..." The Mountie smiled. "Diminishing returns, you know? An Irish terrorist in hand can be no end of trouble, when you think about it. Never mind the legal end of things. We've seen what happens when you lock one up and all his cronies want him out again. We played that number with the GL for quite some time, and now we've got the bloody skinheads on our hands. No thank you."

"And?"

"Two birds, one stone," Grant said. "With any kind of luck, we lose the Irish lads and teach our homeboys a needful lesson, courtesy of Uncle Sam."

"We aim to please."

"I'd make the first shot count from this point on, if I were you."

"Point taken."

Bolan rose, and the lieutenant walked him to the door. "You have my number, if there's anything you need. I'm sorry that I can't provide material assistance, but it comes down to a matter of exposure."

"Understood."

"In any case, I wish you luck."

"It couldn't hurt."

The door snicked shut behind him, and Bolan retraced his steps to the elevator. Down in the lobby, an early-bird traveling salesman was just checking out, scanning his itemized bill with a skeptical frown. The desk clerk ignored Bolan completely on this pass, and that was just fine.

Outside, the newly risen sun was burning off a haze of ground fog from the decorative lawn. The doorman glanced at Bolan for a heartbeat, then ignored him as he returned to his Jeep.

His first step was to ditch the vehicle and find himself another set of wheels in which to lug his mobile arsenal around. He could attend to that in Montreal, then begin his hunt in earnest.

There were cages to be rattled, urgent warnings to be given and received. And it was possible, he told himself, that all of it would be in vain. If Connolly and friends had left Quebec, then he was wasting precious time, but he would never know until he asked the question where it counted.

If Bolan's prey eluded him in Montreal, he would continue the pursuit, no matter where it led.

The sun was in the Executioner's eyes as he slid behind the steering wheel. It was a brand-new day, with brand-new opportunities.

He wondered, for the briefest moment, whether he would live to see the sun go down.

CHAPTER THREE

Montreal, Quebec

Mack Bolan brought his one-man war to Montreal at 8:05 a.m. The sky was clear, the weather crisp and cool, no clouds or rain to challenge long-range visibility—a perfect morning for a sniper.

The warrior's latest set of wheels, selected for its nondescript appearance, was a spacious van. It gave him ample room to store his combat gear, change clothes, or simply park and hide if he attracted too much heat within the next few hours.

That would be a setback, though, and Bolan had no plans for backing off just yet. He was in blitzkrieg mode, prepared to grab his adversary by the neck and shake him until he rattled, anything it took to put him on the trail of William Connolly.

He parked the van two blocks from his selected target, facing Maisonneuve Park from the south. Grant's envelope of photographs was on the empty seat beside him, but he didn't touch it. He had several faces clearly fixed in mind, and only one of them concerned him now.

He left the driver's seat and slipped into the back of the van. A faded denim jumpsuit lay atop a long metallic tool box, and he slipped it on, adjusting it for comfort on the crotch. The patch on Bolan's chest read "Thomas"; on his back, a larger patch identified his employer as Laval Electronics. If anyone asked, he had a pocketful of rumpled work orders, covered with illegible script.

The toolbox was not light, but Bolan handled it with ease. He locked the van behind him, looked both ways before he crossed the street. His destination was an apartment building he had scouted in advance. The building's air conditioners were mounted on the roof. A narrow metal staircase led Bolan to his chosen vantage point.

It was not perfect, but the Executioner was satisfied. Facing north, across the park, he had an unobstructed view of more apartments, seeming carbon copies of the building he had chosen. As in the States, the architects had obviously valued function and economy above originality and style.

He knelt beside the toolbox, opened it and lifted out a tray of ordinary tools. Beneath, disassembled and swaddled in a blanket, lay a Walther WA-2000 sniper's rifle. Bolan took out the compact weapon and deftly reassembled it, his sharp eyes concentrating on the target roughly two hundred yards away.

It was an easy shot, in terms of distance, nothing to compare with long-range missions he had carried out in Vietnam and subsequently, but the Executioner was not about to take the kill for granted. Overconfidence invited careless errors, and he knew that one mistake could get him killed.

He stretched prone, the Walther's muzzle resting on its bipod, with his cheek against the stock, his right hand wrapped around the weapon's pistol grip. The Schmidt & Bender 2.5 x 10-power telescopic sight brought his chosen killing ground up close and personal.

Bolan focused on the doorway of a nondescript apartment, waiting. He was early, but the wait would not be long. His target kept regular hours, maintaining his pose as a quiet, respectable businessman. The neighbors, the warrior guessed, had no idea that he was also one of the leading radical activists in Quebec.

Jean-Paul Rouard had been part of the FLQ when he was still a college student, serving time for his participation in the bombing of a Montreal department store and sundry other crimes. He used a different name these days and wore a different face in public, keeping his opinions to himself, but RCMP sources verified that he was still involved in revolutionary politics, using his business as a front for criminal activities as well as for the GL separatists in Montreal.

Within the past twelve months, according to the information Bolan got from Rick Grant, Rouard had moved four shipments of cocaine through his bar in Outremont, recycling the profits into arms and ammunition for the cause.

Bolan shifted slightly on the flat, unyielding roof, to make himself more comfortable. The Walther WA-2000 was a bullpup design, measuring thirty-six inches overall. The weapon's barrel was fluted longitudinally for cooling and to minimize vibration when the piece was fired.

Downrange, the door to the apartment opened and a slender, swarthy man emerged. Bolan let him pass and waited for the silhouette behind him to resolve itself in greater detail. Short and muscular, Rouard was decked out in a turtleneck and navy sport coat, with a thick gold chain around his neck. He locked the door behind him, pocketed his keys and paused to light a cigarette.

The Executioner had seen enough. His finger tightened on the Walther's trigger, slowly taking up the slack. The scope's cross hairs fixed on Rouard's nose, allowing for the drop in trajectory over two hundred yards.

The rifle lurched against the warrior's shoulder as 220 grains of death hurtled from the muzzle. The bullet reached Rouard before the shot was audible from his perspective, ripping through his chin and larynx. His face exploded in a splash of brilliant crimson, painting abstract patterns on the door and stucco at his back.

Bolan shifted to his right, tracking with the Walther toward Rouard's associate. The swarthy man looked stricken, gaping at the headless body of his friend, recoiling from the sight and from the echo of a distant gunshot. He was reaching underneath his jacket, hauling out a nickel-plated side arm, when the Executioner squeezed off a second round.

The bullet drilled Rouard's companion through one temple, lifting off the top half of his skull. The explosive impact hurled him sideways, and his corpse rebounded off the blood-streaked wall, collapsing in a lifeless heap across Rouard's legs.

All done.

Bolan dismantled the Walther and returned it to its hiding place. He stood and lifted the toolbox, retracing his steps to the sidewalk and back to the van. He had the vehicle in motion when the first of Rouard's neighbors hit the bricks, responding to the sounds of rifle fire.

Putting the killing ground behind him, he cruised toward the next appointed target on his list.

HENRI BOUCHET WAS NERVOUS, and the feeling made him angry. He had picked up fragmentary snatches of the early-morning violence at the lake, and he knew a dozen of his comrades had been killed. For what? By whom? The questions nagged him, set his teeth on edge.

He was prepared for war, had been since he enlisted in Groupe de Liberté, two years earlier, but it was different than his fantasies, somehow. When Bouchet thought about the struggle that was coming, he imagined grasping the initiative, precipitating great events, emerging from chaos as a hero. In Bouchet's mind, the battle always went his way and risks were minimized. Potential tragedy became a movie script, with Bouchet ranked among the shining stars.

It was a different game this morning, with a dozen bodies filling up the small-town morgue at Lambton and the movement's officers broadcasting an alert throughout the province. They were worried sick, LeClaire among them, and it shook Bouchet to see the men he most admired reduced to hiding from an unknown enemy.

Bouchet was lounging in the back seat of a compact car, outside a warehouse in suburban Outremont. The warehouse had been leased by covert members of the movement for the past six months, its list of merchandise on hand revised from time to time when shipments of illegal arms were passing through.

His superiors were anxious to protect the warehouse and a stash of automatic rifles, stolen from a military base in Massachusetts, which had been received the week before. If unknown enemies could raid the lake house, said LeClaire, they might strike anywhere.

Bouchet was cradling an Uzi submachine gun in his lap, spare magazines beside him in a paper bag. He checked his watch at frequent intervals and wished that it was time for his relief. A van rolled past the warehouse, hesitated at the corner, finally turning left and vanishing from sight. The driver did not spare Bouchet a passing glance, and that was fine.

He felt exposed and vulnerable, wishing he had been selected for the inside team. Three guns were inside the warehouse and another on the roof, but they had wanted him out front, the point man as it were. Bouchet had not considered arguing, because it would have cast aspersions on his manhood and reduced him to a whining coward in the eyes of his companions.

Better to accept the order, spend his time out in the car and hope that nothing happened. He was not a praying man—it ran against the revolutionary grain—but he could always keep his fingers crossed. The unknown enemy aside, it would be troublesome if a patrol car passed and he was spotted sitting in the car. Suppose the officers had nothing else to do and felt like asking him his business?

Bouchet frowned and used his feet to probe beneath the driver's seat in front of him. He thought the Uzi just might fit, if he was forced to hide it in a hurry. Otherwise . . .

His stomach rumbled, a reminder that the call to action had prevented his eating breakfast. Two more hours remained before he got a break, but even then he had to hang around the warehouse, waiting for a call that it was safe to leave.

Bouchet willed himself to relax. The lake house was eighty miles away, and he had no good reason to believe the enemy—whomever that might be—was bound for Montreal. For all he knew, the killings might be drug related, tied into the ugly trade that was the movement's leading source of revenue these days. Colombians, perhaps, or even the Chinese.

He would be glad when the revolution came and they could sever ties with the reactionary bastards who controlled illicit commerce in the province. Come the day of victory, drug dealers would be hounded from Quebec. If they resisted—

The explosion shocked Bouchet out of his reverie. He almost dropped the Uzi, twisting sharply in his seat to face the warehouse, where a cloud of smoke was rising from the roof. A heartbeat later, he heard gunfire, muffled by the intervening walls, at least two weapons, maybe three or four.

He cursed and put the car behind him, doubled back to fetch the extra magazines and stuff them in his pockets. He was moving toward the warehouse when a second blast sent shock waves rippling through the corrugated metal walls. The building seemed to shimmy like a jelly sculpture, raining dust from the eaves.

For God's sake, what was happening?

He mounted concrete steps to reach the deserted loading dock. He passed giant metal doors, closed and locked, to reach a smaller door that opened on the warehouse office. Bouchet stepped cautiously across the threshold, clutching the Uzi tightly.

The sounds of gunfire made his ears ring. There was still another door between the action and Bouchet, but he was close enough to hear familiar voices raised in anger. There was Louis, cursing like a trooper, and Armand, shouting in the baritone that never seemed to fit his runty form.

He crossed the tiny office, gripped the doorknob with a trembling hand and passed into the battle zone. Two steps, and Bouchet nearly tripped across the prostrate body of Guillaume Charteris, lying face-down on the concrete in a spreading pool of blood. A bullet, maybe more than one, had chewed the left side of his skull to pulp.

Bouchet, thankful that he had skipped breakfast, doubled over as his stomach twisted in a knot. The blood was part of it, but mostly he was gripped by sudden, paralyzing fear. It was a different game entirely now, with fresh gore on his shoes, a body stretched out at his feet.

He scanned the warehouse, breathing in the fumes of cordite, spotting Louis as he broke from cover, dodging toward a nearby forklift. He was firing back along the aisle between two stacks of wooden crates, his Smith & Wesson submachine gun spitting flame.

En route to the forklift, Louis seemed to stagger, reeling back on drunken legs, his gunfire high and wide, off target. Someone else was firing now, the bullets ripping Louis from his collar to his navel, spouting blood from ragged wounds. He lost his footing, vaulted backward and fell, hitting his skull on a fender of the forklift.

Footsteps ringing on the concrete brought Bouchet around. He glimpsed a stranger, armed with what appeared to be an M-16, and then Armand cut loose from ambush, pumping bullets at the stranger from his vantage point, on Bouchet's right.

The tall man swung in that direction, leveling his weapon, squeezing off a round from the grenade launcher attached to his rifle. It hardly made a sound at first, a muffled pop was all, but the explosion rocked

Bouchet. Armand was airborne, trailing smoke behind him as his mangled body somersaulted twenty feet and landed in a crumpled heap.

Bouchet recovered long enough to jerk the trigger on his Uzi, but the weapon got away from him, its muzzle climbing toward the skylights overhead, brass jingling around his feet. His panic wiped out all the hours of practice, and he burned up half a magazine of Parabellum rounds before he managed to control the bucking subgun.

Too late.

His adversary fired a short precision burst, and Bouchet's legs exploded, crumpling under him. He sat on the concrete, his stylish slacks full of blood. He lost the Uzi somehow, watched it slithering across the floor, beyond his reach.

Another moment ought to see it done. The stranger had him now. Bouchet would die without a hint of who had killed him or the reason why. He closed his eyes and waited for the ax to fall, his legs on fire with pain . . . but nothing happened.

No, that wasn't right. He heard the stranger coming closer, felt the man's shadow on his face. Bouchet looked up and found the stranger watching him, impassive, studying his face.

"Speak English?" asked the stranger.

"Yes."

"I want the Irishman. You understand me?"

"No."

"Then pass it on. Somebody will."

"The Irishman?"

"That's right."

It was ridiculous, but Bouchet nodded, leaning on his outstretched hands to keep himself from toppling over on his back. He closed his eyes and tried to think of something else to say.

And when he opened them again, he was alone.

"GOD DAMN LECLAIRE," William Connolly said. "I thought he was a man."

"A bloody frog." John Breen was scowling over coffee. "What have his people done worth mentioning, the past ten years?"

The phone call had disrupted breakfast, and the eggs were getting cold. It hardly mattered now, for Connolly had lost his appetite.

Roch LeClaire had ordered him to leave Quebec. Not asked him, the way a friend would in his time of trouble. *Ordered* him, for God's sake, like a stooge.

"We're going then?" Breen asked.

"We might as well. This lot is hopeless on security."

In fact, they could have gone the day before, but Connolly had waited, giving Scotland Yard and MI-6 a chance to spin their wheels while he was safe in Canada. Except he wasn't safe.

Not anymore.

Breen poked his cooling eggs around the plate and frowned. "What makes the bastard blame us for his troubles?"

Connolly looked grim. "Some bastard asked about me when he kicked their ass, the last time. Says he's looking for the Irishman."

"It doesn't sound like FBI."

"I couldn't care less who it is. They've spooked LeClaire, and that's the end of it. He wants us out."

"It's just as well," Breen said. "We've got work to do at home."

"I don't mind leaving, John, but being driven off is something else."

"What, then? You said yourself we have to go."

"There's going," Connolly replied, "and then there's going."

"I don't follow you."

"We had a bargain with LeClaire," Connolly said. "He took his pay up front, the bastard. I expect to get my money's worth."

"How's that?"

"The way I see it, John, he broke our contract. In any court I ever heard of there's a penalty for pulling stunts like that."

"What kind of penalty?"

"I'm thinking, Johnny boy."

It was the kind of problem Connolly was good at, coming down to violence in the end. He simply had to pick his target, then choose the proper time and place. A deadline made it awkward, but Connolly had worked under deadlines before. It was the nature of guerrilla warfare that the underdog was forced to action by events beyond his control. He had to take advantage of the opportunities as they arose, bend circumstance to his advantage where he could.

"You have a contact in the city for supplies?" he asked.

"Without LeClaire, you mean?"

"That's what I mean."

"We might not have our pick of merchandise."

"Do what you can. I want a package, six or seven pounds."

"How soon?"

"There's no time like the present, Johnny."

"I'll be going, then."

"You do that, lad."

It gave him time—perhaps an hour—to choose the perfect target. Connolly was not so much concerned with symbolism at the moment as he was with practicality. The target had to be accessible and large enough to justify the risk involved. Beyond that, Connolly would let the media take over with their lights and cameras, ensuring further scandal for LeClaire and, possibly, a headline for the Sword of Erin.

Pushing back his breakfast plate, the Ulsterman considered his anonymous pursuers. He was wanted in the States by agents of the FBI, the New York State Police, and U.S. marshals. Any one of them would gladly shoot him dead on sight, but Connolly was not persuaded they would chase him into Canada and murder native radicals to find him.

The CIA, perhaps?

At one time he would certainly have blamed the company, but much had happened during recent years. The cold war was a fading memory in Europe, and the CIA was under constant scrutiny for covert operations and expenditure of "secret" funds. Above all else, the Company had grown adept at covering its tracks and steering clear of scandal in the press.

He thought about the Brits, then, knowing that the SAS would bend or break established law as it saw fit, with any lame excuse. Gibraltar proved that to the world, and they were killing Irish patriots each week in Belfast, keeping up the score.

It might be SAS, thought Connolly, and then again...

He sipped his coffee, found it cold and left the rest. It did not matter where his enemies had come from, in the last analysis. The Sword of Erin had a two-edged blade, and it was razor-sharp. It cut both ways, and anyone who tried to wrest that weapon from his hand was in for a surprise.

It would be good to see his native land once more. Despite the danger, even with an occupying army in the streets, he longed for home. The thought of small thatched cottages and rolling pastures made his never-ending war worthwhile.

Someday, he thought, the battle would be won. He might not live to see it, but he had a role to play in Ulster—and wherever the oppressors of his people went about their daily business unmolested, banking on the fact that distance somehow made them safe.

He had a job to do, and he was going home.

But first, he had a parting message for the weaklings in Quebec.

LeClaire had failed him, proved a coward when the chips were down. As for the faceless enemy, well, Connolly had wrath enough to go around.

His war was everywhere. Quebec was but a sideshow to the main event, a chance to flex his muscles, but he would not underestimate the enemies.

There would be time enough for letting down his guard when they were dead.

CHAPTER FOUR

It was pushing 10:00 a.m. when Bolan drove his rented van across the Jacques Cartier Bridge, westbound. Ten minutes from the bridge brought him to Longueuil, facing downtown Montreal across the St. Lawrence River.

Bolan's next stop was an "abandoned" factory northwest of town. The neighborhood had long since gone to seed, light industry evacuating in the face of rising taxes and declining income, low-rent housing falling into disrepair. Many of the vehicles that Bolan passed at curbside had been stripped to their rusting skeletons. They sat on naked rims, graffiti-scarred, hoods yawning over vacant engine bays. In more than one, he spotted crouching figures, nursing cans of beer or jugs of bargain-basement wine.

The factory occupied the north end of a block where junk cars had been cleared away, as if in preparation for some new arrivals. Faded placards in the plant's ground-floor windows declared it was For Rent, but there appeared to be no takers.

Bolan circled the block, scanning for lookouts. He could not believe they would let the plant stand unprotected, but any guards on the street were hidden with care. The Executioner would have to take his chances going in.

He left his rental in a narrow alley on the factory's blind side, stepping in back long enough to exchange his blue denim for olive-drab fatigues. He left the M-16 behind this time and chose an Uzi submachine gun, slotting extra magazines and a selection of grenades into the pouches of his combat harness.

The warrior locked the van and pocketed the keys. There was an outside chance that thieves might happen on the vehicle while he was otherwise engaged, but he would have to take that chance. There had been no time to connect alarms or booby-trap the van.

Behind the factory, a combination parking lot and courtyard was enclosed by chain-link fencing. Vandals had been working on the fence with cutters, giving Bolan easy access to the yard at several points, and he was grateful for their help.

Another plus: somone had painted all the windows black, as if to screen the inside of the musty hulk from prying eyes. There could be pinholes in the paint for lookouts, Bolan knew, but there was no way in without the risk of an approach.

The painted windows were a matter of security, but prowlers would not be his adversaries' first concern. According to the information Bolan had obtained from Rick Grant, the ancient factory had been converted to a cutting plant, where shipments of Colombian cocaine and heroin from Southeast Asia were routinely "stepped on" prior to packaging and distribution on the streets.

It was a far cry from the bygone days when radicals had shunned all contact with the system they regarded as reactionary and corrupt. Times change, and revolutionaries all around the world had learned a basic lesson of survival: money talks. It paid for weapons, hideouts, travel documents and protection.

Money made the world go 'round, and once a man convinced himself ends justified the means, his source of income suddenly became irrelevant.

The only thing that mattered was results.

It was a point of view that Bolan understood from living on the edge and waging one-man war against the savages.

He slipped inside the fence and huddled in the shadow of a rusty Dumpster garbage container, considering his options. On the north, across a side street, red brick tenements kept watch with vacant eyes. The place was probably condemned, but even so, it made a handy sniper's nest.

He drifted toward the south and found his angle of attack, a narrow path that ran beneath a fire escape. The ladder was down, dangling a foot or two from the ground.

Not perfect, but it was the best that he could hope for, in the circumstances.

Bolan made his move, a scuttling rush that carried him across the littered courtyard to the south side of the plant. With every step, he half expected gunfire to erupt and cut him down, but he reached his destination unopposed.

He slung the Uzi, scrambled up the rusty ladder to the fire escape and muttered curses as it groaned beneath his weight. If anyone was listening . . .

The factory was four stories tall, and Bolan's information placed the cutting plant on number three. The skinny might be wrong, but Rick Grant had seemed convinced, and the Executioner estimated it was worth a shot.

He gained the third-floor landing, crouched there and pressed one ear against the glass. Nothing.

The warrior took a lightweight gas mask from his belt and slipped it on, adjusting it for comfort with a tug on the retaining straps. He palmed a stun grenade and jerked the safety pin, stepped back a pace and huddled on the fire escape. It was an easy pitch from twelve feet out, a looping overhand. The target window shattered, raining jet-black shards of glass. He ducked and started counting.

The stunner detonated with a blinding flash and thunderclap that dissipated in the open air. Inside the plant, he knew, its impact would be numbing, flattening the opposition long enough for Bolan to achieve his entry.

After that, it would be anybody's game.

He plunged in through the window, tracking with the Uzi, checking out the scene in front of him. A pair of folding picnic tables had been set up end to end, supporting scales and cardboard boxes, plastic sandwich bags and heaps of powder—drugs and baking soda, baby laxative, whatever they were using to dilute the stash these days.

The stun grenade had raised a blizzard in the cutting plant, and Bolan listened to a couple of the groggy workers choking on their product, stripped of their surgical masks by the blast. A fatal overdose was probable, but the Executioner came up short on sympathy.

He heard the outside gunners coming, shouting back and forth with angry, frightened voices, boot heels pounding in the corridor. They jostled one another coming through the door, two shooters packing automatic rifles, while their backup braced a sawed-off 12-gauge at his hip.

The Uzi met them coming in, a blazing figure eight that caught the gunners as they gaped at the scene of chaos. They fell together in a twitching heap, the shotgun artist squeezing off one aimless blast that cleared another windowframe of glass.

The rest was cleanup. He primed a thermite can and dropped it on the nearest table, dodging toward the open window and retreating down the fire escape. He made the second floor before all hell broke loose above him, white-hot phosphorus consuming drugs, flesh and anything at all within its reach.

No message this time, but it hardly mattered. He could always phone it in.

The Executioner was blitzing on.

THE PEOPLE'S BANK of Montreal occupied a prestigious corner lot on Mont Royal, a short block north of Boulevard des Laurentides. It catered to the kind of customers who never asked the price of houses, cars or yachts because they didn't need to ask. No sticker price was ever high enough to leave them short of ready cash.

The very name was a pathetic joke to William Connolly. What kind of "people's" bank would cater to the likes of oilmen, fat-assed lawyers and the owners of suburban shopping malls?

"No reason you should do this job yourself," Breen told him, frowning from his seat behind the gray Toyota's steering wheel. "Why don't you let me take it in? Or Fergus?"

"Never mind. The day I can't do something simple for myself, I'll pack it in."

He reached between his feet to lift the heavy briefcase. He placed it on his lap and opened it, hands steady as he reached inside to set the timer. Even wrapped in plastic, the blocks of Semtex explosive gave off a faint odor of almonds, reminding Connolly of marzipan.

Some treat this lot would be, he reckoned, for those greedy bastards in the bank.

He gave the timer seven minutes, long enough to get him in and out, no extra time for meddling good Samaritans to get themselves involved. He used a tiny silver key to lock the briefcase and left it on the dashboard as he stepped out of the car.

A bus rolled past, trailing diesel fumes, and Connolly crossed the street in its wake. The People's Bank of Montreal was fitted with revolving doors, all glass and close to eight feet tall. Inside, he crossed the spacious lobby, moving toward an island where deposit and withdrawal slips were laid out for convenience of the customers.

He set down the briefcase and nudged it farther underneath the counter with his foot. As casual as could be, he picked up a deposit slip, took one of the ballpoint pens secured to the desk with a chain and pretended to fill out the slip.

Three minutes gone, and counting.

Connolly moved toward the nearest cashier's cage, hesitating en route and glancing at his watch, looking for all the world like a man who has just remembered a critical appointment. Shaking his head and muttering distractedly, he turned and left the bank. He picked up speed as he hit the sidewalk, crossing the street against traffic with blaring horns at his back.

Breen had the engine running, waiting for him, one hand covering the automatic pistol in his lap. He flashed a crooked grin at Connolly.

"All clear?"

"Let's wait and see."

He checked his watch again, and started counting down from forty-seven in his mind. The detonation, when it came, spewed shards of tinted glass and smoking, twisted office furniture into the street. Was that a body draped across the center traffic island? Half of one, at any rate.

"That's it, then?"

Breen had the car in motion, no dramatic peel-out to distract attention from the bank, where oily smoke was pouring from the shattered windows. Cars were slowing across the street, some of them pulling over, drivers checking out the damage.

Eight miles to suburban Dorval and Mirabel International Airport. Flying home was a risk, but their forged travel documents were all first rate, and Connolly was counting on audacity to see him through. If nothing else, the bombing would distract his enemies, a telephone call to the metropolitan police directing their suspicion toward a certain band of traitors who called themselves Groupe de Liberté.

When he was safely home, there would be time enough to set the record straight...or maybe he would leave this project on LeClaire's account. It served the bastard right for posing as a man and acting like a sniveling coward when there was trouble to be faced.

They would be watching out for Connolly in Belfast, not just uniforms, but former friends and lifelong enemies among the paramilitary factions. Even so, he reckoned they would count him too intelligent to show up at the front door with his bare face hanging out. What kind of slinking terrorist would risk himself that way?

The thinking kind.

It was a gamble, granted, but he had the Sword of Erin standing by to cover any bets. The word was out, and he would be expected by the only men on earth he truly called his friends and allies.

Soldiers in the holy cause.

He worried more about the Ulster Volunteer Force and their ilk than a reception party from the SAS or RUC. But most of all, he was concerned about the Provos, knowing they would kill him any time and anywhere they could.

It had been tried before.

He leaned back and closed his eyes. No point in worrying now, when their options were behind them.

William Connolly was hurtling toward the point of no return, and God help anyone who tried to slow him down.

DRIVING INTO BOUCHERVILLE, the Executioner was ready for a shift in strategy. At first, he had been hopeful that GL would give up its Irish allies if he applied sufficient heat. Thus far, there had been no return on his expenditure of energy and ammunition, forcing Bolan to reconsider his methods.

Knowing William Connolly—albeit secondhand, from records that included psychological evaluations—Bolan recognized his ingrained lack of trust for others, most especially for those with personal agendas he could not control. He would allow GL to hide him, but Connolly would always have a backup plan on tap, prepared to cut and run if things went sour.

At the beginning of his blitz in Montreal, Bolan had believed GL was merely hanging tough, committed to resist with everything the organization had. In retrospect, he thought it much more likely that the "friend" from Belfast had performed a crafty disappearing act, leaving his hosts to face the grim music alone.

Connolly's fade, if such it was, left Bolan with a hard choice on his hands. He could proceed with his harassment of GL, in hopes that someone, somewhere, had some answers, or he could regroup and seek another angle of attack. Whichever path he chose, it meant more time, the one commodity that he could least afford right now.

On top of everything, the recent bombing at the People's Bank of Montreal made Bolan's job more difficult. The GL had claimed credit for the blast, and while the Executioner had doubts, his RCMP contact, Rick Grant, was showing signs of strain.

The bombing and his recent strikes in Montreal were almost certainly related. He was no believer in coincidence, especially where wholesale murder was concerned.

The bank bombing had claimed eleven lives, so far. Another twenty-seven victims had been rushed to hospitals in Montreal, at least a third of those so badly injured they were not expected to survive.

The body count made up Bolan's mind for him. If he could not find his Irishman by rattling the Québecois, at least he could repay the bombers for their latest crime against humanity. And if, as he suspected, GL was not responsible, well, there was still a lesson to be learned.

Next time the Sword of Erin or another group of outside terrorists came knocking, asking for a helping hand, the locals would think twice.

For such a special lesson, there was only one place he could go.

This time, the Executioner was starting at the top.

Roch LeClaire had come up through the ranks and managed to escape the heat that sent so many of his comrades to prison. Suspected of complicity in several homicides and other acts of terrorism, he had skated through the raindrops, leading the authorities down one blind alley or another for the past two decades. Creeping up on forty-five, he was the old man of the revolution, still committed to the cause, still dangerous.

The guy was slick, no doubt about it.

He was also running out of time.

The house in Boucherville was larger, more expensive than you might expect for an outspoken socialist and closet revolutionary. The guards were unobtrusive, but Bolan saw them on his drive-by, one on each side of the house, attempting to act casual while crouching under cover of a decorative hedge.

Perfect.

Bolan circled the block and parked his rental in the driveway of a house that stood behind LeClaire's, on a diagonal approach. He wore his faded overalls and had a line of patter ready for the tenants—gas leak in the yard, and so on—but he caught a break when no one answered the bell. He tried again, then knocked just in case.

Nobody home.

The side gate had a latch, but no one bothered with a padlock. Bolan whistled softly for the dog, got no response and let himself into the spacious backyard. A sturdy redwood fence screened the yard from LeClaire's.

He walked to the fence and peered over, standing in the shade of an expansive maple tree. Sliding glass doors at the back of LeClaire's house fronted a concrete patio, but the curtains were drawn. Ditto on what seemed to be a bedroom window, off to Bolan's left. From where he stood, the lookouts were invisible... which meant that he would be invisible to them.

But he would not assume that they were deaf.

The toolbox at his feet gave up a military harness, heavy with its load of ammunition, Desert Eagle side arm and grenades. The Uzi was a good, familiar weight on Bolan's shoulder as he scaled the fence and touched down silently on enemy terrain.

First, the sentries.

He drew the sleek Beretta 93-R from its shoulder rig and cocked the hammer, coming up beside the lookout on the north side of the house. The guy was squatting on his haunches, staring at the street, a riot shotgun propped against the hedge. He never heard Death coming for him, barely registered the silenced Parabellum round at any conscious level as it drilled a hole behind one ear and turned his brain to mush.

It was a gamble, circling back around the house to bag the other outside man. He had to cross the patio, but it was either that or leave the sentry at his post, prepared to slam the door on Bolan once he stepped inside the house.

No choice at all.

He came up on the gunner's blind side, squeezing off another muffled round from fifteen feet away, his target going down like so much dirty laundry on the grass. A neighbor with binoculars might pick out the prostrate bodies, but recognition was another thing entirely and the numbers were falling now.

He listened at the sliding doors and heard music, some kind of easy-listening collection, instrumental versions of Barry Manilow's greatest hits. As Bolan had suspected, they had left the sliding door unlocked, no doubt for the convenience of the sentries in the yard.

He eased it open, just enough to slip inside, and spent a moment shrouded in the drapery before he found a gap and risked a glance into the parlor. On the couch, perhaps ten feet away from where he stood, a chunky man sat with his eyes closed and a beer can in his fist, head back, relaxing to the sounds of music. It was not LeClaire.

He was armed, a pistol sitting on the coffee table just in front of him. The Executioner stepped up behind him, kissing close, and let his 93-R whisper in the sleepy gunner's ear.

Three down. How many left to go?

He followed sounds of conversation to the kitchen, where two young soldiers were rattling pots and pans as they attempted to prepare lunch. The taller of the two saw Bolan and lunged for the shoulder holster draped across a wall hook. A Parabellum round bored through his cheek and dropped him facedown on the floor.

The other would-be chef scooped up a heavy carving knife and threw himself at Bolan with a high-pitched yell. He saw the bullet coming, ran to meet it and was thrown back by explosive impact into the wall.

The Executioner retraced his steps and moved down a hallway toward the bedrooms, hoping that the gunner's dying shout had been eclipsed by the music from the parlor. He was prepared to check each room in turn, kill anyone he met...and then he caught a break. Behind the door immediately to his left, a toilet flushed.

The warrior did not stand on ceremony. Barging in, he caught Roch LeClaire with his pants down—literally. The terrorist fumbled with his trousers, lunging to his feet.

"Sacre—"

The 93-R cut him off in midcurse, two rounds ripping in on target, slamming him back. LeClaire wound up inside the shower, bringing down the plastic curtain as he fell, his feet protruding from the stall, gray trousers bunched around his ankles.

Death with dignity.

And it was time to leave.

Retreating through the charnel house, Bolan already had his mind fixed on the problem of picking up Connolly's trail. It would require some thought, perhaps a knowledgeable contact on the street.

It meant that he would have to have another talk with Rick Grant.

CHAPTER FIVE

"You've had a busy day," Rick Grant commented, as Bolan settled in the Chrysler's shotgun seat.

"So far."

Their meeting had been hastily arranged, Grant waiting for him in the parking lot of a suburban shopping mall. The Executioner had half expected lights and sirens, but he trusted Grant and hoped that trust was mutual.

"I'd recommend you take a breather. Try a change of scene."

"I haven't finished what I came for," Bolan answered.

"That's the problem, friend. We've reached the point of what I think you'd call diminishing returns. The cost is getting too damned high."

"You think GL set off that bomb downtown?"

"It doesn't matter what I think," Grant told him. "The press is running with it now. There's too much heat. I have my orders."

"Namely?"

"End it. Pull the plug. As far as anyone can tell, we've never met. There's nothing in the files, and never will be. Any debt my boss owed your people has been paid in full."

"You've got unanswered questions coming out your ears," Bolan said.

"And it wouldn't be the first time," Grant replied. "If the papers want to sort it out, they're welcome to it. As it stands right now, the bombing is a GL event. As for the rest of it, we leak a story that the radicals are dealing drugs to fatten up their bank account, it comes out looking like a gang war. Everybody wins."

"Not quite."

"You still can't let it go about the Irishman?"

"Could you?"

"Perhaps he ditched GL following your little firefight at the lake house."

Bolan nodded. "I've been thinking that, myself."

"He could be anywhere by now. Across the border, even on a plane."

The same thought had haunted Bolan for the past few hours.

"Right," he said. "Thing is, I can't afford to let him go."

"Who says you have a choice?"

"We all have choices."

"At the moment," Grant informed him, "mine are strictly limited. You haven't hurt us yet, but if the word gets out my people are cooperating with some kind of vigilante effort from the States, well, you can visualize the headlines. My instructions are to offer all assistance necessary for your swift departure from the country. Are we clear on that?"

"As crystal. I was thinking, though..."

"I don't believe I like the sound of that."

"If Connolly *is* gone, I don't believe he'd try the States again this soon. His face is on the wall at every border post between New York and Washington."

"Where, then?"

"In his place," Bolan said, "I think I'd head for home."

"There's nothing I can do to help you there. Try Interpol or Scotland Yard, the Special Branch."

"If Connolly's gone home or means to go there," Bolan said, "he'll need a means of transportation."

"So?"

"With the alert, I don't expect he'll use his given name."

"So what?"

"He lost one bogus passport when they grabbed him in New York. He'll need another if he hopes to make it out of Canada by air."

The Mountie hesitated, frowning. "So?" he asked again.

"So, I suspect you have a line on paperhangers in the province, maybe someone with political connections left of center?"

"It's a possibility."

"It might be worth our while to visit this person."

"My instructions are to wrap this up and see you on your way."

"Exactly," Bolan said. "You want me out of here, and I want to go. The trouble is, I need a destination. If I had a clue where Connolly was going..."

"Belfast, you were saying."

Bolan shrugged. "That's just a guess. To pin it down, I need a solid trail. Now, if I knew what flight he took, the name he used..." Bolan watched as Grant grimaced.

"Think of it as a going-away present," the Executioner suggested. "One for the road."

"And we're quits, then?"

"I'm following Connolly," Bolan assured him. "I don't see his pals coming back anytime soon."

"Amen to that," Grant muttered. "Never would be too damned soon for me."

"You'll help me?"

The Mountie thought about it. "I'll have to make a call or two," he said at last.

"Feel free."

"All right, let's take a ride."

"I'll follow you. My things are in the van."

Grant frowned but made no protest. Bolan left him, walked back to the waiting van and slid behind the wheel. When the RCMP officer pulled out, he followed. The warrior trailed in the Chrysler's wake until they reached a service station, stopped and Grant got out to use the public telephone. More waiting while he made three calls.

It had been close, Bolan thought, gambling on Grant to help him in the face of orders from above. The Mountie would have been within his rights—indeed, he would have been much safer—to reject the Executioner's suggestion and insist he head back to the States. An escort to the nearest border crossing would have been in order.

Still, you paid your money and you took your chances. This time, it had worked.

Rick Grant emerged from the phone booth. Bolan cranked his window down and watched the Mountie approach. "It may not help," he said to Bolan, "but I've got a name."

THIRTY MINUTES out of Belfast the flight attendant approached with her pale green antiterrorism cards, required of every traveler to Northern Ireland. She looked slightly sheepish, handing them to Breen and Connolly, as well she might.

Who would suspect two Catholic priests of being mixed up with the IRA?

It was a laugh for Connolly, traveling in padre's garb. The last time he had set foot in a church with praying on his mind, he had been twelve years old. A short week later, there was Bloody Sunday, gas and gunfire in the streets, troops battering his people to the ground and shooting those who ran.

It was the onset of The Troubles, and the end of life as Billy Connolly had known it for his first twelve years. The IRA was looking for a few good men—or boys—to carry messages, plant ticking parcels on selected doorsteps, carry the dismantled guns and ammunition for their snipers.

Connolly worked his way up through the ranks. He learned to build the bombs, instead of simply carting them around. The first time that he killed a British soldier, firing from a sniper's nest along the Crumlin Road, it was the high point of his life.

And there had been no looking back.

The last time Connolly had been inside a church "on business" as he called it, he was carrying a firebomb in a paper sack. The aging priest—one Father Flaherty—had spoken out against the liberation struggle and ignored suggestions that he find other sermons. There had been no fatalities on that occasion, but it hardly mattered.

Connolly had burned his bridges with the church.

Until today.

He finished filling out the antiterrorism card with flagrant lies and passed the ballpoint pen to Johnny Breen. His signature left "Father Michael Dermott" open to a charge of perjury, but that would be the least of Connolly's problems if he was caught in Northern Ireland. There were murder charges waiting for him, plus the rest of it—enough to put him in prison for several hundred years—but they would have to catch him first.

The clerical disguise included gray around the temples, wire-rimmed glasses, plus a bushy salt-and-pepper mustache. There were brand-new creases in his face, cosmetically applied, together with a faint scar underneath one eye, which he had never seen before that afternoon.

He hardly recognized himself, and that was fine.

Breen had a younger look, but he was also changed. His sainted mother might have known him in a pinch, but Connolly would not have bet his savings on it.

Overhead, the seat belt light winked on. The flight attendant made another pass, collecting green cards and stereo headsets. The aircraft was circling into its final approach, green fields giving way to the familiar urban sprawl of Belfast down below.

It should have felt like home, but Connolly had mixed emotions. Where was home, these days?

The plane touched down and taxied slowly toward the terminal. He made a point of resting easy in his seat as other passengers scrambled for their luggage in the overhead compartments. They would all arrive together, and he saw no need for haste.

"You feel all right?" Breen asked.

"I'm getting there."

They waited for the aisle to clear, and Connolly retrieved his satchel from beneath the seat in front of him. The flight attendant offered him a parting smile and Connolly returned it, wishing her a pleasant day.

And meaning it.

The terminal was crowded, with several flights arriving close together. That could only help, he thought, and if the bloody pigs were waiting for him, it would slow them down.

He showed his passport at the checkpoint, smiled and told the immigration officer that he was looking forward to a two-week church retreat in County Antrim. Pushing through the turnstile, Connolly waited for Breen to catch up. Together, they moved toward the luggage carousel to collect the bags they had checked through from Montreal, for appearance' sake.

Committed terrorists—especially the suicidal Palestinians—had long been known for traveling light and booking one-way tickets in the interest of economy. It was possible to program air line computers to flag suspicious bookings from high-risk points of origin, Northern Ireland included.

Some of the radicals never caught on, but William Connolly was nobody's fool. For the price of a round-trip ticket—actually cheaper than the one-way fare on many routes—his soldiers could travel the world in comparative safety.

Except coming home.

They passed two members of the Royal Ulster Constabulary, top-heavy in the armored vests they were required to wear on duty. Not that any vest would save them from a bomb blast or a clean shot to the head.

He kept up the facade of conversation, nodding to the officers and smiling, hoping it looked more natural than it felt. One of them smiled back at him, then raised two fingers to the bill of his cap in a tidy salute.

Stupid pigs.

He had been watching for surveillance since they cleared the airplane, anything at all to tip him off that they were being shadowed. If the enemy was tracking them, he had to give them credit for their methods. Nothing showed, and Connolly was starting to relax as he approached the baggage carousel.

A nun was waiting for them, rising from a bench and moving out to intercept them. Nineteen months had passed since Connolly last saw her face, and even in the penguin suit she took his breath away.

"How kind of you to meet us, Sister Mary."

"Not at all."

He wondered how the other passengers would feel, what they would say, if he gave in to temptation and embraced her where she stood. Mary Ann Doherty was a sight for sore eyes, and no mistake. The fairest flower of the movement, if he had to say so. Shaking hands with her, he could have sworn he felt a hot electric spark pass between them.

"I hope you had a restful trip," she said, including both of them in the remark.

"It's good to stretch my legs again," Connolly replied. "No problems here?"

"Not one," she told him, wiping off the smile to show him she was serious. "As soon as we pick up your bags, we're on our way."

"That's good to hear."

She stepped closer to him, smiling, dropping her voice to a whisper. "Would you like to know exactly what I'm wearing under this tent, Billy?"

"I'm afraid it wouldn't help me at the moment," he replied.

She laughed and stepped back, turning toward the baggage carousel. "Can you describe your suitcase for me, Father Flaherty?"

"I'll know it when I see it, Sister Mary."

"Grand," she said. "I hope it won't be long."

"You'd be surprised. It's getting longer as we speak."

THE PAPERHANGER WAS Jerome Laurent, a habitual felon with multiple forgery convictions on his rap sheet. Passports were his specialty, but he had also turned a buck on everything from bogus checks and drivers' licenses to stocks and bonds. He had no personal convictions when it came to politics, and his religion was the Holy Dollar.

Laurent lived two blocks south of Broadway, in the northern part of Montreal, and did his printing in a rented loft nearby. He walked to work most days, unless there was a blizzard in the offing, and he jogged on weekends. In another month he would be forty-six years old, but he was still in shape and proud of his physique. He could still attract women with nothing but a smile.

This afternoon he had been working on a relatively simple job, a dozen phony drivers' licenses for members of a local motorcycle gang. He did not know what they intended for the documents and did not care, as long as he was paid on time.

There were attendant risks to dealing with the underworld, of course. Most of those who made their living on the wrong side of the law were bad losers. If someone placed a call to immigration and a runner got arrested at the airport, it was not unknown of his compatriots to blame Laurent, suggesting that his documents were somehow inadequate. In such a case, he never gave the money back—it was his only hard, fast rule—but he occasionally sought to calm a major customer with discounts on some future job.

Thus far, he had been lucky. Dealing with the radicals was worst, because they were completely unpredictable. Without a solid profit motive, living in the world of slogans and ideals, they were often more impulsive than the true professionals he dealt with day to day. They treated him with thinly veiled contempt because he tried to turn a dollar, then complained that he did not work fast enough to meet their needs.

To hell with them.

The job was done, and with a bit of luck he would not hear from them again. The next time they came knocking, if there was a next time, he would quote a price so high the idiots would either stalk out in disgust or come up with sufficient cash to make the aggravation worth his while.

He double locked the loft behind him, passed the elevator and started down the stairs. Four flights, and every bit of exercise was beneficial, keeping up endurance. While Jerome Laurent did not regard himself as a fanatic, he was serious about his body—all the more so since he measured barely five foot four in stockinged feet.

The afternoon was waning as he hit the sidewalk, moving with a steady gait along the boulevard. It tickled him to pass the straight-laced businessmen and women, wondering what kind of secrets they concealed behind bland faces, shifting eyes.

If any of them knew what *he* knew, they would be amazed.

The notion brought a smile to Laurent's face.

He climbed the narrow stairs to his apartment, opened double locks with different keys and secured the door behind him once inside. Too late, his nostrils caught the pungent odor of tobacco in the living room, where no one was allowed to smoke.

He turned back toward the door, had one hand on the knob, the other on the dead bolt, when a strange voice spoke behind him.

"Don't run off, Jerome. You just came in."

Laurent turned back to face the prowler, spotting two of them. The smoker leaned against the breakfast counter in his smallish kitchen, while another, larger man stood watching from the bedroom door. They did not look like thugs, but the taller man had solemn, graveyard eyes.

A killer, certainly, but Laurent could not guess on whose behalf.

"Who are you?" He started with the basics, hoping that he sounded calm.

The smoker made a pass with some kind of ID and badge, too far away for Laurent to identify. "Police," he said. "We need a moment of your time."

"What happened to the warrant, then? Did someone scrap the constitution since I left for work this morning?"

"It's your work we want to talk about," the smoker said. "A short talk, really. Warrants take up so much time and energy."

"May I telephone my lawyer?"

"Maybe later."

This was bad, but Laurent kept his cool. He had no way of knowing whether these were actually police— and he had known a few policemen who were worse than any thug. He would have to keep his fingers crossed and find out what they wanted.

"So." He crossed the room and sat down in his favorite easy chair. "What do you want from me?"

"A bit of information," the smoker said. He moved closer, stopping just in front of Laurent. His large companion sat down on the couch beside Laurent.

"You've tried directory assistance, have you?" Humor in adversity was a sign of courage.

"That's a good one, Jerry. Actually I've checked your file instead. It makes good reading. I noticed you're a three-time loser, for example. Next time out, the court is bound to add an extra fifteen years for the habitual offender."

"Next time?" Laurent kept the tremor from his voice. "I haven't been charged with anything that I'm aware of."

"Fifteen years, assuming that it ever gets to court," the smoker went on. "A case like this, it's not unknown for someone on the street to settle it himself, before the matter ever comes to trial."

"I won't pretend to follow what you're saying."

"No? Well, maybe we should spell it out for you."

The smoker glanced at his companion, and the large man scooted forward, bracing elbows on his knees. "Groupe de Liberté," he said.

"And what are they to me?"

"They gave you a referral," the smoker said. "Maybe more than one. We're looking for the Irishman."

"Is that supposed to be a name?" He felt the perspiration trickling underneath his arms but did not let it show.

The smoker palmed a sheaf of photographs and spread them on the coffee table. Laurent saw five faces. Two of them were familiar at a glance.

"I don't suppose your customers are big on names," the smoker said. "I'll bet you always get to see them, though. Right, Jerry?"

"This is flagrantly illegal," Laurent complained.

"That means we've struck a nerve," the smoker said to his companion.

Turning back to Laurent, he instructed, "Just you pick the faces, now, and fill us in on what you sold them."

Laurent shrugged. "I'm sure I don't know what you mean."

The smoker sighed and cast a rueful glance toward his friend on the couch. "That's it, then," he declared. "I've done the best I can."

Without a word, the large man rose and approached Laurent. He placed the muzzle of the automatic pistol in his hand against the forger's temple and cocked the hammer.

"One more time," the tall man said.

It might have been a bluff, but Laurent did not think so. He had looked into those killer eyes and seen his death.

"All right," he blurted. "Wait. The two men on the right. I don't know who they are. They didn't give their names."

"But you provided them with new ones, am I right?" A sly smile played across the smoker's face. "What was it, Jerry? Passports? Visas?"

"Passports."

"I'll want those names," the smoker told him, fishing in a pocket of his sport coat for a pen and notebook.

Leaning forward cautiously, the pistol hovering an inch or so behind him, Laurent tapped the photo of the younger man. "He's traveling as Michael Dermott. The older one has ID in the name of Joseph Flaherty."

"Did they mention where they might be going?"

Laurent shook his head, imagining a bullet ripping through his skull. "My customers don't normally confide in me."

"A good thing, too," the smoker said. "You're no great shakes at keeping secrets, are you, Jerry?"

Both men were on their feet now, no guns showing as they drifted toward the door. The large man stepped outside before the smoker, his companion turning back to have a final word.

"I'm thinking you might want to file a grievance, Jerry. It's within your rights, of course. With any luck, I might get called out to investigate the charge." His smile was predatory. "Have a nice day, Jerry. I'll be seeing you."

CHAPTER SIX

Belfast, Northern Ireland

It was down to counting days for Sergeant Jason Hardwicke now. The first six months in Belfast, it was hard to think of going home in concrete terms. You went out on patrol and did your job, continually looking forward to relief, but with a year to serve in Northern Ireland it was self-defeating to allow distracting thoughts of home. The second six months, winding down, you started checking off the weeks, and finally, with thirty days to go, the chance of going home alive assumed a measure of reality.

There were enough who never made it, Hardwicke realized, and some of them had been his friends. A rifle shot from nowhere with the column on patrol, and when you looked around to check your men, there was a body lying in the middle of the street. Or maybe it was gasoline bombs cascading from a rooftop as soldiers passed on foot. Perhaps a pound of plastique with a radio receiver, stuffed inside the corner mailbox, waiting for a spotter in a flat across the street to beam a signal on command.

He was disgusted with the whole damned country, bitter toward the people on both sides of its enduring struggle. As a subject of the queen, he was expected to support the loyalist Protestants, but it was hard to tell the terrorists apart in Belfast, once you stripped them of religious labels.

Theoretically he had only to fear the nationalist IRA and its affiliated groups, all Catholic, since the Protestants supported British intervention. At the same time, he had dealt with victims of the Ulster Volunteer Force, the Ulster Defense Association and similar Protestant groups. In Hardwicke's view, it made no difference who pulled the trigger on a pistol or pressed the drill bit through their kneecaps.

"Keep your intervals back there," he warned the troops spread out behind him. Seven young men, two of them green rookies, waited for instructions from the sergeant who had seen it all within eleven months of duty.

They were coming up on Old Lodge Road from Carrick Hill, the barracks well behind them on North Queen Street. This was the heart of enemy territory, where British soldiers were concerned. How many troops had fallen on this very street to snipers' bullets, flying shrapnel and the like since 1969?

No matter. Hardwicke brought his mind back to the present. Distraction in this neighborhood of Belfast was the quickest way to buy himself a one-way ticket back to Yorkshire in a body bag. A foot patrol in Paddyland was not the place to think about your dirty laundry or the girl you left behind.

He saw the station wagon from a block away, outside a pawnshop, and he frowned. The shops on both sides of the street had closed for the night, and parking was forbidden in this district due to the pervasive threat of car bombs. Any unattended vehicles were subject to removal or destruction, at the military's option, and a driver sitting in his car at curbside for more than five minutes could expect a grilling and possible arrest.

He raised a hand to halt the column, stabbed a finger three times toward the far side of the street. Without a spoken word, three members of his team peeled off and took the other sidewalk, holding their position, waiting for the order to advance.

From where the sergeant stood, no occupants were visible inside the station wagon. There was no one loitering along the curb, and no one visible in any of the nearby shops. He felt the first small worm of dread uncoiling in his stomach and determined not to let it get away from him.

Cars stalled, in spite of posted rules and regulations. Christ, if he had gone to jail each time his ancient Beamer threw a fit back home, his record would have rivaled any gangster's out of Birmingham or Manchester.

Still, this was Belfast, and a British soldier who took anything for granted was a dead man walking.

Hardwicke started forward, motioning his troops to follow him with care. He paused again, with half a block to go before they reached the station wagon, checking out the shops and darkened windows on the upper stories, left and right.

He ought to call the bomb squad now, but he did not want to panic, look the fool in front of his subordinates. A glimpse inside the wagon wouldn't hurt, and he could tell if there were any bulky packages or drums of homemade gelignite inside. Once he completed the reconnaissance, there would be time enough to call the barracks for advice and have them send a tow truck or the demolition team, whichever they preferred.

"I'm going to have a look," he said to Corporal Smythe. "You lot stay put and watch yourselves."

"Yes, sir."

It was not any kind of macho power trip that urged him forward. Rather, Hardwicke had a rule of never asking his men to do a job he would not do himself. The rookies in his squad would still be his responsibility for three more weeks, until he went back home, and this would show them that their sergeant had the balls to do a job himself. The next time out, when Hardwicke ordered one of them to check an empty car or scout an intersection where the streetlights had gone out, they would have no cause for resentment of the task.

Another moment brought him to the station wagon. Peering through the windows, front and back, he saw no parcels or suspicious objects in the vehicle. Of course, there were a hundred different ways the bastards could disguise a bomb—it might be underneath the seats, or strapped beneath the chassis, near the gas tank. Hardwicke found that he was standing rigid, like a statue, barely breathing, and he made himself relax.

It was a tow job, from the looks of it, but he would let headquarters make the call.

He turned back toward his men, stepped off the curb and felt a giant fist slam dead between his shoulder blades. The flak vest saved him, but the bullet's impact pitched him forward on the asphalt with sufficient force to crack his teeth together, warm blood spurting from his nose.

Goddamn it! Sniper!

By the time he heard the echo of the rifle shot, the sergeant knew that they had walked into a trap. Not one man with a rifle, that would be too easy. From his awkward vantage point, he heard the sound of several weapons firing overhead, one of them fully automatic, pouring fire into the street below.

His men were trying to return fire with their XL-70 ES Individual Weapons, aiming short bursts toward the buildings around them, scoping on bright muzzle-flashes, but two of them were already down, unmoving on the pavement. Hardwicke started worming back toward the station wagon, knowing it was simply bait to set them up. If he was quick and smart enough, he might surprise the bastards, use their own stage prop to save himself.

He hoped that Marston had been able to radio for help. The barracks wasn't that far off, in terms of mounting rescue efforts. They could send a Saracen or two for cover, with an ambulance. The snipers would not tarry long if there was any danger of arrest.

He wormed his way beneath the station wagon, breathing easier with solid steel above him. All he had to do was wait now, for the cavalry to come and save the day.

With all the gunfire in the street, he barely heard the whirring of the fuse eight inches from his head. It hardly mattered, either way, for there was nothing he could do, nowhere to run.

The sergeant's Belfast tour stopped short with twenty-seven days remaining, as the fuse ran down and seven pounds of plastique fastened to the station wagon's gas tank exploded in his face.

"I WAS AFRAID the seminary might have spoiled you, Father, but I see it hasn't damaged you at all."

There was laughter in Mary Ann Doherty's voice, and something like fatigue. She rolled away from

Connolly and reached out for a glass of water on the nightstand by her bed.

"I think I've gone to heaven," Connolly replied.

He had removed the makeup and his priestly garb as soon as he arrived in Mary Ann's apartment. There was still a trace of artificial gray around his temples, but the better part of it had come out in the shower, where they grappled in a swirl of suds before retiring to the bed.

"You put the fear of God in me, and no mistake," she told him, rolling back to face him, round breasts flattening against his chest. "I think you missed me just a little."

"Rubbish." But he smiled and drew her closer as he said it, and she knew that he was playing with her, teasing.

"Can you stay this time?"

"I don't know yet," he told her honestly. "I doubt it."

"Will it never end?"

"When the bloody Brits go home," he said, "and we have time to settle up a few old scores." .

That said it all. The British were his enemies, of course, but they were not alone. Before he had a prayer of living peacefully in Belfast, Connolly would have to purge his other enemies—not only Protestants, but members of the Provo camp who marked him as a traitor to the nationalist cause.

"It would be nice to have some time alone," Mary Ann said, "without the rest of it to think about."

"You're going soft, girl."

"So are you." She giggled, reaching for him underneath the sheets.

"You have to let me catch my breath."

"You never have a chance," she answered, turning solemn. "Seamus wants you worse than any Brit that I can think of."

"That's no lie."

Seamus Mulavey was the Provisional IRA's brigade commander in Belfast, a former comrade of Connolly's, sworn to destroy him after Connolly defected to create the Sword of Erin. More than three years had passed since the former friends had seen each other, face to face, and each was pledged to kill the other on sight.

"He came to see me, Billy."

"When?"

"The day we heard about your good luck in the States. He reckoned I might know when you were coming home."

"It's lucky you're alive."

"He doesn't hold a grudge with me, the way he does with you. It's so damned personal."

"He thinks I sold him out. I know the truth."

"Which is?" She knew the answer in advance, but asking it was almost mandatory, in the circumstances.

"That he's let the movement lose direction, lose momentum. Christ, it's not just twenty-five or thirty years," he said. "The IRA's been running in the same rut since the Easter rising."

"I could set him up for you, I'd bet," Mary Ann said.

"I'll think about it."

Seamus was a problem, granted, but he was not the priority. Mulavey and his Provos were a constant danger, like the British street patrols, but neither held the key to victory for William Connolly. Fresh out of jail and on the run, he needed something more dramatic to regain the ground that he had lost, these eighteen months.

The boys were out that very moment, waking up the Brits, but that was just for starters. In the next few days, he meant to shake their house down, pay them back for all the aggravation he had suffered, sitting in a prison cell.

They did not know who they were dealing with. Not yet.

But they were bound to learn.

"You haven't told me your plans," Mary Ann said.

"That's right, I haven't."

"So, we're keeping secrets now?"

"I wouldn't want to ruin the surprise."

She made a show of pouting. "I'm supposed to be your revolutionary equal, am I not?"

"I trust you with my life," he said, and meant it. "When we're ready to begin, I'll let you know."

"It won't be long, I hope."

"Not long."

Her fingers teased him. "Maybe I was wrong," she said. "You've not gone soft at all."

"One more surprise," he answered, reaching for her.

"Mmm. It's right then, what they say."

"What's that?"

"A hard man's good to find."

A DRIZZLING RAIN was falling over Shankill Road as John Breen's raiding party motored north between the rows of darkened, silent homes. Breen rode the shotgun seat and held a folding-stock Kalashnikov across his lap, a double magazine secured with electrician's tape. Behind him, in the back seat of the stolen Volvo, two young soldiers from the Sword of Erin smoked and kept their automatic weapons close at hand.

They were deep behind enemy lines at the moment, a distinction that amounted to the difference of a city block or two in Belfast. Catholics and Protestants in Northern Ireland had been waging war on one another with relentless zeal since 1969, their basic conflict dating back three centuries to Sir Arthur Chichester's ouster of the original Gaelic rulers. Any thought of peace was so remote that it was banished to the status of a dream. Whole generations in the neighborhood had grown up knowing nothing but war.

The Shankill Road had earned its bloody reputation as a "no-go" area for Belfast Catholics and a breeding ground for fledgling members of the paramilitary Ulster Volunteer Force. In the 1970s, a gang that called itself the Shankill Butchers killed and mutilated some two dozen Catholic victims lifted off the streets at random in a gruesome sideshow to the never-ending holy war.

The Butchers were in prison now, their leader executed in a drive-by shooting by the IRA, but they were not alone. The very name of Shankill Road was uttered almost as a curse in Catholic circles, and it had been Breen's idea to strike here, in the heart of Orangeland, as a token of the Sword of Erin's strength.

"Up there," he told the driver. "Next block, on your right."

The pub was called O'Leary's, and it catered to the kind of toughs who staffed the UVF and UDA. There were at least a score of taverns like it in the city, Protestant and Catholic, where the hardmen gathered over pints of stout to recount their latest victories, plot future raids and vote death warrants on their enemies.

"Make sure you keep the engine running, Tommy."

"I know how to do it, John." The driver, a dedicated soldier of the cause with two kills to his credit, would be nineteen if he lived to see his birthday in September.

"Sure, I never doubted it at all."

Breen flicked off the safety on his Kalashnikov and reached for the inside handle of his door. The car was slowing through the intersection, braking gradually, until it double-parked outside O'Leary's, flanked by streetlights. Passersby would have no trouble making out the license plate, and that was fine—it had been stolen from another vehicle.

Breen swiftly yanked his knit cap down, the built-in ski mask covering his face. In fact, he didn't give a damn if he was seen and linked to this night's work, but there were young men present, and he had to serve as an example.

Stepping from the car, he waited for the others to flank him. They stepped up to the curb, three men abreast, their weapons leveled at the pub.

"Let's do it."

As he spoke, Breen squeezed the trigger of his AK-47, raking the front of O'Leary's tavern with a stream of 7.62 mm bullets. On his left and right, the youngsters cut loose with an Uzi and an M-16, respectively, their bright, sharp muzzle-flashes stabbing the night. He saw the blacked-out windows of the pub implode, a swarm of divots etched across the oaken door and brick facade. Spent cartridges made clear metallic music at his feet.

Inside the bar, he had a glimpse of bodies falling, patrons diving from their stools or sprawling limp as bullets ripped their flesh. A neon sign behind the bar exploded in a shower of sparks, the ranks of bottles detonating in a cataract of alcohol.

The Kalashnikov's first magazine was spent within four seconds of intensive fire. Breen took a heartbeat to reverse it, cock the AK-47, shifting slightly for a better view of the interior.

Behind the bar, a bearded giant hauled himself erect and aimed a stubby shotgun toward the street. Breen met him with a burst that ripped his face off, spinning him and dropping him from sight.

As the youngsters reloaded, Breen stepped in closer, looking for a solid target. There was movement in the murky room, but it was hard to tell which patrons had been only wounded in the first barrage.

He saw a man and woman huddled near a capsized table and raked them with a burst that set their bodies twitching on the floor. Across the pub, a wounded man was hobbling toward the toilets. Breen unleashed a burst that cut his legs from under him.

The youngsters opened up again, their weapons hammering in unison, dismantling the tavern's jukebox, chairs and tables, ceiling fixtures, knocking great holes in the bar. Breen did not have to check his watch to know that they were pushing it, endangering themselves by lingering too long.

"Grenades!" he barked, retreating two long paces toward the car.

The youngsters reached inside their jacket pockets for the NATO-issue fragmentation grenades that had been stolen from a base in Spain and traded to the Sword of Erin by the Basque separatist ETA movement. They pulled the pins, wound up and pitched in unison, the round eggs vanishing inside O'Leary's.

"Right! Let's go!"

They scrambled for the Volvo, piling in, the car in motion by the time Breen slammed his door. He watched his mirror, grinning fiercely as the twin explosions lit the street, a cloud of smoke and dust erupting from the tavern's shattered windows, blanketing the sidewalk.

"We taught the bloody Prods a lesson this time," Joey Flynn exulted. "They'll remember this awhile, the bastards."

"So they will," Breen agreed, but even as he spoke the smile was fading from his face.

It was a start, and nothing more. There was a chance that they had tagged some members of the UVF or UDA, but no one lying back there in the rubble of O'Leary's would be irreplaceable to the Protestant cause. More to the point, the Prod paramilitaries were only a peripheral issue in the grand scheme of things, when it came to plotting strategy for the Sword of Erin's future.

Britain was the major enemy, her occupying troops the shield that kept a hated and repressive regime in place, daily flaunting discrimination against Ulster's Catholic population. Before the government could fall, the troops would have to go.

The key, he had agreed with William Connolly, would not be found in Belfast. For a quarter century the IRA had tried to wear down the British by sniping soldiers in the streets or planting bombs in London at the Christmas rush. Breen himself had participated in that sort of thing—and would again, he had no doubt—but it would take a more substantial blow to make the British abandon their colonial pursuits.

In Breen's opinion, it took a clean shot to the heart . . . or perhaps the head.

When they had taught their enemies that no one was safe, regardless of rank or station, then they might allow the inevitable vote to let the northern counties run their own affairs.

That day was coming, and the Sword of Erin was prepared to strike the telling blow to hasten its arrival.

Breen's smile reappeared, relaxed now, lacking the ferocity of his expression moments earlier. He felt himself at peace, but there was also a persistent thrill of yearning. Sweet anticipation.

The terrorist could hardly wait.

CHAPTER SEVEN

Dublin, Ireland

The one advantage of a transatlantic airline flight, Bolan thought, was the chance to catch up on his sleep. With seven hours in the air from Montreal to Dublin, there was nothing he could do in concrete terms to prep himself for his arrival on the Emerald Isle.

He slept and dreamed of disembodied faces—some familiar, others vague and strange, belonging, he felt certain in his dream, to people he would never know. He did not know if they were ghosts or victims yet to be. Their silence left him feeling empty, at a loss for answers to the questions their imploring eyes appeared to ask.

He woke when his ungainly seatmate rose to use the rest room, gouging Bolan with an elbow. There was no apology forthcoming, but the warrior did not mind. It was a definite relief to be aroused from such a dream, and he was glad to put the silent faces out of mind.

The in-flight movie had concluded, and the lights were on again. His fellow passengers were stirring restlessly, while flight attendants made the rounds with soft drinks, juice and candied peanuts. Bolan smiled and shook his head, and the snack cart passed him by.

According to his watch, they had another forty minutes left before they touched the ground at Dublin Airport. He would be glad to put the flight behind him, but what followed was uncertain. Apprehension gnawed at the corners of his mind.

For starters, he was traveling unarmed. He could have pulled the necessary strings in Washington to land a military flight, but that meant driving back to the United States and wasting time he did not have to spare. Aer Lingus took a dim view of its passengers transporting military hardware, and he knew about security in Dublin. Secrecy was part of Bolan's plan, and his strategy did not include alerting every member of the Garda Siochana in the city to his presence.

He was only passing through, in any case. The capital of Ireland was a launching pad for his campaign, and nothing more.

It would have saved time for him to land in Belfast, but he had decided on the roundabout approach for reasons of security. It cost him several hours, but he hoped that it would ultimately help him reach his destination unobserved.

Brognola had arranged for his reception by a member of the SAS—the British army's elite Special Air Service, which had become the front-line unit in combating terrorism anywhere in the United Kingdom. It had taken some debate, from what he gathered, to convince the Britons that they should help an American hunt federal fugitives on Irish soil, but Brognola was at his best when cutting deals and pulling strings.

Bolan wondered how he would be received. Elite units like the SAS—or the American Delta Force, for that matter—were notoriously protective of their powers, jurisdiction and authority. Cooperation ran against the grain, and handing over carte blanche to a stranger was unprecedented in the Executioner's experience.

He hoped that he could find a common cause with his appointed watchdog, get the officer to trust him— or, at least, to stay out of his way.

His last, best hope revolved around the common enemy. The Sword of Erin had been on a roll the past few years, its members slipping through official dragnets for the most part, no more than a handful killed or captured by authorities. When William Connolly was taken in New York, it was regarded as a major blow against his band of terrorists. His escape had been a bitter pill to swallow.

The British government had lived with Irish terrorism, one way or another, since the Fenians brought dynamite to London in the middle of the nineteenth century. It was an old game, with attrition on both sides, but outlaw radicals were often better at maintaining their morale. They had a holy cause to fight for, a commitment to the hoped-for day of victory, and they replenished thinning ranks with new recruits from neighborhoods where fratricidal warfare had become a way of life.

Such men would not negotiate, and they could rarely be converted to another point of view. That left the killing option, if the people and their government were willing to pursue the fight to its conclusion.

Sometimes, when they faltered, it was Bolan's job to pick up where the law left off.

A disembodied voice announced that they were starting the approach to Dublin and another quarter hour would see them on the runway. Bolan shifted and peered out the window, seeing only clouds. He could not see the North Atlantic, much less any sign of land.

How long from Dublin to the border? His guidebook made it close to sixty miles, another forty-something from the border checkpoint on to Belfast proper. If his tour guide was a halfway decent driver, they could make it in two hours, with a bit of time to spare.

The clouds were breaking as they descended from their cruising altitude of thirty thousand feet. Below him, cultivated fields and grassy meadows were divided by ancient stone walls, dotted with the ant-sized shapes of grazing sheep and cattle. Here, a horse-drawn wagon toiled along a one-lane road while motor vehicles pulled off to let it pass. A few miles farther on, their fleeting shadow fell across a farmer working in his field, his vintage tractor looking like a Matchbox toy.

Dublin Airport was located seven miles north of the city, separated from the capital of Ireland by a pleasant taxi ride through rolling fields and residential suburbs. That was in the opposite direction from his final destination, though. With any luck, he would not have to backtrack into Dublin with his escort.

Bolan latched his seat belt when the light came on above him, and heard the aircraft's landing gear descend and lock in place. He would not have to wait much longer.

Once his feet were firmly planted on the ground, he knew, the killing game would start anew. No quarter asked or offered by his enemies.

WHEN HE RECEIVED his orders for the meet at Dublin Airport, Captain Darren Finch had not been pleased. He had no grudge against the Yanks, but there was work enough for him to do in Belfast and environs without baby-sitting foreign tourists.

One thing had peaked his interest, though—a reference to the Sword of Erin and its leader, William Connolly. Finch knew about the screwup in New York, where Connolly had left the FBI and U.S. marshals with egg on their faces and brains in their laps. It was the kind of insult the Americans took seriously, and their first reaction was to reach out for the men responsible with clutching hands.

Finch sympathized with that reaction, though his training and assignment rarely gave him any opportunity for venting private anger or frustration. Propaganda headlines and the whole Gibraltar mess aside, his unit rarely confronted the paramilitary troops of either side in Northern Ireland. Most often, Finch and company were sent on wild-goose chases, seeking arms dumps, hostages, a rumored bomb or two. They came up empty more than half the time, looking like idiots.

It would be satisfying, he agreed, to seize one of his adversaries by the neck and shake him until his fillings rattled. William Connolly would be a perfect candidate for some rough justice, but wishing it and seeing something done about the problem were two very different things.

His orders from the major had surprised Finch. He had been instructed to provide the Yank—one man, for God's sake—with all possible assistance in his search for Connolly and friends. When Finch had asked to have the order clarified, he was informed it meant exactly what it said.

That whet his appetite, no doubt about it, but he still had reservations. Being turned loose on the enemy was one thing; being saddled with a Yank who didn't know his rosy rectum from a gopher hole was quite another. Finch had already decided he would cut the stranger loose before he put his own life on the line in some misguided grandstand play.

He checked the wall clock in the terminal against his watch and was rewarded seconds later, when a voice announced arrival of the Aer Lingus flight from Montreal. He drifted toward the immigration line, avoiding the security equipment with a flash of his ID. There was no point in taking chances, even in a building known for its security. He trusted the Beretta automatic in his shoulder holster more than all the Gardai stationed in the terminal.

Finch had no photograph of his connection, just a brief description from the major, but he wore a white carnation in his buttonhole for purpose of recognition. Let the mark find him, and if they somehow missed each other, that was that. It might be better all around if—

Captain Finch was checking out the crowd when one man caught his eye. The new arrival had an athlete's build, a solemn face with eyes that made you take a second look. He wore an understated business suit and had a raincoat draped across one arm. A well-worn leather satchel hung from his hand. The sharp gray eyes homed in on Finch's white carnation, and the tall man veered toward the captain.

"Mike Belasko," the stranger said.

"Darren Finch." Their handshake was a brief formality. "Good flight?"

"As long flights go."

"Do you have luggage?"

"This is it." Bolan held up his satchel.

"Right. My car's outside."

The name would be an alias, of course. Americans tacked code names onto everything. It was a kind of mania that gave them the appearance of omniscience, even when they had their information upside down and backward.

Finch devoutly hoped that his companion was not from the CIA. It was a long shot, granted, but the Company involved itself in terrorism now and then, investigating different groups, arranging for arrests on foreign soil.

This blighter, though, was not about to slap Will Connolly in irons. If Finch's brief instructions from his major had been accurate, the Yank had rather different—and more final—plans.

He meant to step on Connolly the way you would a bug—with Darren Finch providing "all assistance possible."

It did not trouble Finch to be involved in what amounted to a murder plot. He had already seen what happened when the likes of Connolly was jailed awaiting trial. Rough justice from the barrel of a gun was all a terrorist deserved, in his opinion, but it galled him that his government would give the job to Yanks and take a secondary role to an operation in their own front yard.

If the prime minister's office or the palace wanted William Connolly removed, they could have called on Finch. He could have saved them all the cost of ferrying a Yank across the Atlantic and acquainting him with unfamiliar territory.

Not to reason why, Finch told himself as they emerged from Dublin terminal and caught an unexpected ray of sun. His car was in the nearest lot, a sticker on the window. He walked around the driver's side, slid in behind the wheel and opened Bolan's door.

Emerging from the parking lot, Finch paid his ticket and motored right around the airport, picking up the northbound highway at its proper exit. As they cleared the airport, he kept one eye on the rearview mirror, watching for a tail.

All clear.

"We ought to reach the border in an hour," he announced, "unless you need to stop for anything."

"I'm fine," Bolan replied.

"First time in Ireland?"

"No."

"Some of the others in my regiment have grown to hate the country, but I'm rather fond of it, myself. You can't blame everybody for a handful of fanatics running wild."

"True."

Finch hesitated, feeling like the odd man out at some pathetic cocktail party.

"You're American, they said."

"That's right."

"I thought there might be some mistake," Finch said.

"How's that?"

"The Yanks I've met before, the only way to stop them talking was to pour a fresh pint down their lug hole. Reckon you're the silent type we hear so much about but seldom see."

That brought a smile to Bolan's lips. "I had a question, now you mention it, but I was waiting for the proper time."

"No time like the present," Finch replied.

"Okay. I came across without equipment. My connection told me I could pick up what I needed here, from you."

"I've got a bit of hardware waiting for you in the trunk, right now," Finch said. "We can find whatever else you need in Belfast, as you go along."

"Sounds fair."

"My pleasure," the captain said, letting just a trace of cynicism creep into his tone. "You're doing us a favor, I'm informed."

"Let's wait and see how things turn out. It might not look that way tomorrow."

Finch frowned and came directly to the point. "You reckon Connolly's come home?"

"Unless he swapped his latest phony passport to a ringer back in Montreal, I'm positive. He came in late last night as Father Joseph Flaherty. John Breen was riding with him—make that Father Michael Dermott."

"That's a hot one. Well, they won't be saying any kind of Mass today. You'll have to root them out from under on their own home ground."

"Or find someone to do it for me," Bolan answered.

Having said that much, he leaned back in his seat and closed his eyes.

THE BORDER CHECKPOINT seemed to come up out of nowhere, rubber cones and barricades arranged to choke the flow of traffic down to one lane headed north. It might have been a typical construction site, except for all the soliders in the Kevlar helmets, camouflage fatigues and flak vests, checking out each car in turn with fingers on the triggers of their automatic weapons. Bolan watched as a Toyota three cars up the line was pulled aside and soldiers started poking through the contents of the trunk.

"About that hardware," Bolan said.

"No worries," Finch assured him. As he spoke, the SAS commando slipped a hand inside his sport coat and withdrew a laminated card. He waited while a sergeant with an automatic rifle came up on the driver's side.

"Passports, please."

Finch handed him the card and said, "This ought to cover it."

The soldier examined the card, glanced at Finch, then craned his neck to get a better look at Bolan in the shotgun seat. His mustache could not hide the makings of a frown.

The sergeant moved back along the line and huddled with an officer near the barricades. Bolan fought the urge to question Finch, returned the searching stares and watched the sergeant make his way back toward their vehicle. He bent down and gave the laminated card to Finch.

"That's all we need, sir. Thanks." Before he straightened, the sergeant grinned and said, "Good hunting."

They rolled past the checkpoint, moving north past villages that gradually merged, becoming suburbs, running into Belfast on the highway that became Botanic Road.

"Might as well get used to the surroundings," he remarked. "We're coming up on Donegal Square just ahead."

They passed a Saracen armored personnel carrier, with two RUC squad cars following the larger vehicle like ducklings trailing their mother. British soldiers and uniformed police were visible around the square, but numerous pedestrians ignored them as they went about their business. If not for Gaelic street signs and the placards hung in front of several shops, the tableau could have passed for any blighted inner city in the States. Around them, walls were daubed with bright graffiti—not the revolutionary slogans Bolan was expecting, but attacks on Jews and blacks, complete with swastikas, inverted pentagrams and SS lightning bolts. Among the shoppers, secretaries, businessmen and tourists, strutting skinheads glowered from the curb and drank from bottles camouflaged by paper bags.

"Not quite what you expected, eh?" Finch said.

"You read my mind."

"We used to have two or three groups taking shots at each other, the Prods and the Catholics," Finch said. "Today, it's a dozen at least—vigilantes, the skinheads, what have you. God knows where they come from. They drink themselves stupid and go out to look for a target."

Moving on, Finch treated Bolan to a tour of the more traditional hot spots in Belfast—Shankill, Crumlin Road, Falls Road, the army barracks on North Queen Street, the Courts of Justice at Chichester and Oxford. Portions of the Protestant and Catholic enclaves had the look of postwar Germany, with burned-out vehicles and fire-scarred, soot-stained buildings. Here, the slogans painted on the walls were vintage Northern Ireland: Up the IRA! Brits Go Home!

They passed the sites of bombings, drive-by shootings, riots and assassinations. Finch kept up a running commentary through it all, directing Bolan to points of interest. At more than one, they were met with hostile stares. It was the kind of frank hostility to strangers found in neighborhoods where residents were used to living with violence.

Along the way, Finch also pointed out the favorite lairs of local paramilitary groups—the Provos, UVF and UDA, the Sword of Erin. Bolan memorized the shops, cafés and pubs, row houses and apartment buildings where ready targets could be found at need.

"So what's the program?" Finch asked Bolan as they circled back toward Grosvenor Street.

The Executioner was ready for the question. "How much do you really want to know?"

"Your choice. My orders are to help you out the best I can."

"I'll need a place to stay, some unobtrusive wheels and the hardware that we talked about."

"No problem. We've got several quiet flats around the city and a fair reserve of vehicles for stakeouts. Weapons shouldn't be a problem."

"Fine."

"It's up to you, of course," the captain said, "but it occurs to me it might be easier for me to help you if I knew what you were doing."

Bolan thought about it for a block or so before he spoke. "You know I'm after William Connolly?"

"They told me that much when I got my orders."

"And I'm not concerned with extradition or arrest."

"He's made his bed," Finch replied. "The lot of them can go to bloody hell for all I care. I'm more concerned with how you plan to pull it off."

"My information is that Connolly and his boys from Sword of Erin have been feuding with the Provos."

"That's an understatement. The IRA has had a contract out on Billy for the past two years. My guess would be they hate him worse than any British soldier in the country. He's a renegade and traitor to the Provies, right enough.''

''So, that's my handle,'' Bolan said. ''Divide and conquer, or at least upset their apple cart.''

''Sounds risky. It could run away from you unless you're careful.''

Driving past a warehouse, Bolan focused on a mural that depicted men in stocking masks, with automatic rifles raised above their heads. The lurid caption told him Provies Rule!

He turned back toward his escort. ''That's a chance I'll have to take.''

CHAPTER EIGHT

Belfast, Northern Ireland

Bolan waited for nightfall to make his first move. In the meantime, he had checked the flat off York Street, in a neighborhood that passed for neutral, moving in the bags of ordnance Finch provided from his covert stash. Selected items of the hardware stayed in Bolan's latest car, a compact Ford.

He had a list of targets, complete with photographs, addresses and telephone numbers, including members of the PIRA, Sword of Erin and the major Protestant terrorist gangs. The latter were none of Bolan's concern, but he would not hesitate to deal with them in kind if any of them crossed his path.

This evening, his first stop was a Provo safehouse in The Pound, a short block off Falls Road. The Pound had been a Catholic ghetto and the scene of numerous religious riots since the 1850s. British troops patrolling in the neighborhood were used to ducking bricks and bottles filled with lye or gasoline. When soldiers or the RUC came in to lift suspected terrorists, the women of The Pound turned out to beat on garbage cans to warn the targets.

A stranger walking through The Pound by day was marked before he covered half a block, his progress followed by suspicious eyes. The darkness helped, but even so, the Executioner was conscious of the risk he faced on what essentially was hostile turf.

He did not buy the argument that most of Belfast's citizens, Catholic and Protestant, supported terrorism. The problem with a country under siege was the enforced mentality of "Us versus Them," a state of mind that drew a sharp line in the dust and dared the moderates to step across. When children came of age with violence in the streets and in their homes, the future was a dreary wasteland, sudden death a self-fulfilling prophecy.

He drove around the neighborhood for fifteen minutes, watching for a tail, and finally parked in the tiny lot behind a service station that had closed for the day. The night was cool and damp, and Bolan wore a navy peacoat on top of simple workman's garb.

The coat concealed his mobile arsenal.

In lieu of the familiar Baretta, Bolan wore a Browning BDA-9S—the double-action version—in an armpit sling. Beneath his right arm, on a swivel rig, he packed a Heckler & Koch MP-5 SD-3 submachine gun with a built-in silencer. The pockets of his peacoat carried extra 30-round box magazines for the folding-stock SMG.

The Provo safehouse was in the loft of a building with a butcher shop downstairs and apartments on the three floors in between. Bolan walked back from the darkened service station, pacing off an alley lined with battered garbage cans. The back door of the target building had a simple lock, and the warrior slipped it with a knife blade, waiting in the shadows while he listened for sounds from within.

When he was satisfied that he was not about to encounter an ambush, Bolan slipped inside the murky hallway, lit by one faint bulb. There was a staircase on his right, and the warrior started climbing, counting off the flights.

On three, he paused again. One floor to go, and anything could happen in the next few moments. He had no idea how many terrorists were present in the loft, if any, or what kind of weapons they possessed. There might be lookouts in the corridor whom he would have to deal with.

Or he might be looking at an empty flat and wasted time.

He swung the submachine gun from underneath his peacoat, thumbed off the safety and crept upstairs, hesitating momentarily before he rushed the fourth-floor landing with his weapon leveled from the hip.

The corridor was vacant, yawning in the face of Bolan's stealth.

He hurried toward the solitary door. Another pause to listen, poised outside the door, before he raised his foot and slammed a solid kick above the knob. The doorjamb splintered with a ripping sound of aging wood, and Bolan charged the threshold, dodging to the right as he went in.

The spacious loft had been divided with partitions into several smaller rooms. The first, where Bolan stood, was furnished with a table, folding chairs and a decrepit sofa. Two young men were seated at the table, playing cards. A third was stretched out on the couch.

All three of them were galvanized as Bolan burst into the room. They scattered, lunging for weapons on the sidelines. The Executioner cut loose with short bursts from his subgun, working the room from left to right.

The shooter on the sofa was the closest to his piece, an M-1 carbine propped against the nearest wall. A burst of Parabellum manglers caught him on the fly and stitched a line of bloody holes along his rib cage, spinning him and dropping him behind the couch.

The cardplayers broke in opposite directions, one fumbling for a pistol in his waistband, hindered by a flapping shirttail, while the other tried to reach a shoulder holster hanging from a wall hook on his right. The nearest gunner had his piece in hand when Bolan hit him with a 4-round burst across the chest.

He caught the third man inches form his goal and helped him get there with a burst between the shoulder blades. His target stumbled, the crushing impact hurling him facefirst against the thin partition. It was strong enough to hold him, but it rattled loudly, rippling like a sheet of plywood in a gale. The dead man toppled backward, leaving crimson smears on the partition where his face had smashed against the wood.

How many left?

He started on a hasty search, had one room finished when a sound of scuffling feet alerted him to danger at his back. The warrior turned to see a tall young man emerge from a cubicle. The automatic pistol in his fist was already cocked and searching for a target.

Bolan took a chance and dropped the muzzle of his weapon, cutting the Provo's legs from under him with slashing Parabellum rounds. The young man went down on his face, the pistol bouncing from his fingers as a cry of agony escaped his throat.

Before his adversary could recover, Bolan crossed the room with loping strides and kicked his gun away. He knelt beside the wounded Provo, rolled him over on his back and shoved the subgun's muzzle in his face.

"You want to live?"

"Depends on what it costs me," the Provo answered, still defiant.

"I need someone who can get a message to Mulavey. Can you handle that?"

"What message?"

"Tell him Billy Connolly is tired of living like a refugee. He's paying back his enemies with interest. Are we clear on that?"

"I hear you, traitor."

"Just make sure you get it right."

"I'm not forgetting anything, I promise you."

"That's fine. Is there a telephone in here?"

"Back there," the Provo said through clenched teeth, nodding vaguely toward the section of the loft where he had come from.

Bolan hesitated long enough to knot a simple tourniquet around the young man's left leg, where a Parabellum slug apparently had grazed the femoral artery. That done, he went and found the telephone, equipped with a long extension cord, and carried it back to the main sitting room of the loft. He left it several feet beyond the young man's reach and turned to leave.

"You haven't heard the last of this, you bastard!"

"I'm counting on it," the Executioner growled.

HIS TURN ON SENTRY DUTY always felt like wasted time to Pat O'Hanlon, but he did his bit like everybody else. It was better, now that Connolly was back and they were on the move again.

It was a good time to be Irish, all in all.

O'Hanlon knew that standing watch was necessary. There was danger from the bloody Brits and Orangemen, as well as an alphabet of enemies—the SAS, the

UVF, the UDA. The Provies were another problem, having branded Connolly a traitor to the nationalist movement when he broke away and formed the Sword of Erin years before.

O'Hanlon was a high-school sophmore back in those days, but the movement had consumed his life. He had three kills behind him—one of those across the water, in the enemy's backyard—and he was proud of who and what he had become.

The day was coming when his family and friends would thank O'Hanlon for his contribution to their freedom from the British yoke. There would be parties in his honor then, perhaps a statue like the one that he was certain they would raise to William Connolly.

His job, this evening, was to wait outside the Shamrock Club while Johnny Breen conferred with several ranking members of the Sword. In fact, Breen had not reached the tavern yet, but he was due at any moment. Pat O'Hanlon would be there to greet him, standing watch, the Ingram submachine gun weighing down an inside pocket of his army-surplus jacket.

George McCullough, owner of the Shamrock Club, had closed it for the evening "to repair a broken water pipe." In fact, McCullough was a stalwart member of the Sword who held the rank of captain under Connolly and Breen. Aside from drawing pints, his major talent lay in building bombs to kill the Prods and British soldiers on patrol.

Another hero. There would be no end of candidates for statues, come the victory.

O'Hanlon lit a cigarette and flicked his match into the street. It had begun to drizzle, and he kept well back beneath the Shamrock's awning to avoid getting wet. He might be standing there for hours, and it would not do to have his clothes soaked through.

The Ingram was a comfort, but he had been cautioned not to use it unless there was no viable alternative. If an official raiding party came along, he was supposed to warn the others and evade arrest. There was to be no firing at the Brits or RUC tonight unless they had him cornered. It was more important to preserve the Shamrock's cover than to score a hit on some half-witted corporal marking time until he got his orders for a flight back home.

The Prods or Provies were a different matter. O'Hanlon knew that they would come in shooting, and he meant to pay them back in kind. He saw no contradiction in a feud between the Sword of Erin and the IRA, blood brothers killing one another in the streets. A soldier made his choice and lived or died according to his own abilities. If one side was correct, all others had to be wrong.

And being wrong, in Pat O'Hanlon's world, was tantamount to being marked for death.

The first three gunshots sounded like a gavel banging wood, a call for order at a public meeting, but it made no sense at all. The sound had issued from inside the Shamrock, and he swiveled toward the double doors, one hand inside his army jacket, groping for the Ingram.

More shots rang out, and he could not mistake the sound of it up close... but what the hell was happening? He knew that Breen was late, five minutes give or take, but that was no cause for the troops to fall apart and shoot each other.

He was pushing through the swing doors when a shock wave hit from the other side and pitched him back six feet. He landed on his backside in the middle of the sidewalk, wincing with the pain that rippled up his spine.

Now, what the hell!

The explosion came a heartbeat later, smoke and plaster dust cascading through the doorway, swirling like a cloud. O'Hanlon struggled to his feet and fanned an arm to clear his vision, biting off a sneeze as dust got in his nostrils.

All that phony talk about the plumbing, now the bloody place was falling down around their ears!

Still shaken, he did not grasp the full significance of what had happened for another instant. He was heading back inside the tavern when he heard a burst of automatic fire and realized that this was not an accident or natural disaster. They were under fire, and it had gone down while he stood his watch out front, oblivious to danger creeping up behind.

That made it Tommy's fault, but something told O'Hanlon that his young friend, Tom Moran, would not be hearing any lectures from the leadership where he had gone.

O'Hanlon went inside the pub and scanned the smoky room for signs of life. He picked out bodies sprawled in chairs, across a sturdy table, stretched out on the floor beside the bar. The blast had gone off near the toilets, at the back, and left the rest room without a door.

O'Hanlon started calling out familiar names and got no answer. If the men he sought were still alive, they had to be stunned or lying low, to dupe their enemy.

And speaking of the enemy, where were they? Pat O'Hanlon had a score to settle with the bastards who would pull this kind of sneak attack.

He took another step, and never felt the arm until it locked around his windpipe from behind. Some kind of weapon chopped against his wrist and sent the Ingram skittering beyond his reach. O'Hanlon was prepared to struggle when the gun slid behind him, probed the hollow of his knee and pumped a bullet through the joint at skin-touch range.

He went down screaming, clutching at his wounded leg. The pain exceeded anything he could have dreamed from watching others kneecapped in the past. Hell, he had pulled the trigger once or twice on jobs like that, himself, but it was different now.

Somebody had him by the hair and was twisting, causing new pain at a different source. O'Hanlon's eyes snapped open to behold a stony face, mere inches from his own.

"I hope you hear me," the stranger said.

"I hear you." In the circumstances, O'Hanlon felt fortunate that he could speak at all.

"I've got a message from the Provos, for your boss."

"My boss."

"He's marked. You tell him that. This stop is just a little welcome home. He should get used to the attention."

Pat O'Hanlon had begun to fade. Another sharp jerk on his hair brought him around.

"I hear you, Jesus."

"Play it back."

He gave a fair approximation of the message, and his tormentor seemed satisfied.

"You'll live," the stranger said, "but I suspect your disco days are over. Pass the message on the way I told you, and I might not have to visit you again."

He was getting killed by a comedian, O'Hanlon thought, and closed his eyes to let it happen in the dark. Another moment passed, and then he realized that he was still alive, alone inside the Shamrock Club with half a dozen lifeless heroes of the movement.

It was then that he began to scream.

THE WAREHOUSE WAS an ancient fixture of the Belfast docks, facing the Queens Island shipyards across the dark waters of the River Lagan. It was small by modern standards, overshadowed by its newer, grander neighbors, but the structure had some life left in it yet.

Or so the owners thought, at any rate.

The warehouse was on Bolan's hit list, its proprietor identified by sources in the RUC and SAS as an enforcer for the Provisional IRA. It was widely suspected—but never proved—that shipments of weapons flowing into Ulster from America, the Middle East and Eastern Europe had been held there, before the guns were passed around to dedicated terrorists. Search warrants had been executed at the site at least a dozen times, and there had been illegal searches after dark— all failing to produce the evidence required for trial.

From the beginning of his private war on Savage Man, the Executioner had enjoyed two huge advantages over his soul brothers in deputized law enforcement. First, he was not bound by arbitrary rules of evidence and did not have to prove his case before a judge or jury members who were bored, distracted, bribed or terrorized. Second, once he executed judgment on a target, there could be no wrist-slap of probation or parole, no second coming of a human predator with scores to settle and a taste for blood.

The buck stopped here.

He had no reason to believe there would be weapons in the warehouse, and he did not plan to look. It was enough for him to damage the prestige and property of any terrorist within his reach, destroy their confidence and leave a message that would drive a deeper wedge between the rival factions battling in Belfast.

No one observed him as he parked his compact Ford behind a warehouse neighboring his target, then lifted a heavy satchel from the shotgun seat. He took the MP-5 SD-3 submachine gun with him, tucked beneath his peacoat, but he hoped to make the raid a simple in-and-out if possible.

The place was dark and quiet, doors locked all around. He chose an access door in back and shattered the lock with a 3-round burst from his subgun, stepping into the silent interior with every sense on full alert.

A pencil flashlight showed him rest rooms on the left, a narrow hallway leading to the warehouse proper. Bolan followed it, surveying rows of wooden crates and cardboard cartons, some labeled in English, others in Gaelic. He paced off the hundred-foot building to reach a small office in front, the work space separated from the warehouse floor by six-foot fiberglass partitions.

No one home.

He scattered the incendiary charges more or less at random, one to get the office going nicely, others here and there among the crates of merchandise to spread the fire around. The charges were composed primarily of thermite, with explosive detonators, generating heat enough to melt refrigerators, forklifts, even portions of the concrete floor. By the time firefighters arrived at the scene, there would be little left for them to save.

Outside, Bolan took a can of spray paint from his satchel, lingering long enough to write a message on the blank side of a van nosed in against the warehouse loading dock. Three words said it all to Bolan's Provo adversaries: Sword of Erin.

He walked back to the Ford and climbed behind the wheel. Driving away, he saw light flare behind the frosted windows of the warehouse, growing brighter by the second, spreading like the break of day.

Ignition.

It was small potatoes in comparison to some of the objectives still on Bolan's target list, but he was speaking in the only language terrorists could understand—harassment and attrition, heaping pressure on your enemies until they cracked and either fled the battlefield or launched themselves into a suicidal grandstand play.

In Belfast, history and fratricidal warfare made his mission that much easier. From the beginnings of the modern Irish republican movement and the Easter rising of 1916, nationalist factions had been splitting up and quarreling with one another, charging treason to the movement, killing one another's leadership and members of the rank and file. It was a weakness that the loyalists and British troops were quick to use against the IRA and its competing factions.

Now, the Executioner was doing likewise...with a vengeance.

By the time he reached the far end of the block, it was apparent that the warehouse was on fire. He still had time, though, given the deserted docks at this time of the evening. It would take a larger blaze or a coin-

cidental passerby to bring the fire brigades just yet—
and even so, they would have found themselves too
late.

He hoped the van would not explode, but if it did,
there would be other chances to convey his message to
the Provo leadership. The word was spreading even
now, and Bolan knew that once a finger pointed at the
Sword of Erin, every violent act that followed would be
lumped together in a gut reaction, fueled by private
animosity.

Divide and conquer.

The fire was spreading, and Bolan was about to add
more fuel.

CHAPTER NINE

"Two blocks," Frank Ryan announced, peering through the windshield of the old Volkswagen, checking street signs. "Everyone be ready now."

As Ryan spoke, he reached between his feet to check the cardboard box that held four gas bombs, wine bottles filled with gasoline and laundry soap to make it stick, wicks fashioned out of shredded handkerchiefs.

"I'm ready for the bastards," Jack Brady told him, speaking from the car's back seat. He held an L-2 A-3 Sterling submachine gun in his lap and cocked the weapon as he spoke.

Beside him, Peter McGill was fiddling with the safety on his Browning automatic shotgun, leaning forward so his chin was nearly resting on the driver's shoulder. Young Sean Devlin had the wheel, a Colt .357 Magnum wedged behind the buckle of his belt.

"We're on a stopwatch from the second that we leave the car," Ryan told them. "Anybody tries to stop us is fair game, understand?"

There was a general murmur of assent from his companions in the car. The troops had heard it all before, and they were ready for the leap from words to action. Ryan reached inside his denim jacket and pulled out his SIG-Sauer automatic pistol, snapping back the slide to put a live round in the firing chamber.

Ready.

Ryan and his three companions were an active service unit of the Provisional Irish Republican Army. Their mission in the predawn hours of this Tuesday morning was retaliation versus IRA opponents in the rival Sword of Erin clique. Provo blood had spilled within the past few hours, and Ryan's team had hit the street with orders to exact a fitting retribution.

It would be only a start, but Ryan meant to stay the course.

Their target was Ernest Kennedy, a Sword of Erin triggerman who occupied a row house off the Old Lodge Road. Kennedy had been marked for death three years earlier, a warrant issued in closed session by the PIRA's Belfast brigade commander, but he had proved elusive. His execution had been deferred with the arrest of William Connolly in the United States. Now Connolly was back in Belfast and the Sword of Erin had initiated new attacks against the IRA.

The time had come to settle his account.

"Right here."

The target's address had been painted on the curb outside his row house. Devlin mashed the brakes and Ryan hit the sidewalk with the SIG-Sauer in one hand, the carton of gas bombs clutched under his arm. Brady and McGill fell into step behind him, moving toward the stoop. They mounted concrete steps, and Ryan triggered three quick rounds from his pistol into the front door's locking mechanism, followed with a kick that put his team inside.

The stairs were on their left, and Brady led with his Sterling SMG to clear the way. Kennedy's second-floor bedroom was on their right at the top of the stairs. There were thrashing sounds as someone, aroused by Ryan's gunshots on the street, struggled out of bed. A woman's voice called out to someone who did not answer.

Brady went in firing, Ryan and McGill close behind, fanning out to cover the open bedroom door. A pistol flashed twice from a corner of the darkened room, and Ryan fired three shots in that direction. McGill, meanwhile, was pumping buckshot through the flimsy wall, cutting a new door of his own. Return fire drilled the plaster, whining over Ryan's head.

He dropped to one knee, set his pistol on the floor and palmed a lighter, lifting one of the gas bombs and setting the flame to its wick. He craned forward, feeling the heat on his wrist as he wound up the pitch, his missile streaking like a comet through the darkness to explode above the bed.

He followed with a second bomb and a third, flames racing up the walls and gnawing at the wooden floor. A woman shrieked, and Ryan saw a human shape engulfed by fire, limbs thrashing as it tumbled off the bed and rolled across the burning floor.

"Pull back! We're out of time!"

The gunman in the bedroom—Kennedy, presumably—was still returning fire as they fell back in the direction of the stairs. A bullet smacked the wall near Ryan's head and he ducked lower, scuttling down the steps. They reached the bottom of the stairs together, Ryan pausing long enough to light his final bomb, turning back to lob it toward the landing.

Kennedy was still alive upstairs, but with any luck the flames would trap him there. It was the best that they could do without remaining on the scene until police arrived.

Outside, the double-parked VW waited with its engine running, Devlin shouting at the three of them to hurry up. Bright flames were showing through the bedroom window. Someone smashed the glass and fired two shots down into the street.

"Goddamn it!"

Piling in, they screeched off from the curb with smoking tires. If Kennedy was firing at them, his shots went wild and Ryan could not hear them. In his mirror, flames were leaping from the shattered upstairs window, lighting up the quiet residential street.

"You think we got him, Frank?" McGill was breathing like a distance runner, sitting forward with the Browning shotgun gripped between his knees.

"Unless the bastard's got asbestos underwear," Ryan said, hoping it was true. He didn't need a failure in the new campaign, his first time out.

"We got his woman," Brady interjected. "Jesus, did you hear her scream?"

"It's time they learned a lesson," Ryan said. "You play with fire, you're going to get burned."

THE CLOCK STRUCK 6:00 a.m. when Edward Twoomey parked his car and stepped out into drizzling rain. He glanced up and down the one-lane rural track, and scanned the trees directly opposite before he turned back toward the house that was his destination.

You could never be too careful in the middle of a war.

The farm was three miles west of Belfast in the open countryside. The gently rolling scenery felt alien to Twoomey, born and raised in Belfast, schooled to hate the British occupying army at his widowed mother's knee. Besides his father, caged and murdered in Long Kesh, he had also lost two brothers to the nationalist cause—one shot down by a military sniper on the

Crumlin Road, another knifed and bludgeoned by a flying squad of UVF commandos in The Pound.

The rural countryside was Ireland, in its way, but Twoomey was a city boy and always would be. Not for him the placid world of sheep and cattle, plows and fertilizer. There were many loyal men in the countryside, but the vital contests of the struggle would be waged on urban streets—in Belfast, Derry, London and beyond.

It had been relatively simple for a time. The enemy was obvious—the British troops and Ian Paisley's paramilitary Protestants, regardless of their chosen names. When Twoomey ventured out at night to make a killing in those days, he knew exactly who should occupy his rifle sights.

These days, the list of enemies had grown. It wasn't only Brits and Prods you had to watch in Belfast now, but bloody traitors to the nationalist cause who went off on their own and tried to change the rules around to suit themselves. There had been half a dozen spin-offs from the IRA in recent years, but none was more persistent than the Sword of Erin.

It had seemed all settled, in the States, when Billy Connolly was pinched and held for extradition back to London. Life inside would be the only verdict he could hope for once the British courts got hold of him, and it would be a relatively simple thing to sort out the other Swordsmen when they had lost their guiding light.

Except old Billy never made it to his London flight. Instead, he had escaped from the United States and back to Belfast, where his troops had launched a violent new campaign against the IRA. Blood called for blood, and Twoomey had no doubts about the reason he was summoned here this morning.

Edward Twoomey was a hunter of men. If Seamus did not mean to send him after Connolly, he would be very much surprised.

Mulavey was already waiting for him on the porch as Twoomey stepped around his car and moved along the flagstone path. "Good morning, Seamus."

"Not so good," said the brigade commander of the Belfast IRA.

Inside the house, Mulavey poured two steaming mugs of coffee, tipped a dash of whiskey into each and handed one mug to his guest. They sat in the parlor, facing each other across an oaken coffee table.

"You're aware of what's been happening in town," Mulavey stated.

"Of course."

"We're hitting back already, but it isn't bloody good enough. You know exactly what we need."

"Billy Connolly."

"That's right."

"Just give the word."

"You always were a scrapper, Eddie."

That was true enough, but Twoomey waved the compliment aside. "The bastard has it coming, Seamus. It's a pity that he's lived this long, to lead so many patriots astray."

"You'll do it, then?"

"With pleasure. It could take some time, of course. He's like an eel, our Billy."

"Make a proper job of it," Mulavey said. "That's all I care about."

"I might not have the chance to catch him on his own."

"To hell with that. A friend of Connolly's is no good friend of ours."

"We understand each other, then."

"As always, Edward. Do the movement proud."

"I should be getting back to town." Twoomey stood to leave.

"You have a place to start?"

"We've got a file on Connolly, his friends and such. It ought to put me on his trail."

"Just tell me if there's anything you need."

"I will, indeed."

"Good man."

Mulavey closed the door behind him, letting Twoomey return to his car alone. It was a relatively short drive back to Belfast, but he needed time to think.

The coming hunt could make or break him in the IRA, assure his future or reduce him to the status of an also-ran. He had no fear of letting down the side, however. He'd never missed a target yet, and did not plan for Billy Connolly to be the first.

The bloody traitor was as good as dead.

He simply didn't know it yet.

THE SNIPER'S RIFLE WAS a Heckler & Koch G-3 SG/1, a specialized version of the same firm's excellent assault rifle. Chambered in 7.62 mm, it weighed in at eighteen pounds with a loaded 20-round box magazine in place. The Zeiss 6-power telescopic sight was guaranteed accurate to a range of some 600 yards.

This Tuesday morning, Bolan's shooting range was less than half that distance, limited by the geography of downtown Belfast. He would happily have worked from farther out, but the warrior's military skills did not include the power to see through brick and concrete walls.

He stashed the rifle inside a duffel bag, with two spare magazines. The backup was overkill, he realized. If Bolan hung around the target long enough to squeeze off sixty rounds, police would have him boxed in from the street.

The proper method for a sniper was to strike and fade, repeat the process frequently, until your enemy was decimated or demoralized. In urban conflicts, certain limits were imposed by the terrain, but sudden, unexpected hits could still play hell with enemy morale.

It was coming up on 8:00 a.m. Bolan's target was a sixth-floor office on Donegal Street. It was rented by Sinn Fein, the political arm of the Irish Republican Army, which formed a bridge of sorts between paramilitary action in the streets and evolutionary action at the ballot box.

The Executioner was not a politician, and he did not normally take sides in a political campaign, unless his outlaw targets sought to sway the outcome with brute force. In this case, though, while there was no election pending, he had picked Sinn Fein as a connection to the Provos, one more way of driving home his point.

And he was operating with a difference here, today.

If possible, he planned to rattle his opponents without spilling any blood.

His sniper's nest was situated in a vacant flat, 250 yards southwest of the Sinn Fein offices on Donegal. The SAS had taken out a one-year lease and used the smaller apartment as a spotter's post, recording faces of the party staff and visitors on film and tape. Bolan had the flat all to himself this morning.

Opening a window that would let him watch the Sinn Fein offices, he scanned the target first with his binoculars, examining the layout, spotting desks and doors, the rest rooms, filing cabinets, all of it. That done, he took the sniper's rifle from its duffel bag and loaded it, sitting well back from the open window as he adjusted the sight. No point in giving witnesses downstairs a clear view of his weapon braced against the windowsill.

When he was satisfied that he could make the necessary shots, locating members of the staff and memorizing faces, Bolan reached inside the duffel bag for a final piece of equipment. Cellular telephone in hand, he tapped out the number of the Sinn Fein office, waiting while it rang twice at the other end.

A young man picked it up on three, his face life-sized in Bolan's field glasses. He had light hair, blue eyes and a sprinkling of freckles on his nose and cheeks.

"Sinn Fein, g'morning to ye."

"William Connolly."

The young man frowned, unsettled. "Sorry, sir?"

"You heard me right. He's kicking ass and taking names. You lot are on the list."

"Say, who is this?"

A dial tone answered him, the cordless telephone discarded as Bolan picked up the rifle. Sighting quickly through the scope, correcting for distance and deflection by the windowpane, he set his cross hairs on the young man's coffee mug. It was a trick shot, almost showing off, but even if he missed it, the result would be the same.

He took a shallow breath and held it, then gently stroked the trigger, absorbing the weapon's minimal recoil as 180 grains of death sizzled downrange. His bullet struck the office windowpane at a velocity of 2,100 feet per second, exerting 1,800 foot-pounds of destructive energy on impact. With its full-metal jacket, the projectile drilled a relatively tidy hole and kept on going, smashing the Sinn Fein staffer's coffee mug to smithereens.

The young man sat there, gaping for a moment at the window and the dripping mess upon his desk, finally grasping the significance of what he saw and diving to the floor. Bolan chased him with another bullet, toppling a stack of plastic stationery trays, then shifted to his right in search of other targets.

Counting off the doomsday numbers in his head, he gave himself an arbitrary thirty-second deadline, spotting targets swiftly, grateful for the rifle's self-loading action to reduce his firing time. In swift succession, Bolan nailed the office water cooler, potted shamrocks and a filing cabinet, two framed landscapes on the wall and a coffee machine with a pot on the boil. Three members of the Sinn Fein staff were huddled under desks before he finished, and he left them there, unscathed.

For now, it was enough to link the Sword of Erin with another strike against the IRA. He had no reason to believe these secretaries were involved with acts of terrorism, other than the editorial support they lavished on the Provos in their publications, and he had a list of other targets waiting for him, men with fresh blood on their hands.

He did not plan to keep them waiting long.

RAGE WASHED OVER William Connolly in crimson waves, obscuring vision, nearly blotting out the voices of his several companions in the room. He understood what fiction writers meant by "seeing red" and fought to shake it off, regain enough of his composure to respond intelligently in the movement's hour of need.

"Enough!" he rasped. "Shut up for Christ's sake, will you?"

Johnny Breen sat back and clenched his teeth; the others muttered briefly and were still.

"All right." He stabbed an index finger at his chief lieutenant, aiming like a pistol. "Run it down."

Breen cleared his throat, eyes lowered, concentrating on the fingers tangled in his lap. "We started taking hits last night, all over Belfast," he said. "We've counted seven dead so far, including Ernest Kennedy. The bastards torched his flat and burned up his lady."

"Which bastards?" Connolly demanded.

Breen was scowling now. "It has to be the bloody Provies, doesn't it? I mean, we've got O'Hanlon from the Shamrock. They were bold enough to drop Mulavey's name."

"Not 'they.' O'Hanlon saw only one man."

"So what? The neighbors right across from Ernie's flat saw three men climbing into a car and driving off. We don't have any names, but I'll be knackered if it's not a Provie active service unit."

"What about the bloody SAS?" asked Paul McNerney, leaning forward on the sway-backed sofa.

"Not their style," Breen replied. "You know those bastards like to frame a case and take full credit in the papers. This is something else."

"That fucking Seamus." There was steel in Connolly's voice. "We'll have to deal with him, and no mistake."

"Just say the word," Breen offered.

"Patience, John. I'll not let anything divert us from our course."

The master plan took precedence for Connolly, but he could not afford to let the PIRA murder and harass his troops while they were moving toward that final day of victory.

Tim O'Malley took a long drag on his cigarette and blew a plume of smoke toward the ceiling. "What's the program, then?" he asked.

"We're not about to take this lying down," Connolly stated. He turned to Johnny Breen. "You have the list of Provie names and hangouts?"

"Current as of late last month."

"No point in starting at the bottom, then. If we can get a line on Seamus, take him down. If not, go after any of his cronies you can find. The higher the ranks, the better. When you go to kill a snake, cut off the head, I say."

"And what about our own?" McNerney asked. "A few more hits like last night, and we'll have to pack it in."

"Like hell! We've got the whole machinery in place, and nothing is about to put us off. This business with the Provies is a sideshow."

"But we're losing people, all the same," O'Malley argued.

"Because they caught us unaware. We won't make that mistake again."

"I had another thought," McNerney said.

"What's that?"

"It could be someone from the States. They want you bad, back there. You had that trouble with the Frenchies, up in Canada."

"Some kind of vigilante squad, you mean?" Connolly asked. He thought about it, frowned and shook his head. "It sounds farfetched to me."

"So, what about Groupe de Liberté?"

"They deal in poison," Connolly replied. "God only knows what kind of scum they're doing business with. Colombians, Chinese, you name it. If you ask me, they've been shorting someone on their money, and the bill came due. It was a damn sight easier to put the blame on me than own up to the trash they call their friends. I felt obliged to leave a thank-you note for everything they'd done."

"We heard about the bomb," O'Malley said. "You still don't think the Yanks had any hand in what went on?"

"I've told you what I think. We're still on schedule for the main event, and I'm not canceling while I have legs to stand on or a finger for the trigger."

"Even so," McNerney said, "we have to deal with problems here at home."

"Agreed," Connolly said. "Beginning now, a state of war exists between the Sword of Erin and the IRA. Pursue the list of targets when and where you can, with all dispatch."

The troops looked satisfied, but Connolly was wise enough to recognize that he had only calmed their apprehension temporarily. If he could not turn the tide of battle soon, reverse their recent losses, he would lose face with the men whose loyalty was essential to his master plan.

The Sword of Erin's leader would not let that happen.

For the moment, for his own security and peace of mind, he would be carrying the battle to his enemies. Mulavey and his people had a grim surprise in store, a lesson none of them would soon forget.

CHAPTER TEN

The snatch came down to Paul McNerney. He was left to choose his own team from the men available, selecting Robert Kehoe, Terry Rourke and Dickie O'Hearn. He knew them all as stalwart soldiers who had proved themselves in killing situations, and they would do whatever was required.

Abduction was a different matter from assassination. When you went out on a killing mission, it was relatively simple. All you had to do was choose your spot, wait out your prey and get it done. Kidnapping was another problem, most especially in broad daylight, when you were supposed to keep from damaging the target.

Connolly had been specific on that point. If anything went wrong and they were forced to kill the woman, it would eliminate her value as a chip for bargaining. She had no value to the movement or McNerney in herself, but with the proper handling she could be very useful to the Sword of Erin in its present difficulty.

"What's the address?" Rourke was driving, leaning forward, checking numbers painted on the curb or walls.

"Two-sixty B," McNerney told him. "West side of the street."

"Suppose she left already?" Kehoe asked from the back.

"We're early," McNerney said.

"Anything can happen."

"If we miss her this time, we can always grab her after work."

"I'd like to get it over with," O'Hearn said. "We're like a fucking spider on a wall out here."

"Just keep your shirt on, Dickie. Nobody's giving us a second look."

"You hope."

McNerney swiveled in his seat to face O'Hearn. "I picked you out for this because I thought you had the nerve to see it through. Don't make me out a liar."

"You think I'm scared?" O'Hearn bristled at the very thought.

"I think you ought to concentrate on what we're here for," McNerney told him, "and forget about what might go wrong."

"Don't fret about me holding up my end."

"We're almost there," Rourke announced.

"Look sharp," McNerney said. "We need a place to park. Not here, though. She'll be walking north on that side of the street."

"I'll have to go around the block," Rourke stated, speeding up a bit and passing through the intersection, down another block to circle back, approaching their objective from the north. By sheer dumb luck they found a curb space three doors from the target's address.

Turning back toward Kehoe and O'Hearn, McNerney told them, "When we see her coming, I'll get out and walk in that direction, pass her by and swing around to take her from behind."

O'Hearn was grinning. "Sounds all right to me."

"Wise up," McNerney snapped. "You fellows wait until she's even with the Morris Minor there, and head her off. She won't have anyplace to run from there. We tuck her in the back, and off we go."

"Suppose she cuts up rough," Kehoe asked.

"She's a lass, for Christ's sake, not a bloody kung fu expert. If the three of us can't get her into the car, we need to pack it in."

"The neighbors hereabouts don't care for screams and fighting on their sidewalks in the morning," O'Hearn said.

"That's why we had you pinch the license plates," McNerney told him, scowling. "You remember that?"

"I just don't want the bloody RUC for breakfast."

"You've got your Armalite back there, Dickie," McNerney said. "Have you forgotten how to use it?"

"Not a bit."

"Well, there you are. Let's take one problem at a time—or would you like to talk about what happens if the fucking British army comes along?"

O'Hearn retreated into silence, lighting up a cigarette and staring out his window with a bland expression on his face. Whatever thoughts were trapped behind his eyes, he kept them there.

A slim brunette stepped into view and turned in their direction, pacing off the sidewalk with athletic strides.

"That's her," McNerney said, already opening his door. "Look smart, and no mistakes."

He tried to keep it casual, not even looking at the woman as he approached her, passing three feet to her left. She did not seem to recognize him, busy with her own thoughts as she moved along the sidewalk. Counting off the paces in his mind, McNerney turned and fell into step behind her, swiftly closing the gap.

Another moment, and she would be even with the car, O'Hearn and Kehoe waiting for her. She would have no chance against the three of them, and if she tried to fight, McNerney had a blackjack in his pocket. Just a tap behind the ear, and her resistance would evaporate.

McNerney started walking faster, one hand in his pocket, wrapped around the leather blackjack. He imagined how the sap would feel on impact with her skull, and almost hoped she would struggle, give him an excuse.

The bitch deserved it, after all.

The corners of his mouth turned upward in a wicked smile.

THE SUN BROKE THROUGH gray clouds as Lucy Mulavey emerged from her apartment house, but she had no interest in the weather. She was frightened for her brother, worried by reports of violence overnight that indicated grim new problems for a city long at war.

It was not bad enough they had to fight the British, RUC and Protestants from day to day. Now they were locked in battle with the very men who should be helping Seamus and the others liberate her homeland from the foreign yoke.

Her brother, Seamus, was brigade commander for the IRA in Belfast, and as such, he spoke for all the nationalists pledged to overthrow oppressive British rule. It was a travesty that traitors like William Connolly and his pathetic Sword of Erin should conspire against the movement, when they should have joined a firm, united front against the common enemy.

From childhood, Lucy had been schooled in nationalist politics at home. Her late paternal grandfather had been among the rebels of the Easter rising, spending several years in prison for the "crime" of hoping that his children would be free. Her father was an IRA commando in the lean days of the 1950s, skirmishing repeatedly with British troops in the long border campaign. When brother Seamus joined the Provos at age seventeen, he was carrying on an established family tradition.

Lucy played no active part in the guerrilla war, per se, but she was no less dedicated to the cause than Seamus or the rest. She carried messages from time to time, and more than once had sheltered fugitives in her apartment, while they waited for a chance to travel south. On one occasion, she had risked a charge of perjury to swear an alibi for a suspected sniper. Never mind that it had soiled her reputation in the eyes of the police and certain neighbors; Lucy's family understood, and they approved.

Sometimes, she wished she was a man, that Seamus and the rest would trust her with a mission where her zeal would count for something, let her strike a blow against the hated enemy. And yet...

For all her dedication, Lucy felt squeamish sometimes when she watched the news on television. So much blood and pain in Belfast, Derry, even in the south. She grieved on cue for martyred soldiers of the cause and made appropriate excuses when a British soldier or Protestant commando was assassinated, but of late she had begun to think about the other casualties. Men and women, even children, caught in the cross fire of a war that was the last thing on their minds until a bomb exploded in the local grocer's or a bullet ripped their flesh.

She did not question the legitimacy of her brother's cause, nor had she given voice to any doubts about the Provo tactics...yet. She sometimes felt embarrassed at the weakness in herself, when news of maimed and murdered children brought a tightness to her throat, a stinging to her eyes. Was there some natural deficiency within herself, or was it part and parcel of her sex? Was Seamus right, with his infuriating attitude that women never made good soldiers?

But she knew that for all its innate chauvinism, the movement boasted its fair share of heroines through the years. They did not always carry arms, but many had, and they were known as fierce, determined fighters.

Why could Lucy not be one of those, instead of harboring belated doubts?

Still, she had no doubts that the Sword of Erin and its leaders were an obstacle to Irish unity, striking off on foolish tangents, risking all in the commission of atrocities that ultimately failed to help the movement or the Irish people in their long, hard march toward liberty.

The Sword would strike her brother down if given half a chance, and she owed more to Seamus, in her own way, then she did the movement. His had been the strong arm that protected her from schoolyard bullies and the ruffians who sometimes prowled their neighborhood in search of Catholic girls to torment and abuse.

If she could find a way to help him in this time of trial, she would not hesitate.

This Tuesday morning, though, they were expecting her at work as usual. She held a secretary's job downtown, answering phones and typing letters for a middle-aged accountant who stared at her with lustful eyes.

She passed a slender man with sandy hair and glanced at her watch. In front of her, the back doors opened on a dark sedan and two men emerged onto the curb. She felt the first, small stab of apprehension as they moved to block her path.

She hesitated, was about to turn around and see how they reacted, when a firm hand gripped her arm above the elbow. Lucy glanced across her shoulder, staring into pale blue eyes beneath a shock of sandy hair.

"You won't mind coming with us for a wee ride, will you, lass?" The stranger smiled. "No trouble, now, or someone might get hurt."

IT WAS A LONG SHOT, going for the woman, but the Executioner had won on long shots before. He had no concrete plan beyond communication—meet Mulavey's sister, play the rest of it by ear from that point on. If nothing else, the woman could relay a message to his enemies, his very contact with her serving as another goad to reckless action from the IRA.

The name and address came from Finch's master list. Bolan found the apartment house on his second try, missing the side street on his first drive-by. He was driving slowly south, half looking for a place to park the Ford, when he spotted Lucy Mulavey emerging from her apartment house. She paused for a moment, then began walking north.

Downrange, he saw a man emerge from a car at the curb, moving as if to intercept the woman, belatedly passing her by. No sooner was the man behind her, though, than he reversed his track and fell in step with his apparent target, swiftly gaining ground. The woman seemed oblivious to him, her mind on other things.

Bolan slowed his progress to a crawl, watching as two more men climbed out of the car. These moved to block the sidewalk, halting Lucy's progress. She hesitated, seemed about to make a swift retreat, when the first man came up from behind, grabbed her arm and spoke.

At first, it seemed she might comply with his instructions, but the moment passed. Instead of moving toward the car as she was clearly meant to do, the woman slammed a knee into her captor's groin and shook her arm free of his grasp. A sharp push sent him sprawling, and she raced back toward her flat.

The Executioner had seen enough. These men were not police, or one of them would certainly have shown a badge by now. He stood on the accelerator and his car surged forward, blocking the enemy vehicle as it began to pull out from the curb. He drew the Browning BDA-9S and stuck it out the window as he came abreast of the sedan, its muzzle lined up on the driver's face.

He was a young man, startled at the sight of Bolan's pistol, mouthing silent curses as he tried to reach his own. The Browning bucked in the Executioner's fist, two Parabellum rounds exploding through the window, drilling flesh and bone. The wheelman's head snapped back, a splash of crimson on the glass behind him, and his foot slipped off the clutch. His vehicle collided with the car in front of him and stalled.

The sound of gunfire startled Lucy's three pursuers. One of them had almost overtaken her, the second close behind, while number three was hobbling in their wake and favoring his wounded genitals.

The third man, nearest to the source of danger, swiveled in a crouch to face the Executioner, one hand still cupping his privates while the other disappeared inside his jacket, reaching for a weapon. Bolan shot him in the chest, and the explosive impact lifted him completely off his feet and slammed him against the plaster wall behind him. He was dead or dying as he slithered down the wall into a seated posture, crimson streaks marking his passing.

That left two.

The runners turned to find out what was happening behind them, but Mulavey's sister had to have thought the kidnappers were firing at her. Far from slowing or halting in her tracks, she picked up speed, feet flying as she ran. Instead of ducking into her apartment house, she kept running down the sidewalk, heading for an intersection fifty yards beyond.

The gunners, first.

They were staring at Bolan, openmouthed, immobilized by shock. He fired two bullets at the gunner on his right and watched him crumple in a lifeless heap. The other reached his piece but never cleared the holster. The warrior's Parabellum mangler drilled through his forehead with the impact of a hammer blow.

That left the woman, almost to the intersection now and running hard. It would be all for nothing if he let her get away without a chance to talk, and as he watched her run, he had the sudden makings of a plan in mind.

He stood on the accelerator, cranked the wheel and set off in pursuit. In front of him, his quarry made the corner, veered hard right and disappeared.

He had her in another moment, tires squealing in protest as he took the corner without slowing. The woman glanced across her shoulder, showing frightened eyes, dredging up a reserve of strength that somehow gave her more speed.

Still, she was no competition for the Ford, and Bolan passed her in a heartbeat, swinging in to block the curb. She had excellent reflexes, pivoting on one heel to reverse her track, but he was too close and too swift. A strong arm snaked around her waist, the other blocking Lucy's elbow as she struck back toward his face.

"Hold on!" he snapped. "I'm not one of them. I got them off your back."

"You say!"

"I'll walk you back to see the bodies, if you like, but the police might not approve."

She hesitated. "Who are you?"

"We should really talk about it on the road."

"Where are you taking me?"

"I'd like to meet your brother," Bolan said.

"For God's sake, what are we supposed to do when women get the best of us?" A scowl carved furrows in William Connolly's cheeks and etched a cleft between his eyes.

"I can't believe the woman took them out," Johnny Breen said.

"Mulavey?"

"Well, it stands to reason he would have his sister under guard."

"McNerney should have seen the bastards coming, damn it! Even if they had an ambush waiting, he'd been out on jobs enough to watch his back."

"Sometimes—"

Breen hesitated, shook his head. He'd been about to offer an excuse for McNerney and the others but thought better of it. They were dead, all four of them, and pissing Billy off would do the living no damned good at all.

"What happened to the bitch? Anybody got a clue?"

"The RUC is looking for her now, from what I hear. I'd say they missed her clean."

"Which means that Seamus has her stashed away by now, and he'll be laughing at us over whiskey."

"Don't be too surprised if he comes looking for your head. This makes it personal, you know."

"I meant it to be personal," Connolly growled. "I take it personally when the bastard puts a price tag on my head. It's time he found out what it feels like."

"Even so, this business with the Provies stands to slow us down. I'd rather concentrate on London, if I had a choice."

"Mulavey didn't give us any choice. He hit us first this time, remember."

"That's the funny thing," Breen said.

"So, share. I need a smile right now."

"We have our ears out on the street, all right? I'm hearing that the Provies took a hit or two last night before we did. They've got men dead we can't account for with our raids since midnight."

"So?"

"So, this. We know Mulavey wants you dead. The bastard hates us all for walking out. But let's suppose somebody else stirred up the pot this time."

"The bloody Prods, you mean."

Breen shrugged. "It could be, but they normally aren't shy on taking credit for their kills. So far, we haven't heard a peep from anybody in the UVF or UDA."

"They could be getting smart," Connolly said. "Stir up a fuss and watch us going head-on with Mulavey's people."

"I'm not sure."

"What's on your mind, John? Spit it out."

Breen frowned. "Suppose it wasn't just Mulavey hitting back at us because the Orangemen hit him first. Imagine someone else hit both of us to start things off, and made each think the other was to blame."

"But not the Prods?"

"It wouldn't have to be."

"Who, then?"

"I'm thinking back to Canada," Breen told his friend.

"The goddamn GL?"

"Whoever hit them there, in Montreal."

The smile felt strange to Connolly. "Old son," he said, "I think you've played this game too long. You're getting bloody paranoid."

"I hope you're right."

"Remember what the old man said—when you find hoofprints in your flower bed, think horse, not zebra."

"Meaning?"

"Meaning we've got all the enemies we need right here in Belfast. With the Brits and bloody Protestants, Mulavey's boys, we don't need an imaginary bogey-man to make things worse."

Breen thought about it, frowning. "The SAS has pulled some nasty tricks before, you won't deny."

"It doesn't sound like their kind of game," Connolly said. "But if they're meddling in our patch, it makes the payoff that much sweeter. I'd like to see their smarmy faces when we pull it off."

"You don't think we should concentrate on first things first?" Breen asked.

"You said yourself, Mulavey's on our back. We might have trouble getting one without the other."

"Then we need to do it right. Quit mucking with the small fry and go for the bastard in charge."

"Just like I mean to do with the Brits."

"It's settled, then. I'll put the word out on Mulavey. He's an oily bastard, but we still have people who can spot him, even when he's lying low, like now."

"I'd like to see his eyes, old Seamus, when we put a bullet in his stinking guts," Connolly said.

"I wouldn't recommend the personal approach," Breen warned. "The Provies will be watching for you high and low."

"I don't care who pulls the trigger," Connolly replied. "As long as it gets done."

"Then London?"

"We're on schedule. I'm not about to let Mulavey slow us down."

If anything, Connolly thought, disturbances in Belfast might provide a good excuse to move their schedule up, but he was wise enough to hold his tongue. There was no point in agitating Johnny unnecessarily.

"I'm off, then," Breen informed him. "Any luck, we'll have old Seamus taken care of by tonight."

"I'll keep my fingers crossed."

But not his trigger finger. In a few days, he would be needing that one for a very special job.

CHAPTER ELEVEN

They were driving south on York Street when she found her voice. It sounded strange in her own ears, as if another person had devised some way of speaking through her lips, and Lucy cleared her throat to try again.

"I can't take you to him," she informed the stranger at the wheel. "You must know who my brother is, or else you wouldn't want to see him after...after that, back there."

"I know exactly who he is," Bolan replied.

"Well, then, you understand about security. I don't drop in like that, without a word of warning, and I'd never get a total stranger past his men."

"You have his number, though." It did not come out sounding like a question.

"Yes."

"So, make a call."

"Not yet," she told him stubbornly. "I need some information first."

"You mean, beside the fact that someone wants your brother bad enough to kidnap you?"

She almost laughed out loud. "That's politics in Belfast, Mr.... See, now, I don't even know your name."

"Mike Belasko."

"Mike. It's more than a coincidence, I'd say, you being in the neighborhood that way, just when I needed help."

"It wasn't a coincidence at all," he told her. "I was dropping by to say hello."

"To me?"

"You're one Mulavey I could find."

"Who are you, really?"

"I just told you."

"Not your name. I mean who sent you? What's your business? You're not Irish, anyone can tell that much. You sound American."

"Is that the kiss of death?"

She smiled despite herself. "Not necessarily. Are you a copper?"

He responded with a laugh. "Not even close."

"You could be lying."

"True enough."

"So, tell me something I can trust."

"Suppose I was a copper from America," he said. "I'd have no jurisdiction here, no right to carry firearms. Taking out those goons back there would leave me open to a list of felonies, including murder."

"I suspect the charges are the same for a civilian," she replied.

"I don't intend to stick around for any trial."

"What do you want with Seamus?"

"Have a chat, for starters. See what comes from that."

"Not good enough. I won't do anything to put his life at risk."

Bolan thought about that as he waited for a traffic light to change, and spoke only when they were moving again. "We have a common enemy," he said at last.

"I'm betting he's responsible for what just happened on your doorstep."

"Billy Connolly," she said. It felt as if a stone had settled in her stomach.

"So, you know him?"

"More or less. I've met him, but we never spent much time together. Billy's not the social type, you see."

"He wasn't feeling social when he sent those goons to pick you up just now. My guess is he was looking for a pawn."

"To reach my brother?"

"One way or another."

Lucy had been flirting with the same idea, but hearing it expressed in words was chilling. From the way he spoke, it was apparent that the American reckoned Billy Connolly would take her any way he could—dead or alive. Her death would be a blow to Seamus, but a hostage in the traitor's hands would do more damage to her brother and the IRA. If Seamus was compelled to bargain with the Sword of Erin, it would place him at the mercy of his mortal enemies.

"I ought to go away," she said, speaking more to herself than the man at her side.

"It's your choice. I don't know if the Sword has a clear way to track you or not, but it won't help your brother, your running away. At least help me meet him before you take off."

"Suppose I refuse?"

Bolan shrugged. "I can drop you off back at your flat, or wherever you say."

"Just like that?"

"Don't confuse me with Connolly, Lucy. I'm asking for help. You say 'no,' it means 'no.'"

"It's not the wisest thing to trust a stranger, is it?"

"Maybe not. But if I intended to coerce you, we'd be sitting in a basement somewhere, playing twenty questions."

"Even so, you've killed three people."

"Four," he said, correcting her.

"I didn't see a fourth."

"The driver."

"Oh."

"Don't let it worry you. The blood's not on your hands."

"You make it sound so easy."

"It's a fact of life. I don't suppose your brother loses any sleep."

She stiffened, wanting to stand up for Seamus, knowing Belasko spoke the truth. It seemed to make a difference, killing when you had a cause. But then, for all she knew, the stranger had one, too.

And that was what disturbed her at the moment—owing him her life, when he could be an enemy.

"How long have you been watching me?" she asked.

"I wasn't. It was pure coincidence their showing up like that when I dropped by. It happens."

"Even so, you had my name and address."

"Right."

"I don't like being spied on."

"No one does, except an exhibitionist."

She paused. "If I say yes, what then?"

"I can talk to your brother, and maybe we'll work out a deal. All I want out of Belfast is Connolly, maybe a few of his friends."

"For the coppers they killed in the States?"

"Close enough."

"You have no jurisdiction here, remember?"

"That's okay," he said. "I'm not arresting any-one."

"You mean to kill him?"

"How much do you really want to know?"

He was right. Up close, the details made her blood run cold.

"You see that petrol station up ahead? Pull in there, would you?"

"Right." He sounded weary and resigned. "Your choice."

"I'll only be a moment," Lucy said. "I have to make a call."

THE NEWS OF LUCY'S near-abduction reached her brother seven minutes after the event. Her flat was in a solid Catholic neighborhood, which meant that many of her neighbors shared at least some sympathy with Seamus and the IRA. A number of them were committed loyalists, and three of these had telephoned in swift succession by the time an RUC patrol arrived to cart the bodies off.

Four dead, and there was still no sign of Lucy. She had been glimpsed running from the scene, a compact car in hot pursuit, but that was all Seamus could discover of her fate.

The men shot down outside her flat were something else entirely. They had names, all right, and three of them were known to Seamus as defectors from the PIRA to the Sword of Erin, pledged to William Connolly. McNerney was the oldest of the lot, late thirties, and a cool hand on a sniping mission when he was not in his cups. O'Hearn and Kehoe had been average soldiers, not afraid of much, but no great thinkers when the chips were down. Mulavey did not know the youngster, Terry Rourke, but it was safe to bet that he was also part of Connolly's menagerie.

It infuriated him to think that Connolly would strike at him this way, through Lucy, but he felt no great surprise. It was the kind of slimy, underhanded trick he would expect from traitors to the cause, and he was also angry at himself, for failing to provide security when Lucy was at risk. The violence overnight had been directed toward his men, the front-line soldiers of the IRA, and it had lulled him into thinking noncombatants were exempt from harm.

Mulavey would not make the same mistake again.

He would have liked to pay the bastards back in kind, by striking at their kin, but Connolly had no surviving relatives that anybody knew, and Johnny Breen had come up from the south somewhere, a name so common you could never hope to sort them out without a printed family tree. The last thing Seamus needed at the moment was to be distracted by the task of stalking every Breen in Ireland.

He could spend his time a damn sight better killing off the enemies he recognized, but he would have to find them first. And he would have to find his sister, too, before he could achieve some peace of mind.

He paced the kitchen of his farmhouse, wishing he could have some word from Twoomey, find out how the hunt for Connolly was going. Seamus knew that it was early yet, too soon for any kind of definite results, but he was anxious for an end to the infernal game of cat and mouse.

It wasn't bad enough that Connolly and his supporters had defected from the IRA and trampled on their sacred oath. Instead of merely dropping out like other cowards through the years, they had to strike off on their own, attacking targets that were unrelated to the British occupying army or the bloody Protestants who dominated Ulster politics. They struck at random, stirring up a hornet's nest of outrage in the name of revolution, later droppng out of sight to let the heat fall on the IRA.

And even that was not enough for Connolly, the scheming bastard. Now he had to make war on Mulavey, on Mulavey's flesh and blood, without distinction to the target's age or sex. It was the kind of thing Mulavey would expect from Arabs or the bloody Japanese, but there was no denying Connolly his roots in Irish soil.

If Seamus had his way, the bastard would be planted in that soil before another week was out.

The jangling telephone distracted him, but Seamus left it to the officer in charge of his security around the farm. With Connolly at large, he had diverted several gunners from the streets to mount guard duty at his rural home. It was a temporary measure, just until they traced their enemy and Seamus had a chance to lead the raiding party that would finish him, but in the meantime, having friendly guns around him helped Mulavey sleep at night.

"You'll want to take this, Seamus."

"Who?"

"Your sister."

Brushing past his first lieutenant, Seamus grabbed the telephone receiver. "Lucy?"

"Seamus, I'm all right."

"Where are you, lass?"

"I'm calling from a petrol station in the city."

"Let me have the address. I can send a car around to pick you up."

"I have a ride," she told him, sounding tense.

"Oh, yes? With who?"

"You wouldn't know him, Seamus. He's a Yank."

Mulavey paused, considering that. "What are you saying, Lucy? If he's hurt you—"

"I'm all right, I said. He stopped the others when they tried to lift me."

"Did he now? And what's he asking for the favor?"

"Nothing much. He wants to meet you, have a chat."

"Old chums, is that the game?"

"It has to do with Billy Connolly."

"The bastard's hiring Yanks now, is he? I'm surprised that he can find one willing, after all the bad blood in New York."

"He's not *with* Connolly." Mulavey heard exasperation in his sister's voice. "In fact, I think he'd like to top the lot of them."

"Is that a fact?"

"I'd say it's worth a listen, anyhow."

"I guess your hero has a name."

"Mile Belasko, at the moment. I can't vouch for that."

Smart girl. The name was almost certainly an alias. She had her wits about her, even now.

"What does he have in mind, then?"

"All he seems to want is conversation. Name a meeting place, he'll bring me there, and you can have your talk."

"Suppose I don't like what he has to say?"

"He doesn't seem to mind the risk."

"All right. I'll meet your chum in Antrim, then. Is that too far for him to drive?"

"We'll be there."

"Make it half-eleven, on the street outside that little pastry shop you like, downtown. I won't be on my own, in case the Yank has any fancy schemes in mind."

"I'll let him know."

The line went dead, and Seamus cradled the receiver, frowning. He disliked receiving terms from total strangers, even when they spoke with Lucy's voice, but he was bound to have her back, no matter what the risk.

And there was something else, a sense of curiosity about the Yank who had appeared from nowhere in his sister's hour of need. Mulavey knew it had to be some kind of setup—Lucy's neighborhood was not the sort of place where tourists went to window-shop—but it was worth his time to find out what the stranger wanted.

Most especially if it would help him to be rid of Billy Connolly.

"What's going on?" his bodyguard asked.

"Get six or seven of the boys together," Seamus ordered, "and make sure they bring their guns. We're going for a little ride."

THE TOWN OF ANTRIM, from which County Antrim draws its name, is ten miles northwest of Belfast, on the shore of Lough Neagh. It was an easy drive on B39, a secondary road that averaged twenty feet in width. When Bolan met a truck approaching from the opposite direction, bound for Belfast, he was forced to brake and yield the right of way by pulling over on the grassy shoulder, swinging into gravel lay-bys when they were available.

His passenger was satisfied to ride in silence, staring out at the countryside unfolding as they passed. She had explained her brother's terms before she lost her voice, and Bolan did not miss her company to any great degree. His mind was focused on the meeting scheduled for eleven-thirty, knowing it could cost his life.

Mulavey's sister had been, quite direct about informing him that Seamus would not come alone to meet a stranger. She was giving him a chance to duck out, Bolan thought, but he had not come all this way to let a golden opportunity slip by.

If Seamus had an ambush waiting for him down the road, he would be forced to deal with it as best he could. Conversely, if the Provo leader let him speak, there was at least an outside chance for them to strike a bargain.

Bolan had no sympathy for terrorists, regardless of their nationality, and that included members of the IRA. He had destroyed a number of them in the past, and several of them in the past twelve hours alone. But he would not flinch from using them if they could help him land his chosen prey in Belfast. William Connolly was Bolan's target at the moment, and Mulavey's Provo faction had good reason to despise the Sword of Erin's ranking chief.

They entered Antrim from the south, and Lucy found her power of speech again, directing him along the crowded streets, past homes and tidy shops, until they reached the central business district. Bolan found a parking lot and took a ticket stamped with date and time for the attendant.

"We're to meet him over there," Lucy said, pointing across the street, in the direction of a pleasant-looking pastry shop.

"Okay. Let's go."

They crossed together, several feet of empty air between them, looking much like lovers who have quarreled and not made up. She reached the sidewalk first, and Bolan moved in closer as she scanned the pastries in the window, counting on her proximity to give a sniper pause.

Her brother stepped out of the tobacco shop next door, approaching Lucy and her escort with a smile that seemed distinctly strained.

"How are you, lass?"

"I'm fine," she replied, and kissed him lightly on the cheek.

"You're sure?" The glance he spared for Bolan held a world of menace for the man who harmed Mulavey's flesh and blood.

"I said I'm fine."

"Why don't you step inside and have yourself a cup of tea, then? Tommy will be glad to keep you company."

"All right." She glanced at Bolan one last time. "I haven't thanked you."

"Never mind."

There was a kind of wistfulness about her as she disappeared inside the pastry shop, and Bolan shrugged it off. He concentrated on the Provo leader standing just in front of him.

"Mike Belasko, I presume."

"It's close enough."

"You know my name."

"I do."

"Let's walk, and you can tell me what inspires a good Samaritan these days."

They moved off down the sidewalk, almost rubbing shoulders, speaking softly with an eye on passersby. The Executioner did not waste time examining the street or upstairs windows for Mulavey's escort.

"I'm no good Samaritan," he said for openers.

"I can believe that," Seamus answered. "You've the look about you, or I miss my guess."

"The look?"

"A killer's look. I see it in the mirror every day, before I take my breakfast."

"So, we understand each other."

"Not just yet. You helped my sister out today. For that, I'm grateful. But it doesn't tell me why."

"I had a feeling she could pass me on to you."

"And so she has. That still leaves why."

He had decided, when the moment came, to stick as nearly with the truth as he could manage, short of burning down his cover at a single stroke. Mulavey and his kind were reared on paranoia, Bolan knew, and it would take no master of persuasion to convince him that America had placed a bounty on the head of William Connolly. The Provo might believe it, and he might not. Either way, Mack Bolan hoped Mulavey would be pleased to find another hunter on his adversary's track.

"We have an enemy in common, I believe."

"Wee Billy. He's been up to mischief in the States, from what I hear."

"And back in Belfast, too."

"The bastard gets around, and no mistake."

"I'd like to take him off your hands," Bolan said.

"Ah. Why don't you do it, then?"

"He moves around, just like you said. I haven't got him spotted yet."

"What's that to me?"

The warrior shrugged. "I helped your sister out. If you were in a mood to repay the favor, you might turn up an address, put me on his trail."

Mulavey's laughter was soft, almost musical. "Suppose I knew where Billy was," he said. "Why shouldn't I have done with him, myself?"

"I'm sure you'd like that," Bolan said, "but think about the drawbacks."

"What would those be, if you don't mind telling me?"

"The heat, for one thing. You've got problems, any way you slice it. Connolly just makes things worse. You take him out, no matter how it plays in ink, you've got the army and the RUC all over you."

"As if they weren't already."

"Fair enough. So, think of me as an insurance policy. If I get busted going after Connolly, you haven't lost a thing. No casualties for your side, nothing comes back to you in the media. You're looking at a no-lose situation."

"Not exactly," Mulavey said. "I lose the pleasure of removing little Billy with my own two hands."

"Is that worth jeopardizing your command? The movement?"

"Bloody lot you care about the movement, Yank." Mulavey's voice had suddenly acquired a razor's edge. "For all I know, the CIA has loaned you out to someone in the bloody SAS, to set us up."

"If that's what you believe, you ought to drop me here and now."

"Don't think I've ruled it out."

"I came alone, just like you said," the Executioner reminded him. "No Saracens or snipers. Frankly if I wanted your head on a stick, I would have done you at the pastry shop."

"And died right there, for all your trouble."

"Everybody dies," Bolan said.

"That's been my experience, as well."

"So can we make a deal or not?"

"I'll go this far, Yank. If you have a number for me, I'll do what I can to keep in touch. Wee Billy might come up for air some time or he might not. A simple hit, we might not want to pass him up. I've got my people looking for him, but that's all I'll say. You want a shot at him, that's fine with me, but I won't jeopardize my brothers for your sake."

"First come, first served?"

"Suits me," the IRA brigade commander said. "You have a tape machine at home?"

"I'll get my messages," the Executioner replied.

"Then, shall we say, let's keep in touch?"

"Let's say that, yes."

"I'm going now," Mulavey told him. "You wait a bit."

"All right."

"And thank you. For my sister."

Bolan watched the Provo turn away and head off through the crowd. A younger man fell into step beside him, halfway down the block, and Bolan lost them when they turned the corner.

Gone.

He had no way of knowing if the terrorist would keep his word, but it was worth the effort. Nothing ventured, nothing gained.

He waited two more minutes, turned and walked back to his car. The war was waiting for him back in Belfast, one way or another.

Bolan had places to go and people to kill.

CHAPTER TWELVE

Kieron Kelly had a birthday coming up. He would be twenty-one on Friday, legal for the pubs—as if his age had ever stopped him drinking in the past. On Friday, he would be a man.

Provided that he lived that long.

But this was Tuesday, and he had a job to do. It was not any ordinary job this time, like mixing fertilizer with your basic household chemicals in plastic drums to make a bloody great explosion. Anyone could build a car bomb if he read the manuals and measured the ingredients to fit. A relatively steady hand was all you needed.

A face-up confrontation with the enemy was something else, though. When you went against the hardmen and they started shooting back, it took a special kind of man to stand his ground and carry out orders under fire.

That kind of manhood came from dedication, training, courage. It had bugger-all to do with age.

This morning's target was the U.S. Consulate on Queen Street, no small order. There were always RUC outside to watch the place, and uniformed Marines inside the wall. A bank was easier, all things considered, but at least he did not have to make his way inside. It was enough to shake them up a bit and let the bloody Yanks know they had picked the losing side this time around.

They way it looked to Kelly, Billy Connolly had picked this target special, as an insult to the Yanks. He had already rubbed their noses in the muck with his escape from custody, and now he meant to drive it home.

It was a glory run, at that, the more he thought about it. How many of Kieron's friends could say they took it to the Yanks this way?

He only hoped that he would live to talk about it afterward.

The young man kept his bulky weapon in a paper shopping bag. It was an MM-1 multiround projectile launcher, with a 37 mm bore and a revolving cylinder that held twelve rounds. The launcher's maximum effective range was roughly 120 meters—about ten times what the current job required. His mixture of explosive and incendiary loads would keep the bastards hopping once he opened fire.

It should be quite a show.

"Two minutes." Bernie Fallon sounded nervous, but he held the Austin steady as he motored into the approach.

"I'm ready."

Kelly eased his weapon from the shopping bag and cocked it, rolling down his window for a clear shot. All he needed was a clear eye and a steady hand. Unless he mucked up with a vengeance in the next few moments, Kelly knew his MM-1 should do the rest.

They cleared the final intersection, rolling south on Queen Street. He saw the squad cars of the RUC, uniformed officers in their caps and bulky flak vests loitering around the front gates of the U.S. Consulate. The coppers were not Kelly's major target, but it would not hurt his reputation any if he shook them up a bit, perhaps sent two or three home in bags.

"Get set."

He flicked an irritated glance at Fallon, wishing he had not been saddled with a know-it-all who had to run the show, but he had to concentrate on the task at hand now.

Twenty meters remained, and he poked the 37 mm launcher's muzzle out the open window, bracing his left elbow on the sill. Fallon held the Austin at a steady pace. One of the coppers turned toward them, a bored expression on his face before his eyes went wide and he began to jabber at his mates.

But the alert came too late. There was no recoil to speak of with the MM-1, but it achieved spectacular results. His first explosive round peeled back the hood of a patrol car at the curb and detonated on the engine block, a fireball shooting upward while the shock wave knocked the coppers sprawling.

Kelly's second round impacted on the high retaining wall around the U.S. Consulate and went off with a thunderclap that made his ears ring. Shrapnel filled the air, but they were past it now and even with the gate. He raised the launcher's muzzle, loosing three more rounds as swiftly as the weapon's firing mechanism would allow. Two of them were incendiaries, with one more high-explosive round to shake up the Yankee bastards.

The Austin veered out into traffic, with a couple of the coppers firing after it from prone positions at the curb. At least two bullets struck the trunk, but Kelly had to laugh at their pathetic efforts. Shooting up a stolen car would get them nowhere in the long run.

Kelly swiveled in his seat and fired a parting shot at them for the hell of it, grinning ear-to-ear as the grenade exploded in the street. A truck veered in toward the curb and struck the second RUC patrol car, caving in the driver's side.

"Take that," he muttered, as he slipped his smoking weapon back into the shopping bag. "Take that, you bastards, and be damned."

IT WAS NOT ALWAYS EASY hunting men, but Edward Twoomey had a lifetime of experience. Nineteen assassinations to his credit, and he did not count the snipings, executions ordered by the drumhead courts, or bombs that he had carried to the very doorsteps of his country's enemies. Those deeds were acts of war, but it was stalking human prey that Twoomey most enjoyed.

It was ironic, he suspected, for a lifelong city boy to turn out as a hunter, but his fate was sealed, and Twoomey had no real complaints. If he could serve the cause and find some small enjoyment in the process, he was doubly blessed.

Stalking Billy Connolly would be no easy task, at that. The sneaking bastard knew his business when it came to lying low and striking out from ambush. He could bait a trap with the best of them, and it only made things worse that some within the movement still had a soft spot for Billy in their hearts. Despite his treason to the movement, he was still a boyo to some of the lads, and there was no changing their minds.

It had been crafty, Connolly's attempt to get at Seamus through his sister, but the team had fumbled going in. That made it Twoomey's turn, but he was working at a disadvantage. Connolly had nothing in the way of family to use for leverage, and all his friends were soldiers in the Sword of Erin, either serving time or burrowed underground with Billy.

Still, if Connolly had no blood kin, his entourage was not so fortunate.

Take Paul McNerney, for example. Barely cold, and what would happen to his wife and children now that he had gone? The Sword had never laid aside a pension fund for widows, as the IRA had done for decades. The McNerney brood would soon run through their savings, if they had a bank account at all.

The row house looked like any other in the Crumlin Road. His face was known here, and he did not fear the eyes that followed him along the sidewalk. He took for granted that there had to be various informers in the neighborhood, but Twoomey's name did not appear on any warrants. He was good at covering his tracks and making sure that any living witnesses were loyal believers in the cause.

McNerney's widow answered on the second ring, little children clinging to her skirt, an infant on her hip. The woman's eyes were dry but haunted, and she cringed from Twoomey as he stood before her, hat in hand.

"I heard about your man, Jane. It's a crying shame."

"You came to tell me that?"

"I came to ask if you'd be after needing anything."

"We're getting on."

"I see you are. Of course, it's early days yet, isn't it?" The hunter flashed his most endearing smile. "I wish you'd ask me in."

"For what?"

"A cup of tea, perhaps. Some talk."

Reluctantly she stepped aside and took the little crowd of children with her. "As you like."

The living room was small and cluttered. Twoomey sat on the sofa, McNerney's widow a chair directly opposite.

"You know what Paul was up to when he had his accident?"

"I never asked his business," the woman said, frowning as she bounced the baby on her knee.

"A wise decision," Twoomey answered with a fleeting smile. "It's hard, though, when a man turns on his brothers. Some might hold a grudge, you know."

"I'm not afraid."

"No, of course not. There's no reason why you should be, lass. I understand your man was led astray by traitors. A mistake in judgment, you might say."

The woman remained silent.

"I could have a word with the brigade," Twoomey suggested. "Make them see the light, I wouldn't be surprised. We have a pension fund, you know."

"Blood money." There was bitterness in Jane McNerney's voice.

"I understand your feelings. It's time to think about the wee ones, though. They can't eat pride, you know."

"What are you asking me?"

"A trifle. Hardly anything at all. We know the who and why, it's just the *where* we have a bit of trouble with, right now."

"It's not as if the lot of them confide in me," she told him, weakening.

"I understand that, Jane. Still, I respect a woman's intuition and her powers of observation."

"There's a consequence for what you're asking."

"Not a bit of it," the hunter said. "You're under my protection, lass. Say what you will, I've never known a ghost to reach out from the other side."

"WHOSE FLAT IS THIS?" Jerry Donahoe asked.

"A friend," Dan Callahan replied. "He got himself locked up this morning at the boozer. He'll be fine as long as we stick to the plan."

So saying, Callahan produced a pry bar from a pocket of his leather jacket, wedged it deep into the jamb beside the latching mechanism of the door and gave a violent twist. Wood splintered and the lock gave way. Another moment saw the two of them inside.

"A break-in." Callahan was smiling. "Nothing they can hang our mate with, anyhow."

"Let's get it over with," Donahoe said. He moved toward the windows and set down his heavy duffel bag, a pair of AK-47 rifles clanking together.

He nudged the ratty curtain back an inch or so and peered across the alley at a carbon-copy flat. The curtains were open over there, lights on, and Donahoe counted half a dozen men engrossed in conversation.

"Anyone worth mentioning?" he asked.

"You mean the boy himself?" Callahan frowned as he shook his head. "We won't sort Seamus out that easily. They're all good Provies, though, make no mistake."

Downstairs, the spotter would be gone by now. He had been watching the Provo flat, waiting for the delegation to arrive. There was no sign of Seamus, but in a war like this, you had to settle for the targets you could find.

The Sword of Erin started at a disadvantage, first in terms of numbers, with the Provos holding a minimum ten-to-one advantage. Supplies were another problem, all the more so since the collapse of the Soviet block cut off Russian subsidies to international terrorists. Still, they managed to get by.

This morning's work should help to level out the playing field a bit.

Callahan unzipped the duffel bag and lifted out a folding-stock Kalashnikov with a banana clip in place. He passed the gun to Donahoe and took its twin for himself, unfolding the metal shoulder stock, cocking the rifle with an easy, practiced movement.

"Take it easy with the curtains, now, Jerry. Once they start to hit the floor, we've lost them."

"Right."

He knew all that, but there was no point telling Callahan to shut his mouth. Donahoe reached out and eased the curtains back, opening his field of fire. The window stuck at first, but he forced it halfway open on the second try. Beside him, Callahan was ready, sitting on the floor, feet braced against the wall beneath the window, sighting down the barrel of his piece.

The first time Jerry Donahoe had shot and killed a man, nine months earlier, it was a British corporal in The Pound. He'd used an Armalite that time, one shot from hiding, bailing out with the echo of the shot still ringing in his ears and barely time enough to see his target fall.

It was a different game this time. The men in front of him had once been friends, and even now he found it difficult to hate them as he did the Brits and Protestant commandos. Still, they threatened Billy Connolly and stood against the Sword, a living obstacle to Irish freedom.

It was time for them to die.

"On three," Callahan said. "I'm tracking left to right. You work the other way."

"All right."

His finger curled around the AK-47's trigger, taking up the slack. The rifle's stock was tight against his shoulder, cool where metal touched his jaw line.

"One."

He concentrated on the weapon and his targets, forty feet away. He knew exactly what the piece would sound and feel like when he pulled the trigger, sending sudden death across the narrow alley.

"Two."

He took a breath and held it, closing one eye, just like on the practice range. The man directly in his sights was balding, sipping beer and pushing wire-rimmed glasses back on his lumpy nose. The old man looked familiar.

"Three!"

The AK-47 lurched against his shoulder, spitting 7.62 mm bullets at a cyclic rate of 600 rounds per minute. Donahoe ignored the muzzle-flash, the shiny brass that rained around him. He was focused on the windows opposite as they imploded, crimson splashing from the profile of his chosen target. Tracking on, he swept perhaps a quarter of the room in the three seconds before his magazine ran dry.

And it was time to go.

They left the windows open and yanked the curtains shut to discourage return fire, scuttling away from the windows and stowing their weapons in the duffel bag. Outside, they found a couple of the neighbors peeking from their flats, but Callahan discouraged them with shouted curses as he passed.

Downstairs, their teenage driver had the engine running. Donahoe piled in the back and Callahan slid in beside the wheelman.

"Shag it, Dennis!"

Donahoe was waiting for the shock to hit him, but it never came. When they had covered half a dozen blocks without the sound of sirens on their trail, he knew that they were free and clear.

It was a job well done, no looking back.

The way it ought to be.

DRIVING BACK from Antrim through a misting rain, Mack Bolan listened to the radio for news from Belfast. Violence had continued in his absence, with a drive-by raid against the U.S. Consulate among the latest incidents. The authorities were having difficulty with the bulk of recent crimes. The army and the RUC were long accustomed to sectarian attacks, a war between religions, but the latest spate of violence was internecine conflict in the strictest sense, the paramilitary nationalists killing one another.

Bolan understood it well enough, since he had put the ball in play, but he was looking at the action from a different angle. His vague agreement with Mulavey and the Provos gave him allies, of a sort, but that was not to say that he had anything in common with the terrorists.

It was a matter of priorities. He had been sent to punish William Connolly—and any others from the Sword of Erin he could reach—for their cold-blooded massacre of federal agents in New York. If he could use the IRA to that end, he would do so. If, conversely, they got in his way, he would not hesitate to fall upon them like the plague.

The warrior had no way of knowing if Mulavey would abide by their agreement; he would have to wait and see. The number he had given to the Provo officer would relay any message through a cutout to an answering machine. A trace by Provos or police would lead his adversaries nowhere. He could replay or erase any messages from any public telephone and never run the risk of being traced.

Meanwhile, he could not bring himself to loiter on the sidelines, waiting for Mulavey's men to finish off the job that he had started. They were squaring off against the Sword of Erin now, still unaware of Bolan's covert role in touching off the latest conflict. He saw no need for further raids against the Provos.

That did not imply, however, that he was ready to back off from his raids against the Sword of Erin. He would do anything to keep the heat on Connolly and friends, to rout them from their hidey-holes.

He thought of Lucy Mulavey, glad that he had seen a chance to help her, and he was not embarrassed at the bargain he had worked out with her brother. Covert war produced all manner of improbable alliances, and he would wind up owing nothing to the IRA when all was said and done.

And what of Darren Finch? His SAS connection had to be aghast at Bolan's tactics in the past twelve hours. Even with the squadron's standing reputation for unorthodox behavior, Finch would likely view his tactics as a step toward anarchy in Belfast, undermining law and order with a vengeance.

And the soldier had a point.

Unfortunately there were times when "law and order" brought the grinding wheels of justice to a standstill and allowed the guilty to escape unscathed.

He hoped that Finch could stand the heat. If not, he hoped the SAS commando would be smart enough to stay out of his way.

If nothing else, the man was trained to follow orders, and Brognola had pulled strings to get the British brass on Bolan's side. He could not picture Finch deliberately interfering with his mission, but there was a world of difference between enthusiastic help and listless, halfhearted "cooperation." He had experienced both in his time, and if the latter was his only choice, he would prefer to see the mission through alone.

No point in borrowing trouble, Bolan thought, as he put the notion out of mind. Finch did not strike him as a slacker, but it made no difference to the outcome of his campaign, either way.

The Executioner had work to do and he would see the job done, one way or another. Rolling through the suburbs west of Belfast, he could almost smell the smoke of battles yet unfought. The war was heating up, and he was coming back to raise the temperature another few degrees.

The radio announcer was reciting body counts, including several casualties among the RUC and British troops. Civilians had been spared so far, but each new outbreak in the city had a grim potential for disaster. Bolan trusted his ability, but with the Provos and their enemies involved, he could not guarantee the safety of innocent bystanders in any particular engagement.

War was war.

The Sword of Erin did not know it yet, but they had gambled with the very lifeblood of their movement when they slaughtered U.S. federal officers and thought to stroll away without a scratch.

They had a debt to pay, and Bolan was preparing to collect.

In blood.

CHAPTER THIRTEEN

It happened, after all, that Paul McNerney's widow held more secrets than she thought. When Edward Twoomey left her humble flat, he had a fair idea of where to go and whom to ask for directions to his target. There was still a job of confirmation to be done, not Twoomey's favorite part, of course, but he took each chore as it came.

The confirmation came from one of McNerney's boozing mates, another stalwart in the Sword of Erin who had been an honest Provo once upon a time. He was a legman—what the Yanks would call a gofer—who was never much at spilling blood, and so he was at home when Twoomey went to visit him. Surprise would be an understatement for the lad's reaction, but he spilled his guts when Twoomey found the proper buttons and applied the necessary pressure.

Afterward, he slit the poor dumb bastard's throat and left him in his kitchen, draped across the table with a steak knife in his chest.

The hardest part, from that point on, was making up his mind if he should run the operation alone or call on Seamus for support. It would be pleasant, Twoomey thought, to deal with Connolly himself, roll up the whole damned Sword of Erin leadership and hand their heads to Seamus as an early birthday gift.

Surprise was critical, and that meant he had little time to waste. They would be looking for his late informant by and by, to run some errand for the tribe, and once his body was discovered, there was every chance that Connolly would seek to relocate his hideaway.

If Twoomey missed his quarry this time, it would be more difficult—perhaps impossible—to find the trail again.

Presented with a choice of now or never, Twoomey did not have to weigh his options. Still, he hesitated to attack a band of armed men on alert without some kind of backup.

In the end, he compromised and bypassed Seamus, placing urgent calls to two young Provos from the neighborhood of Peters Hill. They were available, as he suspected, and he ordered them to bring their guns along.

The target's chosen hideout was a small flat west of Corporation Street, a short walk from the railway terminal. It had been rented by a lady friend of Johnny Breen's, a young divorcée known for her association with the Sword of Erin. She had tried to hide her tracks by giving out her maiden name, but Twoomey was not deceived by such a hackneyed dodge.

The major question was whether he would find Connolly or Breen at home when he dropped by. Sadly there was no way he could call ahead and verify their presence in the flat. He had no choice but to proceed and hope that one or both would fall into his net.

The youngsters, Charley Bell and Richard Seaver, waited for him at the curb outside a restaurant on Carrick Hill. They both wore knee-length coats to hide the automatic weapons that would earn them six or seven years inside if they were picked up by the RUC.

"Where we going, then?" Seaver asked, settling in the back of Twoomey's car.

"We're calling on the boy himself," Twoomey said.

"Connolly?"

"None other, Richie lad. With any luck, we might just end a war this afternoon."

He left his compact in the railway station's parking lot and led the youngsters south on Corporation Street until they reached the intersection he was looking for. A right turn put them in proximity of their intended target, closing on the same side of the street.

"The fire escape for you," he said to Charley Bell. "When we come through the door, they might bail out the back."

"I'll be there waiting," Bell replied.

"Good lad."

They parted company at the alley's mouth, Bell moving off on his solitary errand while Twoomey and Seaver continued toward the front of the house. There was no spotter on the door to challenge them, and Twoomey led the way inside, Seaver on his heels. The young man had his coat unbuttoned, but he did not draw his weapon yet. For Twoomey's part, he took no chances, drawing the Model 61 Skorpion machine pistol from its shoulder sling.

Connolly's flat was on the uppermost floor, with nothing above it but roof and blue sky. If Bell did his part, pinning down the windows and the fire escape, they ought to have the Sword of Erin's finest in an airtight trap.

They reached the fourth-floor landing, Seaver showing off his weapon. Twoomey recognized the Sterling L-2 A-3 submachine gun, doubtless lifted from a British arsenal somewhere.

"You take the door, lad," Twoomey ordered. "For experience."

Beyond the door, a telephone began to ring.

Without hesitation, Seaver took a short step forward, raised one foot and kicked the door in, plunging through to catch the tenants by surprise. A startled curse was torn from someone's lips before all hell broke loose.

"WE COULD HAVE WRAPPED it up by now," Johnny Breen said, "if that McNerney hadn't bitched it with the girl."

"He's paid the tab for that one," Connolly replied. "There's no point crying over spilt milk any longer."

"Even so—"

"We need to concentrate on London, Johnny. Once we pull that off, the rest of it will fall in line."

"I hope so."

"Faith," Connolly said. "I've got it all worked out."

"You reckon we can tag the big boy, then?"

"No man's invincible. It takes a little work to get it right, that's all."

"You still expect to leave Friday morning?"

Connolly was about to answer when the phone rang in the other room. He turned reflexively in that direction, listening, heard Eamon Lemass say "Hello" into the mouthpiece. He was waiting for a hint of who was calling when the door slammed open. Hugh Delaney started shouting curses, and a burst of gunfire swept his voice away.

"For Christ's sake!"

Breen, an automatic pistol in his hand, erupted from his chair and bolted for the bedroom doorway. Connolly hung back to retrieve his own Beretta from the nightstand, ducking as a burst of submachine-gun bullets pierced the wall beside the door. Breen fired a shot around the jamb, recoiling as another burst sprayed plaster dust and splintered wood.

"How many?" Connolly demanded. "Are they Brits?"

"I couldn't tell." Breen squeezed off two blind shots, directly through the door. "No uniforms that I could see."

"That's it then. Time to go."

"The window?"

Breen had barely spoken when another automatic weapon opened up from somewhere on the fire escape. The bedroom window shattered inward, raining glass across the carpet, bullets gouging divots in the ceiling. Connolly threw himself flat on the floor, smelling dust as he wriggled around the end of the bed, digging in with his elbows and knees.

"Follow me!" he commanded, worming his way toward the closet with Breen close behind. He reached up for the knob and threw the door back, rising to his feet when he was safe inside.

As if to mock the thought, a bullet whispered in beside him, smacked the outside wall and burrowed deep into the plaster.

Safe? Not even close.

"Close the door tight behind you," he ordered, as Breen crowded into the closet behind him.

Immediately on his left, a ladder had been mounted on the closet wall. Directly overhead, a trapdoor offered access to the roof. It had been cleverly concealed from observation topside, meaning Connolly was forced to put his weight behind a solid shove to rip through a layer of tar paper, sunlight streaming into his eyes.

He scrambled clear, waiting with pistol in hand as Breen mounted the ladder and lunged through the trap. Connolly lowered the hatch and turned on his heel, striking off toward the north side of the building, away from the guarded fire escape.

"What now?" Breen asked, falling into step.

"We have to make a dash," Connolly replied. "They can't be watching every house along the street."

"We've lost the sodding car," Breen said.

"We'll find another," Connolly assured him.

The next house to the north stood flush against their hideout, and the runners skipped from one roof to another, moving on. When they were three doors from the ambush site and halfway to the next street intersection, they were forced to drop ten feet onto a lower roof. Breen cursed and staggered as he landed, limping after Connolly.

"My ankle! Christ!"

"We're getting there," Connolly said. "Hang on a bit."

He moved to check the building's fire escape, found it unoccupied and scanned the alley. There was no one visible outside the building they had fled, which told him that the raiders were inside or else had retreated to their cars. In either case, he was not going back to check his mates and wait for the police.

A cat was scrounging in the nearby garbage bin when he dropped beside it, gun in hand. The feline blinked at Connolly, gave out a warning hiss, then retreated swiftly with its dignity intact. Breen clambered down the fire escape a moment later, favoring his good leg.

"We haven't got much time," Breen whispered through gritted teeth.

"Does that mean you can run?"

"I'll show you bloody cartwheels, if I have to."

"Right. Let's go then."

Neither of them had a pistol showing by the time they reached the sidewalk, slowing their pace to an urgent walk. It would not be the simplest thing to nick a car in daylight on a residential street, but Connolly and Breen had pulled off more demanding tasks before.

And then, what?

Connolly had other hideouts in the city, other friends he could rely on in his time of need. Wheels first, then a telephone. They had not lost it yet, by any means.

He thought of London, and his target moving through another uneventful day, blissfully ignorant of his own impending death. No simple twist of fate in Belfast was about to frustrate Connolly when he had risked so much and come so far.

The Sword of Erin had been raised to strike his enemies, and it would not be sheathed until the blade had tasted English blood.

THE MOPPING UP TOOK ALL of ninety seconds. Twoomey followed Seaver through the doorway, sweeping with his Skorpion, in time to see one gunner flying over backward in his chair, a burst of crimson spurting from his neck and chest.

A second man dodged toward the sofa, squeezing off quick, aimless rounds at the invaders from an automatic pistol, cursing as he ran. The tag was simple reflex, barely conscious action. Twoomey brought his Skorpion around and stroked the trigger, stitching a line of holes across the traitor's side.

His target staggered, sprawled across the near arm of the couch and came back firing for effect. He was a tough bastard, Twoomey had to give him that, but he was bucking hopeless odds. A second burst of 7.65 mm bullets took him in the chest and blew him over backward, lifeless.

The tiny kitchen was unoccupied. Doors opened off the left and right, one closed, the other ajar. From that direction, someone triggered several shots at Twoomey and his young companion, firing high. The first shot struck a ceiling fixture, smashed one bulb, and plunged the sitting room into a murky semidarkness. Seaver hosed the doorway with his Sterling, spent his magazine and ducked behind an armchair to reload.

Suddenly the other bedroom door flew open and a tall man charged into the room, cursing at Twoomey and brandishing an M-1 carbine. Twoomey met him with a burst that knocked the gunner backward, bounced him off the nearest wall and dropped him on his face.

"Time's wasting," Twoomey snapped. He guessed the Skorpion's magazine to be half-empty, and he left it alone, brushing past Seaver as the young soldier rose from his couch.

The second bedroom beckoned. Twoomey hesitated for the barest instant, kicked the door in and immediately followed through. He almost fired on Charley Bell, just climbing through the window, but he checked himself in time. With Seaver coming up behind him, Twoomey glanced around the room and found it empty.

That left nothing but the closet. Twoomey swung in that direction, raised his Skorpion and emptied the remainder of his magazine in one long burst, directly through the closet door. Wood splintered, sharp bits flying, and a fair hole opened in the center panel as Seaver joined him with a long burst from his Sterling.

Twoomey stepped in close and yanked the riddled door back on its hinges, cursing as the empty closet mocked him.

He saw the ladder, scrambled halfway up and hit the trapdoor with an angry fist. Unmindful of the empty weapon in his hand, the hunter poked his head out through the trap and scanned the vacant roof. There was no sign of Connolly or anybody else. Twoomey knew that he had missed his chance.

"Goddamn it!"

"What?" Seaver asked from below.

"The fucker's given us the slip." Twoomey stepped down into the closet, brushing past the youngsters with a scowl. "Let's go."

Some of the neighbors would be making calls by now, police cars rolling. They had stretched their timing to the limit, and they had to move before they blew it totally.

"Downstairs!"

No faces peered at them as they passed. The tenants in this neighborhood were veterans of the Troubles, and they knew enough to keep their heads down when the guns were going off. It was a matter of survival, and a quarter century of urban war had taught that lesson very well indeed.

They reached the sidewalk unopposed and walked back toward the railway terminal where Twoomey's car was parked. As they were entering the parking lot, a siren started wailing in the middle distance, drawing closer by degrees.

No matter. They were home and dry.

"Will we be going after him?" Seaver asked.

Twoomey frowned. "I'll let you know. Stay near your telephones."

Driving back to drop the youngsters off, Twoomey concentrated on the fallback options, thinking through his strategy. It stood to reason he would hit some snags along the way, and he did not hold himself accountable for letting Connolly escape. The bastard had been slipping in and out of traps the past few years, and he had proved his skills as a survivor.

Even so, his luck could only stretch so far.

It would be Edward Twoomey's turn, next time around.

The hunter felt it in his bones.

DARREN FINCH WAS waiting at the flat when Bolan got there, sitting at the kitchen table with an open can of beer. He had his jacket off, the automatic in its shoulder holster on display. The flat was quiet, and the sound of someone's baby wailing for a bottle drifted through the wall.

Bolan had called ahead to fix the rendezvous. He needed time with Finch to find out if the British officer had picked up any leads since the night before. He also hoped to chart a strategy that would achieve his goals with minimum distraction, preferably within the next few hours.

"It's a funny thing," Finch said. "I never thought of Belfast as a quiet place before you came to town. If this is an improvement, I don't see it."

Bolan sat across from Finch and settled in. "You have to shake the trees," he said, "if you expect to make the nuts fall down."

"You've got a way with words," the Briton replied. "It translates into chaos on the streets."

"Not quite," Bolan replied. "There's a method to the madness."

"What did Seamus have to say?"

"I let him have the cutout number, and he agreed to call if he gets any leads on Connolly. Beyond that, I suppose we'll have to wait and see."

"You haven't heard the latest, then?"

"Why don't you fill me in?"

"I just found out myself," Finch said, "from one of our connections with the RUC. Some shooters dropped in on a Sword of Erin safehouse near the docks. At first, I thought it might have been your show, but then a neighbor told the constables she saw three men slip out a moment after all the shooting."

"Connolly?"

Finch shrugged. "He's not among the dead. We'll have to wait for fingerprints before we know if he was ever there at all. Two men escaped through a trapdoor to the roof, but it's a guess who they were."

"You lay it on the Provos?" Bolan asked.

"I'd say it had to be. It was, for damned sure. If you'd asked me last month, I'd have thought about the UVF, but they've been lying low the past few weeks."

"Okay. Assume they had a shot at Connolly and couldn't pass it up. Mulavey never promised me he'd put his gunners on a leash."

"And if the Provos step on Connolly, it's all the same to you?"

"Not quite."

"I understood you didn't plan to take him back."

"That's right. Ideally I'd prefer to make the tag myself."

"Professional ethics?"

"A matter of taste."

"The way it's going, friend, you might not get the chance."

"That's why I think we need to speed things up. If Connolly starts running, we could lose him. I don't want to have to start over from scratch."

Finch sipped his beer and frowned. "We need an eye inside the Sword."

"Sounds right."

"It may be I can help you there."

"I'm listening."

"We keep tabs on the membership, you know. There might be someone I could squeeze to find out where your rabbit's gone. We'd have to keep it off the record, though. That's final."

"I won't tell if you don't," Bolan said.

"Right, then. I'll make some calls and see what I can see."

Finch rose and went to the telephone and answering machine in the next room. Bolan left him to it, idly listening to the one-sided conversation as he focused on the next step in his personal campaign.

If Connolly was running—and it stood to reason that he would—Bolan meant to head him off by any means available. It might already be beyond his grasp, but he was bound to try.

And if he somehow missed his quarry in the streets of Belfast, he would keep on trying. The one thing Bolan's target could have bet his life on, if he only knew his nemesis, was that the Executioner would never tire nor give up on the chase.

CHAPTER FOURTEEN

Kevin Downey took a last drag on his cigarette and stubbed it out. The big clock on the wall seemed frozen since the phone call. Was it possible? he wondered. Could a piece of bad news really halt the flow of time?

Ridiculous.

He lit another smoke and watched the minute hand lurch forward. There, that proved it. He was not in limbo, and the laws of physics had not been suspended on demand from Johnny Breen.

The news was not entirely unexpected, after all. When he had joined the Sword of Erin, Downey recognized the likelihood that he would be required to take an active role in the impending revolution. Why else had he sworn the oath, if he did not intend to do his part?

A man could not afford to fail his country or his friends.

His hand was trembling as he reached out toward the ashtray, and Downey cursed himself in silence. There was nothing worse than cowardice, and he could almost smell his own fear.

He checked the time against his watch and sat straighter on his stool. The shop was empty, had been for an hour and a half. Nobody was pawning anything or shopping for a cut-rate deal on Sandy Row this afternoon.

Which left him time to answer Breen's urgent call with no great inconvenience to himself.

Like hell.

He walked behind the counter, locked the door and hung the Closed sign. Retreating to the storeroom for his jacket, Downey moved slowly. He had at least an hour before he was expected to report for duty. In the meantime, he could have a drink and try to put his thoughts in order, maybe find his nerve.

It was unsettling, the attempt on Billy Connolly where everybody thought that he was safe. With the man himself at risk, all hands were being called on for assistance. In the past, it had been Downey's lot to watch and wait, occasionally minding weapons, once providing quarters for a fugitive, but these were desperate times. If he was called upon to take a life or risk his own, the young man told himself that he would find the nerve, somehow.

He kept no weapon in the store, but he had guns at home. Each member of the Sword was bound by oath to arm himself and answer to the call of his superiors. One week a year, the least of them were ordered to an isolated farm in County Tyrone, where the neighbors knew enough to keep their mouths shut when they heard a bit of unexpected gunfire.

There was a world of difference, though, between discharging rounds at paper targets and preparing to annihilate a total stranger on the street. He would have prayed for courage, but it struck him as a sacrilege to ask for strength to kill.

He took his jacket off the hook and shrugged it on. It was ten minutes to his flat, to arm himself, and twenty-some to reach the rally point. It would be better, once he had a chance to speak with Connolly—or listen to him, anyway. The man had ways of making anything seem possible, no matter how bizarre it might at first appear.

That was charisma for you.

Feeling somewhat better, Downey glanced around the storeroom, making sure he had forgotten nothing. His cash was in the safe, the burglar alarm set. All he had to do was lock the back door, and everything would be secure.

Inside the shop, at least.

Outside ... well, that was something else.

How many friends had Kevin Downey lost to violence in the past five years? He counted seven before he gave it up and put the ugly pictures out of mind.

This day was different. He was called upon to make a stand, and he would not betray his oath.

His country needed him, to break the British yoke.

He had his keys in one hand, doorknob in the other. For an instant, when he saw the stranger standing before him in the open doorway, nothing registered in Kevin's mind. The danger struck him, then, but he was too late when he started to recoil.

A fist encased in leather rushed to meet him, and the world turned upside down.

"HE'S FINE," said Darren Finch. "I barely tapped him."

Standing on the sidelines, the American looked skeptical. "Let's wait and see."

"No waiting to it," Finch replied. He reached out from his place behind the straight-backed chair and twisted both of Kevin Downey's ears. After about five seconds, the Irishman began to sputter, wriggling in his seat.

He could not rise. The metal cuffs around his wrists and the nylon rope that formed a hobble on his legs secured the captive to his chair.

"I gather you can hear me, Kevin?"

Downey muttered something. Finch stepped around in front of him, his brass belt buckle level with the captive's face.

"I didn't catch that, Kevin."

"I can hear you," Downey said. "You needn't twist me ears off."

"Simply getting your attention, lad. That's all. We need to have a talk."

"Who are you?" Downey challenged.

"God Almighty," Finch replied. "At least, I am as far as you're concerned."

"That's blasphemy."

"What else would you call someone with the power of life and death?"

"A Provie rat, is what I'd call you."

Finch allowed a smile to touch the corners of his mouth. "Not even warm," he said.

Still smiling, Finch lashed out at Downey with an open hand, the slap resounding like a pistol shot inside the crowded storeroom. Downey cursed and strained against his bonds, a livid handprint showing on his cheek.

"I won't be taken for your Provo scum," Finch said.

"A bloody Prod, then."

"Guess again."

The backhand seemed to come from nowhere, catching Downey on the other cheek with force enough to rock his chair. A slender thread of blood crept from his swollen lower lip and dribbled off his chin.

"Once more."

"The RUC?" There was reluctance in the captive's voice, as if he feared the consequences of another slip.

Finch chuckled and shook his head. "You're lucky we're not playing baseball, Kevin. Three strikes and you'd be out. You know that? But enough small talk. I have one question for you. It's a simple thing, no challenge to a man of your abilities. You might not want to answer me right off, but I can promise you I'll keep on asking. All night long and through tomorrow, if it comes to that."

"What question?"

"Billy Connolly," Finch said. "The shooters missed him at his flat this afternoon. I need for you to tell me where he's gone."

"Get stuffed."

Finch reached inside a pocket of his overcoat. The weight of powdered lead in pockets sewn across the palms and knuckles made the gloves stiff and heavy as he slipped them on. He glanced at his companion and marked the vague expression of distaste on Belasko's face.

A squeamish killer?

Never mind.

"It's one thing being loyal," Finch told his prisoner. "I don't much like your chances of surviving as a punching bag."

"Why don't you—"

Finch silenced Downey with an explosive left that opened up a cut above his captive's eye. He'd have to watch it, if he didn't want the bastard losing consciousness.

"Let's make a wager, shall we, Kevin? I'll bet one of us comes up a little short on patience as the night wears on. Who might that be, do you suppose?"

No answer, and he swung again—but lightly, just enough to rattle Downey's teeth. There was a throbbing in his fist, but nothing Finch was unaccustomed to. He reckoned it had to feel a damn sight worse on Downey's end.

"Our Billy," Finch repeated. "Where?"

The captive's voice came thick through swollen, bloody lips. "He'll kill me if I grass."

"Assuming that he gets the chance," Finch said. "Your problem at the moment isn't Connolly, old son. It's me."

"What makes you think they'd tell me where he's gone?"

The man was stalling. Finch could read it in his eyes. He stroked one puffy cheek with armored knuckles.

"Desperation, Kevin. Even if you don't know where he's run to, you can pass me up the ladder. Either way, I'll take what I can get."

When Downey hesitated, Finch wound up and hit him with a hard right to the rib cage. It required some time for him to breathe again and find his voice.

"Don't think to tire me out, old son. I eat your kind for breakfast."

"You'll let me go?"

"When we've confirmed the information, you'll be on your way. No problem."

"So you say."

"Look at it this way, Kevin—have you got a better choice?"

"I took an oath." This time, there was an almost plaintive tone to Downey's voice.

"So be it."

Finch grabbed Downey by the hair, drew back his head and cocked his right fist for a smashing blow. The left cheek, this time, hard enough to crack the bone.

"No! Jesus, wait!"

"I'm listening."

And once the pigeon started talking, Finch discovered, it was difficult to make him stop.

THE SAFEHOUSE HAD a telephone, but Connolly was not about to risk it. Paranoia drove him out to use a public phone booth on the corner, dressed up for the outing in a stocking cap and false mustache.

What a bloody joke that it should come to this, but he was desperate. The Provie troops had almost bagged him at his last stop. If it had not been for the escape hatch in the bedroom closet, he would almost certainly be dead now.

Never mind.

The pricks had missed him once again, and that was all that mattered. He was on his way to greater things, a triumph such as Seamus and his lackeys only dreamed of, and they would never stop him now.

He reached the phone booth, waited for a gray-haired matron to emerge and took her place. The pockets of his jacket were weighted down with coins. He rang the foreign operator, gave the London number that he wanted and began to feed the telephone when she declared the price.

His contact picked up on the second ring. He recognized the voice; no introductions were required. They used no names.

"You're late," the contact said with a heavy trace of Scottish brogue.

"I've had some problems," he admitted grudgingly.

"It's been on the wireless."

"Are we ready?"

"My end, anyway," his contact answered. "I can't vouch for anybody else."

He let the thinly veiled aspersion pass unchallenged. It was no time for an argument across the water.

"What about the mark?" Connolly asked.

"We're following his schedule. It's strictly routine. There's been nothing so far to suggest he smells a rat."

"That's good to hear." He dropped the other shoe. "I'm coming over early."

There was fleeting hesitation on the other end. "How early?"

"Say tonight."

"Well, shit."

"Is that a problem?" Connolly enjoyed the fact that he had wiped away his contact's smug self-confidence.

"Three days ahead of schedule? Why should that be any problem? Drop in any time you like."

"How generous. I don't want any slipups, understand?"

"We're not a bunch of amateurs, you know."

"I hope not, mate ... for your sake."

Any answer from the other end was cut off as he dropped the telephone receiver in its cradle. Never mind the bloody inconvenience to his contacts. They were being paid to do their jobs without complaint, and his success would benefit their cause, as well as Connolly's. If they had any arguments with his approach, a bullet ought to settle the dispute.

He left the phone booth, checked the street in both directions and began to walk back toward the safehouse. It was no flat, like the last time, but an honest row house off the Crumlin Road. There was a back door, just in case, and Connolly's commandos had prepared a tunnel from the basement to the storm drain underneath the street.

He went in through the back door of the building and strode past the lookout, who had an AK-47 in his lap. John Breen was watching television in the smallish parlor, checking out the news and wiping his Beretta with an oily rag. His eyes strayed from the screen as Connolly sat beside him.

"Nothing fresh," he said. "They're mopping up, down by the docks."

"They'll have prints soon. We didn't have a chance to wipe the flat."

"It makes no difference if they don't know where to find us, Billy."

"Right you are. That's why we're leaving."

"We just got here," Breen protested.

"Not the house, John. I mean leaving Belfast."

"Now? Tonight?"

"I called ahead. They're ready for us. Moving up the schedule won't hurt anything. The more I wait around here, John, the more I think we're wasting precious time."

"Okay, then. Are we flying?"

"Too much heat. Mulcahey's taking us across."

"That scow of his?" Breen made a sour face. "We're lucky if he doesn't lose his way and wind up in the frigging Arctic Ocean."

"Never mind. One hour. Pack your things."

He left Breen to it, drifting toward the kitchen for a snack before they left the house. With the decision made, he suddenly felt more relaxed. If there was time, he could have curled up on the bed, upstairs, and drifted off to sleep.

There was no time, however.

He was on his way to making history.

FREDDY MCENROE WAS scowling as he left the public phone booth, moving toward the nearest station for the underground. The bloody micks thought it was simple, loitering around in downtown London waiting for a telephone to ring and hoping no one from the Special Branch dropped by to have a chat while you were hopelessly exposed.

To Connolly and others like him, anything that did not serve the cause of Holy Ireland was a trivial concern, unworthy of consideration. Everyone on earth was planted there to serve the cause, or else stand in as targets when the Irish felt like staging an "event."

For his part, McEnroe was a defiant Scotsman, dedicated to his own cause through the machinations of the Tartan Army. He had no use for the bloody English, and it seemed to him that anyone who gave John Bull a swift kick in the ass was a coincidental ally in the war for Scottish independence.

Hence his brief alliance with the Sword of Erin in a common cause. It ran against the grain, this trusting strangers—foreigners—but McEnroe had given nothing up in his exchange with Connolly. The Irishman had certain cutout numbers he could call in an emergency, but that was all. If things went badly for the Sword, in England or at home, it would not faze the Tartan Army.

Not unless the bloody Special Branch should find them keeping company and open up another file. The last thing McEnroe needed at the moment was another swarm of coppers on his ass.

The underground was typical: a lot of poofs in shiny suits competing for minimal space with the leather-clad scum of the earth, shaved heads or spiky hair in every color of the rainbow. There was no crime to speak of in the underground, but McEnroe was glad to have the French MAS automatic pistol tucked inside his belt, against his spine. He did not plan on shooting anyone tonight, but traveling without a shooter always left him feeling naked, somehow.

It was part of the mystique.

He still knew people, even Scotsmen, who would laugh themselves into hysterics at the very thought of Scottish independence from the bloody "Mother Country." Stupid bastards. When the day came, they would recognize the error of their ways and beg his pardon.

History was written by the winners, after all.

He found a seat between a Hindu man and a fat blond woman. He opened a day-old issue of the *Times,* pretending interest in an article about the blood-letting in the Balkans. Not that anyone would speak to McEnroe without an invitation, but he always strove for the appearance of normality when out in public. Fit in with the crowd as best you could, and never give the bloody coppers reason for a second look.

It was a sad fact that the Tartan Army's war had not been going well of late. First off, nobody took them seriously. Even when they bombed an English bank in Edinburgh or shot a London policeman in the leg, the talking heads on television still made snide remarks and smirked.

He felt pathetic, sometimes, but it helped to know that he was in the right. How many other revolutionary heroes had been mocked in the early days of this or that crusade?

McEnroe's stop was coming up, and he stood in the doorway, moving with the flow of strangers to the platform. Up the stairs and out, he walked north past the T-shirt shops and record stores with music blaring from open doors. His flat was three blocks down and two flights up, a monthly rental giving him a place to hang his hat and be out of the public eye.

He was a half-block from the building, whistling, when two young skinheads blocked his path. He did not give the pair a second glance until the taller of them spoke.

"No hurry, is there, mate?"

"Piss off," McEnroe growled.

"That's not polite," the second skinhead said, sneering.

"I never studied etiquette."

"Suppose we give you a refresher?" the first youth suggested. "Tell you what—we'll only charge you everything you've got."

The punk was grinning like an idiot when McEnroe stepped up and kicked him in the crotch. His partner took a backward step, one hand inside the pocket of his leather jacket, reaching for a weapon.

He gasped as McEnroe reached out and caught him by the throat with one hand, striking with the other in a short, swift jab that broke the skinhead's nose. The Scotsman followed with a rapid one-two combination, and his adversary hit the pavement in a boneless sprawl.

That left the first punk, kneeling on the sidewalk, wheezing curses while he clutched his wounded privates. McEnroe was smiling as he drove another solid kick into the skinhead's pasty face and flipped him over onto his back.

"Thus ends the lesson," he informed them, moving off before some nosy passerby had time to memorize his face.

The bloody coppers would be coming, but he did not plan to wait and join them for a chat. No one was watching at the moment, and he took advantage of the break to reach his goal.

The ancient elevator wore an Out of Order sign that had begun to fade with age, and McEnroe walked up the two flights to his tiny flat. He did not mind; the exercise would do him good.

It helped to stay in shape for what was coming up, the main event.

There would be time enough to rest when he had won his victory.

CHAPTER FIFTEEN

"You're sure you want a piece of this?" Bolan asked.

"Might as well," Finch answered. As he spoke, he slipped a curved 30-round magazine into his Heckler & Koch MP-5 A-3 submachine gun. When he had the weapon primed, its safety set, he tucked it back beneath his jacket. "I've never cared much for spectator sports."

"Well, you won't be sidelined tonight."

"I hope not."

The informant had spilled what he knew, directing them to a row house off the Crumlin Road, not far from the intersection with Duncairn Street. It was a staunchly Catholic neighborhood, where nationalist rioters turned out to stone patrols of British soldiers, and the IRA had long been welcomed there. These days, the Sword of Erin had its outposts in the area as well.

It would be risky, working behind enemy lines, in effect, but Bolan had no choice. It was ridiculous to think that Connolly would choose a hideout in a neutral neighborhood—assuming such a place existed in this city sundered by religious strife.

Bolan drove past the appointed address, turned left and circled the block. No sentries were apparent, but he understood the standing neighborhood watch system, taking for granted that someone would spot them, either going in or coming out.

Assuming that they *did* come out.

"Suggestions?"

Finch was leaning forward in his seat and checking out the street, long blocks of semidarkness between the streetlights.

"Pull in here," the SAS commando said.

It was a narrow driveway for delivery vans. Unless a stray patrol car rolled by and spotted Bolan's vehicle, they should be fine. In any case, a safer berth would give them several blocks to walk between their target and the car. It was the best that they could hope for in a pinch.

"You want the roof or street?" Bolan asked.

"Street. If I meet anyone along the way, I've got a better chance of passing for a local boy than you do."

"Right, okay."

He reached behind the driver's seat to find the CAR-15. It fit beneath the calf-length overcoat that hid his nightsuit and the bandoleer or extra magazines across his chest. He missed the standard military harness, but his borrowed Browning BDA-9S was slung beneath his arm, a British frag grenade in each side pocket of his coat. It would have to do.

He checked his watch. "I have 9:25," he said to Finch. "Ten minutes suit you?"

"Perfectly."

"Good luck."

"Who needs it, mate?"

They moved in opposite directions, Finch off toward the street, while Bolan circled toward the alley in back. There would be two paths to the roof, one from inside the target building, the other from without. To get there unobserved, he had to cross the rooftops of three intervening buildings—an apartment house and two more private homes.

The fire escape was old and rusty. As Bolan climbed, he passed lighted windows, but no one noticed him— not the middle-aged couple sitting down to a late supper in silence, the children huddled in front of a small TV set, or the young woman practicing nude aerobics in her bedroom. That one put a smile on Bolan's face that stuck until he reached the roof and he had to focus on his job again.

The roof was broad and flat. He moved past television aerials and a creaky air conditioner to reach the next house in the row. It was a short hop down, and Bolan took it easy, not wanting to alert the tenants to a stranger prowling overhead. He cleared that row house and the next, his destination just ahead.

There was a simple trapdoor on the roof that let the tenants reach their TV aerials, or to patch leaks, whatever. It would open on an attic storage space, above a bedroom, and the warrior had to take his time, be extra careful with the noise from that point on.

Two minutes were left and counting as he knelt beside the trap and tried to lift it. It was locked inside, of course, to frustrate burglars, and he put the knife to work on the soft wood with urgent strokes. Time was running short when he slipped into the musty-smelling attic.

There was another trapdoor but they had not bothered to lock it. Bolan stooped and listened, his ear against the trap—no voices, no clear sounds of movement from below.

He raised the hatch and peered into a closet, dark, with hangers mostly empty on the wooden rod. Another heartbeat had him standing in the closet holding the CAR-15.

He found the knob and turned it slowly. A wedge of light let him scan the bedroom just beyond. In fact, he saw, the light was coming from a door that opened on a hallway, voices audible from somewhere in the middle distance, possibly downstairs. The double bed was neatly made, unoccupied.

He followed the carbine out to meet his enemies.

IT FELT STRANGE, walking down this street where nearly everyone he met would gladly slit his throat if they had known his mission or his name, but Darren Finch was not afraid. They beat fear out of you in training for the SAS, with drills and exercises that demanded confidence above all else. From there, his field experience had taken over, teaching Finch that he could deal with problems as they came.

Until he missed a cue and wound up in a box.

But not this night.

He wanted Connolly as badly as the Yank had to want him—nearly so, at any rate. It meant a reckless move outside the law, light-years beyond his own legitimate authority, but that was simply what his old instructors used to call initiative.

They had a lookout on the street. He was lounging on the stoop, a slender young man in a sweater and denim jacket. There would be a gun beneath the jacket. As he came up on the row house, Finch had one hand in his pocket, wrapped around the Walther PP automatic with a stubby silencer attached. The "Hochler" submachine gun rubbed against his rib cage in its armpit sling.

Finch forced a smile as he approached the sentry, holding his tongue until he was directly opposite the stoop. He hesitated there, and turned to face the young man seated on the steps.

"You wouldn't have the time, would you?" he asked.

"'Fraid not." The young man's tone was flat, his eyes suspicious.

"Too bad."

Finch shot him through the lining of his coat, the first round slapping home an inch below the sentry's collarbone. Round two drilled through his open mouth before he had a chance to shout the warning. He slumped back on the steps, his body going limp.

There was nowhere to hide him, but it didn't matter. The soldier knew that he was out of time. He left the pistol in his pocket, brought out the submachine gun and took the concrete steps two at a time. The door would probably be locked. He wasted no time fiddling with the knob, but raised one foot and kicked it in, momentum taking him across the threshold in a rush.

A young man standing in the foyer gaped at the new arrival with a dazed expression. He wore a heavy pistol on his hip, well back, and made his move as Finch kicked back to slam the door behind him, closing out the night.

The Hochler spat a 3-round burst that punched the young man backward, crimson spouting from the small holes in his shirt. The submachine gun was not silenced, and its jackhammer racket filled the house.

He swept past the corpse and turned hard right into a spacious parlor. Two men rose from a pair of mismatched easy chairs, and a third emerged from a door on Finch's left as the commando faced them, covering the trio with his weapon. He considered letting one of his opponents make the first move, then dismissed the thought.

His next burst took the short man in the doorway, spinning him out of sight.

Finch spun to catch the next one as he tugged a shiny pistol from a shoulder holster, thumbing back the hammer. He was almost fast enough. A stream of Parabellum bullets stitched across his chest and punched him through a backward somersault, heels over head, the armchair serving as his vaulting horse.

And that left one.

Finch shot the gunner from a range of fifteen feet, the Hochler trembling in his grasp. His target, gut shot, buckled like a straw man, dropping to his knees. A handgun hit the carpet out of reach, but the man kept trying to reach it in the face of mortal pain.

The SAS commando gave him one to die on, taking off the left side of the young man's head. Reloading on the move, he started for the kitchen, long strides taking him across the threadbare carpet. At the kitchen door, he stepped across an outstretched corpse, lying just inside. A blood slick was spreading over the pale linoleum.

No other targets were visible, and he backtracked toward the stairs. Whoever else was in the house would be waiting for him—and for Belasko—on the second floor.

Finch reached the staircase and started up. Almost halfway to the landing, he was confronted by a young man, naked to the waist, who clutched an automatic shotgun. Flame spurted from the muzzle, and a giant fist struck Finch dead center in the chest.

You never hear the shot that kills you, he remembered.

But the thunder made his ears ring as he toppled backward, down the stairs.

BRAD DOOLEY HAD RELAXED a bit, once Connolly and Breen were gone. Their presence in the house was like a magnet, drawing trouble upon the rest. He had only to look at what had happened at the other hideout, or throughout the city in a day's time, since the previous evening, to understand that Connolly had brought no end of troubles home with him from the United States.

Dooley did not know where Connolly was going. That was classified, but he would find out in due time. They all would. When the time was right, and Connolly had finalized his master plan, the bloody world would know about it, right enough.

Meanwhile, it was enough for Dooley just to sit and wait.

No coward, he, but things had heated up so swiftly in the past twenty-four hours that it was frightening. You couldn't stick your nose outside without some bloody Provo sniping from the shadows, maybe cruising past and shooting up the place.

He felt a trifle guilty, hoping to avoid the worst of it, but that was simply human nature. Only madmen longed for death when there was an alternative. Dooley loved his country—or he would, if it was ever free from war and sudden death. His grandfather was still a young man when partition split the northern counties off from Mother Ireland, as a consolation prize to Ulster's Protestants who loved the bloody monarchy. The latest round of Troubles had begun the year before Brad Dooley's birth, and he had grown up as a fighter, like so many others of his generation.

Even so, it felt strange sometimes, being called upon to fight the Provos, when there were so many Brits and Protestants around who needed killing for their sins. It seemed a shameful waste of ammunition, time and energy, but Dooley did as he was told.

A soldier followed orders or he was no good at all.

He did not know how many they had lost since yesterday, but they had paid the Provie bastards back in kind. The day might set a record, after all, but Dooley had no interest in statistics. He was looking forward to the day when British troops left Ulster for the last time, taking all the bloody Orangemen with them for good measure.

The crash as the front door burst open startled Dooley. He jerked upright in bed and faced the open door, as sudden gunfire stuttered in the wake of the initial crashing sound.

Too late, but then, the bastards didn't know that. They were pulling out the stops to smother Billy before he had a chance to put his great plan in effect.

And it was Dooley's problem now.

The shotgun standing at his bedside was a cut-down Browning semiautomatic from the States, and it had maximum efficiency within a range of twenty paces. It would kill at longer ranges, but the spreading shot reduced the chances of a solid hit.

No matter.

Twenty paces would have put Brad Dooley in the middle of the street.

He scoooped up the shotgun and jacked a round into the chamber, moving toward the bedroom door. His chest and feet were bare, his only covering a pair of baggy sweat pants he had worn to bed.

More gunfire, a machine gun, and he hesitated in the doorway, facing the stairs. The raiders were downstairs, at least four of his fellow soldiers there to greet them, and there was a chance the first team could dispose of the intruders.

It did not sound that way, however, with the sudden, ringing silence from below. He waited, frozen where he stood, until the sound of footsteps reached him, moving right across the parlor and the foyer, coming up the stairs.

Still Dooley waited, hoping the intruder would get close enough so it would be impossible for him to miss. Like spearing goldfish in a bowl, he reckoned.

He lunged from cover and strode across the landing. The stranger on the stairs scowled at him, bringing up a submachine gun from beneath his overcoat. The Browning felt like lead in Dooley's hands, but he remembered how to use it, the loud report like music to his ears.

And dead on target, too.

He saw the stranger's clothing ripple to the slap of buckshot, the impact sweeping Dooley's target off his feet.

Dooley started down the stairs behind him, wondering how many others he would have to kill this night.

THE SHOTGUN BLAST was close at hand, a few feet past the bedroom doorway. Bolan crossed the threshold in a fighting crouch and came up on the blind side of a shirtless, barefoot gunner moving toward the stairs.

There was no time for chivalry in this war. Bolan triggered a 4-round burst that caught the shirtless gunner between his shoulder blades and pitched him headfirst down the stairs.

A swift step toward the staircase, and the warrior caught his breath. Below him, Darren Finch was stretched out on the floor, his arms flung wide. Was there a trace of movement in his legs?

A close-range shotgun blast above the waist was generally fatal, but he could not diagnose the Briton's condition from a distance. He would try to help, if help was possible, but first he had to carry out his mission to the best of his ability.

Two bedrooms remained to be checked before he went downstairs, and Bolan started with the one immediately on his left. It was dark and empty, except for three cots. All had rumpled bedding, but the nearest was the only one with sheets thrown back, as if its occupant had suddenly been called away. He guessed that this was where the shirtless gunner on the stairs had come from, while his roomies—if, in fact, they were in residence—were probably downstairs.

He backtracked to the other bedroom and shouldered through the door, prepared for anything. More cots, more scattered bedding, but no occupants in sight. He was about to leave when shuffling noises from the closet stopped him in his tracks. He moved to stand before the closet, at an angle, covering the beige door with his CAR-15.

"One chance," he said, just loud enough for someone crouching in the tiny cubicle to hear his voice. "Step out here."

What he got, instead, were three quick pistol shots that pierced the door around waist level, angled slightly upward, to the left. That told him that his target had to be crouching on the right side of the closet. When he stroked the automatic carbine's trigger, Bolan concentrated on that section of the door and wall.

The 5.56 mm tumblers chewed through flimsy wood and plaster in a heartbeat, leaving ragged tracks. He took it easy, closing in, retreating swiftly as he threw back the door, covering the open closet with his carbine.

He was staring at a pair of naked feet.

The gunner had been young, perhaps twenty, but he had seen his final birthday. Bolan's penetrating burst had drilled his upper chest and neck, one bullet ripping through his cheek an inch or so below the eye.

Case closed.

He doubled back toward the stairs, descending past the body of the shirtless gunner, to where Darren Finch lay stretched out on the floor. His legs were definitely moving now, as were his arms.

Death tremors?

Did he have a chance?

He knelt at Finch's side, surprised to see no evidence of blood. He gave a tug at Finch's shirt, where it was torn in front, and caught a glimpse of Kevlar underneath.

"You wouldn't have an aspirin, would you?" There was pain behind the SAS commando's crooked smile, but he had found his voice.

"Not on me," Bolan said. "If we get out of here, I'll get you some."

"We've got one down outside, one in the foyer, two more in the sitting room, one in the kitchen."

"You've been busy."

"Could have missed some," Finch replied through gritted teeth. "Is Connolly upstairs?"

The warrior shook his head. "I hoped you had him."

"Not among the ones I bagged."

Bolan found the Briton's submachine gun and placed it in his hand. "Wait here."

"Damn. I had in mind to run the bloody marathon."

"Tomorrow."

The Executioner knew that they were running out of time, but still he double-checked the entryway, the sitting room, the kitchen. Bolan found the back door of the row house bolted from inside, no other exits.

Nothing.

Connolly had slipped away once more . . . or had he ever been here?

Finch was on his feet when Bolan returned from his tour of the charnel house. "All gone?" he asked.

"I don't know if he saw us coming, or if we missed him altogether," Bolan answered. "Either way, we're into overtime."

"Agreed."

They went out through the back and left the door wide open. Let the homicide detectives work it out, another puzzle to compound the chaos of the past few hours.

Finch kept up with Bolan on the walk to the car. He kept one hand pressed flat against his solar plexus, but he seemed to have no difficulty breathing, even if it caused him pain.

"Are you all right?" Bolan asked.

"More or less. I've never had a 12-bore hit from fifteen feet before."

"You're lucky," Bolan told him. "Any farther, and the buckshot would have had a chance to spread."

"There's always that."

"You ought to have an X-ray."

"Maybe later. We've got work to do."

"Suggestions?"

"Kevin bloody Downey, for a start. I told him we'd be back to chat if nothing came of his directions."

They had left the Sword of Erin captive trussed up in a closet of the loft where Finch had grilled him. He was hobbled and handcuffed, with duct tape wound around his head to silence him.

"He might not have that kind of information," Bolan said.

"It couldn't hurt to ask. That is, it can't hurt us."

"I'll make some calls. See what I can scare up on my own."

"Suits me," Finch said, as they approached the car. "While you're about it, I'll just see what little Kevin has to say."

CHAPTER SIXTEEN

Kevin Downey knew a great deal more than he had shared with Captain Finch the first time out. A fresh dose of "persuasion" let them know that William Connolly planned operations for London in the next two weeks, with his departure set for Friday afternoon. The Sword of Erin's leader had contrived a loose alliance with a shoestring bunch of Scottish radicals who called themselves the Tartan Army to provide assistance in pursuit of "something big" on British soil.

Unfortunately Downey's ranking in the Sword had not been high enough to rate a briefing on the actual event, and most of what he knew was picked up secondhand from colleagues talking out of turn. Still, it was something, and it did not take a psychic to predict that Connolly might skip town early if the heat grew too intense.

Like now.

The British Midland flight from Belfast Airport lifted off at 8:15 a.m. on Wednesday, with Finch and Bolan booked in coach. The relatively short flight into Heathrow gave Bolan time to plot a basic strategy.

There was a risk, of course, in leaving Belfast on the supposition that his target had moved on. It was entirely possible that William Connolly was still in Northern Ireland, waiting for his trip on Friday. If it worked out that way, Bolan was prepared to take responsibility for any action taken by the Sword of Erin in his absence, since departing Belfast Wednesday morning had been his decision. He did not believe, however, that his quarry was about to cancel London.

Not if there was "something big" in store.

A call from Finch to his superiors had smoothed the way in terms of wheels and hardware, backup if they needed it, with a place to sleep if needed. The SAS and Special Branch were watching Heathrow and the city's other airport, Gatwick, plus assorted trains and ferry lines, in hopes of spotting Connolly and any hangers-on when they arrived.

He wished them luck, without believing for a moment that the net would trap his prey. Whatever else he might be, William Connolly was clearly not an idiot. He had to know that airports and the like were under heavy scrutiny.

The Executioner had no idea how Connolly would make the crossing, and in truth, he did not care. It was enough to know the man was on his way or would be coming shortly. With a line on Connolly's connections in the city, Bolan had at least a fighting chance to track him down and close his show before he had a chance to pull off "something big."

The SAS had not come up with anything that seemed to fit the bill for London in the month ahead. In simple terms, that meant no "signature" events that carried special significance to the Irish Question—no parades, debates in Parliament, or personal appearances by any celebrities with special connections to Belfast.

Of course, there was always *something* happening in London—in the theater, in politics or high society, whatever. Covering the countless possibilities would take an army, and they still might miss the boat for want of a clairvoyant who could read the target's mind.

It was far better, in the Executioner's experience, to ditch the waiting game and strike from an offensive posture, keeping up the pressure until something cracked. If he missed his target, somehow, there was still a decent chance to foul the master plan.

The Executioner would take what he could get.

The flight attendants made a final pass with heated washcloths for the passengers to freshen up. The pilot's voice announced that they were fifteen minutes out of Heathrow, well on time with no expected delays getting down to earth.

"We've got wheels waiting?" Bolan asked.

"All set. They left it in the short-term parking lot and told me where to find the keys."

He did not ask about the rest of it, unwilling to discuss their military hardware with civilians pressing close on every side. For now, it was enough to know that they would not be going in unarmed.

"You'll want the Scotties first, I guess," Finch said.

"It's all we have to start with," Bolan answered.

"Right. We ought to find some helpful information in the car."

And so, it would begin once more. A different city, different faces, but the game remained unchanged. It all came down to finding pressure points and squeezing until your adversary screamed. With any luck at all, he might spill something that you needed to hear.

If not, you found another pressure point and squeezed again. You kept the hellish pressure on until they crumbled in your grip and there was nothing left to threaten decent people on the streets.

It was a cruel, relentless game, and Bolan knew the rules by heart.

LUCY MULAVEY WAS STILL in bed that Wednesday morning, when Edward Twoomey arrived at the farmhouse to visit her brother. She was not asleep—had barely slept all night, in fact—but the fatigue she felt from the day before discouraged her from getting dressed and going out to join the men.

Besides, she told herself, they would have things to talk about that she was not supposed to hear.

The city had been going mad all night. She knew that much from listening to Seamus on the telephone, one-sided conversations with his men in Belfast that had sent him to the whiskey bottle more than once. He also watched the television, switching channels frequently to keep up with the news from Belfast.

All of it was bad.

The Brits had not come under fire last night, from what she could discover. It appeared to be a case of fratricidal warfare, Provos dueling with the Sword of Erin's members anywhere they could be found.

And stalking William Connolly.

Lucy knew that much without being told. Her brother held Connolly accountable for the attack outside her flat, and she had no doubt he was right. The kidnapping attempt had frightened her, of course, but it was worse to think that she was now responsible, to some degree, for further bloodshed on the streets.

Reluctantly she rose and slipped into a terry robe. She had not come prepared to visit Seamus and had nothing in the way of sleepwear. She did not relish facing Edward Twoomey in her underclothes.

Indeed, she did not care to speak with him, regardless of her dress. He made her flesh crawl, that one, with his pasty skin and flat, dead stare.

Still, she supposed he was a patriot, in spite of everything.

The two of them were sitting at the kitchen table, sipping coffee, when she got there. Seamus nodded to her, but he did not force a smile.

"G'morning, love."

"Good morning, Seamus. Mr. Twoomey."

"Edward, please."

She poured herself a cup of coffee and retreated to the breakfast counter, settling on a stool with Twoomey's line of sight in mind, the counter blocking two-thirds of her body from his view. He did not leer at her, exactly, but his gaze made Lucy cringe, as if she sat before him naked, rather than enshrouded by her brother's robe.

The two men had broken off their conversation when she showed herself, and that was fine. It would be perfectly all right with Lucy if she heard no more about the violence for a time. She was mature enough to know that shutting out the Troubles did not make them go away, but she could use a break.

"I'm going to the city in a bit," Seamus announced. "I'd prefer that you stay here."

"All right."

She had already called in sick at work that morning, and they would not mind if she missed two or three more days. It was the first time she had used her sick days in the past four years, while Lucy's colleagues often failed to show on Mondays, stretching out their weekends on a whim.

"I doubt if I'll be back for supper," Seamus told her, "but I shan't be staying in the city overnight, if I can help it."

"Will you call me, if you change your mind?"

"Indeed I will."

He drained his coffee, rose and rinsed the cup before he left it on the sideboard. Always tidy, was her brother. Not like other boys or men his age.

"I'm leaving two men on the grounds," he said. "They have a means to get in touch with others if it's necessary, but you should be fine. We don't get bothered here."

"I'll be all right," she replied, putting on a smile as Seamus bent to kiss her cheek.

"Another day or so, this should be settled."

"Fine."

Twoomey watched them from the sidelines like a mannequin. She wondered if the man was capable of an emotion, thinking she had never seen him frown or smile much less break out in laughter. Lucy tried to picture Twoomey at the cinema, a comedy on-screen, but it was more than she could manage. He would sit there like a lump, she thought, unless some kind of horror film came on. Then, Lucy speculated, she might catch the barest hint of interest in his eyes.

She did not follow Seamus to the door, but waved goodbye from where she sat. He smiled at her again, and Twoomey's features rippled in a kind of grimace that she took for an attempt at parting pleasantry. She thought it must be something like the way he looked when there was no one else around, and he was staring down the barrel of a gun at human prey.

Still, Ireland needed soldiers at the moment, and you could not always choose the most agreeable of men to do the movement's dirty work. If not for Edward Twoomey and his kind, where would they be?

She heard the car start up, tires crunching gravel as it pulled away, and wondered where they were now.

"NICE GIRL, your sister," Twoomey said, when they had cleared Mulavey's farm and reached the highway.

"She is that."

Twoomey shifted gears and changed the subject simultaneously. "Still no word about the second raid last night," he said. "Our people weren't involved, but that's all anybody seems to know. Of course, we're getting credit in the bloody press and all. You won't get anywhere with that lot, splitting hairs."

Mulavey thought about the Yank, Mike Belasko, and imagined that he had a fair idea of who had busted Billy's second home away from home. If he was right, the big American had come up empty, just like Twoomey's raiders in the first attempt. No matter what they tried with Connolly, he kept himself one jump ahead of them and left them looking like a pack of idiots.

"He must be getting short on men by now," Mulavey said.

"Who, Billy?"

"No, Eddie lad, the Pope. Who would you think I meant?"

The hunter's shrug was casual. If he was irritated by the barb, it didn't show. "We reckon he was somewhere short of fifty soldiers when it started. With all the shit since Monday night, I'd say his team's been cut by half, at least."

"That's something, anyhow."

"We've lost our own share, too, you know."

"I'm not forgetting anything."

As if he could. The troops were his responsibility, and every man he lost was one less soldier for the cause. Beyond that, they were like his family, blood brothers, of a sort, who took their chances as they came. Mulavey called the tune, and they got up to dance... sometimes with Death.

It troubled him that he had lost so many of them in the past—what was it? Thirty-seven hours? When he thought about the recent dead and tried to list their names, it felt like days or weeks.

But they were winning now, he felt that, too. The tide had turned against his enemies, and he was traveling to Belfast for the last great push to drive the Sword of Erin from the city. Whittled down by half, their leader hiding in a rat hole somewhere, he did not expect the Sword to offer any great resistance.

"Have we got the targets marked?" he asked.

"All ready," Twoomey answered, concentrating on the road ahead. "I doubt we'll catch them all the first time out, but we've got numbers on our side, and time. The word I get, they're running out of friends. Too much heat from the Brits and RUC since Billy's back in town."

"I'm not surprised."

"It doesn't feel right, somehow, when the soldiers help us out."

"Don't look that gift horse in the mouth," Mulavey said. "Right now, we need all the help we can get."

He thought about the Yank again, debated telling Twoomey, and decided it would be a bad idea. Whatever else he might be, Edward was a loyalist to the cause, fanatical in his commitment to security. It would unhinge him if he knew that Seamus had been meeting with a total stranger—an American, at that, and almost certainly some kind of agent—to facilitate Bill Connolly's demise.

A quarter mile in front of them, the two-lane blacktop narrowed for an old stone bridge. Seamus enjoyed it when the water rushed past underneath his feet and made a sound like liquid silver, coursing over polished stones. But the streambed would be dry this time of year.

Next time it rained, the Provo chief would make a point of driving out to spend an hour or so and put his bloody thoughts on hold.

"You'd think someone could widen out this bloody bridge a bit," Twoomey commented, shifting down from fourth to third, then second, slowing by degrees.

"It's been like this forever," Mulavey told him, smiling. "Anyhow, the country's where you come to take things easy. Where's your soul?"

"I leave it in The Pound when I'm away," Twoomey said, glancing at his chief. "You used to be a city boy yourself."

"It's not a crime to broaden your horizons, Eddie."

"Unless you start forgetting who you are and where you came from, Seamus."

"Nobody's forgetting anything. I like to get some time away, that's all. Don't let it worry you."

"Not me," the hunter said. "I don't believe in worrying."

The timbers of the ancient bridge were solid underneath their tires, the cross ties beating out a rhythmic tune. The car had crossed halfway when something flashed beneath the bridge, inside the weed-choked culvert, and the bridge disintegrated in a rolling cloud of smoke.

Authorities would later estimate the culvert bomb consisted of ninety or a hundred pounds of dynamite—enough, at any rate, to split the bridge along its length and hurl the shattered pieces skyward. Jagged shrapnel and the shock wave ripped the compact car apart and punched it through a looping somersault. The secondary blast occurred on impact with the earth, the fuel tank detonating like a napalm bomb, incinerating both men.

That afternoon, a phone call from a self-styled Sword of Erin spokesman claimed the fatal bombing as an act of war. Thus would the revolution deal with Ireland's enemies, wherever they were found.

THE IMMIGRATION CHECK was quick, and their luggage passed through Heathrow customs without incident. Darren Finch waited as Bolan cleared the passport desk, and together they proceeded through the crowded terminal. Outside, Finch got his bearings, pointing toward the short-term parking lot, perhaps a hundred meters away.

"We're over there," he said, "against the fence. A Buick, gray."

"We'll need a second car," Bolan reminded him.

"It's waiting at the flat. I didn't want to start this off with a parade."

"Okay."

The day was overcast and cool, perhaps a threat of rain. To Finch, it felt like home.

He did not like to think about his mission here on native soil, but there was no way to avoid it. It had been decades since London and the country at large were immune to assault by determined terrorist foes. The British empire was a fading memory, and with it went the smug belief in Anglo-Saxon invincibility. For some, that meant the same as sitting back to let yourself be robbed and pillaged, but Finch had a different idea.

Times changed, but right and wrong were still identifiable positions on the moral scale. You chose one angle or another for yourself and tried to make it work. The folks who wound up sitting on the fence were easy prey for any jackal with an appetite.

They found the Buick nosed in to the chain-link fence. Finch retrieved a small magnetic box secreted inside the left-rear wheel well, worked it open and palmed the keys inside. Another moment saw them in the car with their bags stowed in the trunk. Then he was wheeling out of Heathrow toward the city proper.

"Have you ever been to London?"

Bolan smiled and said, "A time or two."

"We've got a flat on Bateman Street, in Soho," Finch explained. "Not much on peace and quiet, but the locals mind their business, and they're used to stranger sights than us. Beyond that, it's a good location, fairly centralized. A couple of your targets are nearby."

Your targets. After Belfast, he had nearly made it *our,* but Finch still harbored reservations when it came to Belasko's private war. It was a different game in Northern Ireland, bending rules or chucking them entirely out the window when you had to, but it had a different feel in London. Not that Finch opposed a touch of vigilante justice for the terrorists, far from it, but the thought of bringing Belfast's war to London gave him pause.

Except that it was not his doing, not his choice. The IRA and Sword of Erin were responsible for bringing Irish acts of terrorism onto English soil. He would defer the policy debates to politicians and professors, but the fact remained that there were killers on the prowl, already stalking targets here, perhaps within his reach.

"What kind of hardware do we have on tap?" Bolan asked.

"Pretty much the same as Belfast," Finch replied. "The basic standards. Nothing traceable directly back to my firm, as you might expect."

"Of course."

"One thing you ought to keep in mind."

"What's that?"

"We haven't got a fix with Scotland Yard on this. No understanding with the locals like we've worked out with the RUC in Belfast, right? We share some information with the Special Branch, of course, and MI-6, but that's surveillance for the most part. The business we're about is well beyond the pale."

"In other words, I'll have to dodge the cops."

"To say the least."

"No sweat."

Finch glanced at Belasko as they drove east on Bayswater Road with Hyde Park and Kensington Gardens to their right. The tall Yank seemed relaxed, at ease, no apprehension as he entered yet another urban battlefield.

The SAS captain wondered who he was, what sort of background had prepared him for this day? How many lives had those hands taken, and for what offense?

He stopped himself, aware that he would have a hard time passing a similar test. It had occurred to Finch that anyone who scanned his file at headquarters could easily regard him as a murderer, depending on his or her point of view.

Yet Finch knew that he might be forced to kill again before the day was out—and that was fine. He was committed to the destruction of his country's enemies.

If that meant tracking terrorists in Soho, he was ready.

Starting now.

CHAPTER SEVENTEEN

London, England

Connolly was early for the meeting, checking out the shops on Westbourne Terrace to kill time. A block west of Paddington Station, the Bayswater district was known for its once stately town houses, converted into midprice and budget hotels. The shops were a mixed bag, more conservative than those in Soho, less exclusive than Chelsea or Mayfair.

It was neutral ground, and Connolly did not feel out of place. He wore a sport coat and a dress shirt open at the collar, rubbing shoulders with the window-shoppers and pedestrians, smiling now and then, avoiding eye contact whenever possible. No one who passed him by would guess that he was carrying a Heckler & Koch P-9 S automatic tucked into his belt at the back.

If things went well, he would not have to use the gun. Not yet.

It was a heady feeling, moving past his enemies, the very Brits he hated with a passion that eclipsed all other feelings in his life. He would have loved to draw his pistol, kill a few of them at random, but that kind of chaotic violence was self-defeating. It would throw his master plan offtrack, and nothing must be done to interfere with that triumphant strike against the enemy.

Across the street, a record shop was doing steady business, patrons equally divided between the young and middle-aged. He picked the Scotsman out on his approach, a man whose tweeds and close-cropped beard gave him the look of a professor from a small-time college somewhere in the countryside.

His contact from the Tartan Army.

Waiting for the light, he crossed Westbourne Terrace and entered the shop behind his ally. They had never met, but Polaroid snapshots had been exchanged through channels, burned once they were memorized. He had no fear that McEnroe would fail to recognize him.

It was the rest of it that troubled Connolly.

Third parties always complicated matters, all the more so when they came from foreign cultures. It could blow up in your face without a moment's warning. He would have to watch himself at every step along the way, leave nothing to chance.

Connolly browsed through the classical albums, waving off a young employee who inquired if she could help him. McEnroe was sorting through a stack of heavy-metal records, glancing up as the Irishman approached.

They did not speak. He moved around the Scotsman, spent a few more moments pretending to study the albums in front of him. In fact, he was checking out the other customers, alert to any hint of treachery. He saw no evidence that anyone had followed McEnroe, but there was still a possibility that someone— the police or worse—could have been tipped to arrive in advance.

When he had satisfied himself that no surveillance apparatus was in place, he turned and left the shop, dawdling outside until McEnroe emerged moments later. They moved down the sidewalk in tandem, Connolly pausing yet again to check his backtrack, using the reflective windows of a dress shop as his mirror, before they reached the intersection of Westbourne Terrace and Chilworth Street, where they finally stood side by side.

"Satisfied?" the Scotsman asked.

"For now. Is it set?"

"We're to be there in an hour. With the subway, we've got plenty of time. We can stop for a bite on the way, if you like."

"I'm not hungry. Which way?"

"Come with me."

They walked to the Bayswater underground station, then down broad concrete steps to the platform below. They purchased tickets from a vending machine and waited several moments for the next train to arrive.

"We're off to Euston Square..." McEnroe said.

The name meant nothing to Connolly, but he stood quietly with hands in his pockets until the train pulled in. Its doors hissed open, and they jostled through the crowd of disembarking passengers to find their seats.

The ride took most of twenty minutes, and they passed the time in silence. Connolly stood when his guide rose to leave, trailing McEnroe to the nearest exit from the car, onto another platform and upstairs to the street. Except for different advertising posters on the walls, it looked almost the same as Bayswater Station.

"This way."

It had begun to rain while they were underground, a listless pattering of drops with no real energy behind them, nothing worth the trouble of unfurling an umbrella. Euston Square was nondescript. Drab hotels were clustered around the railway station, and Mc-

Enroe led him to one of these, past a bored-looking doorman and into the lobby.

"We've got thirty minutes to kill," the Scotsman announced. "They don't care for early birds here."

"So, let's go for a walk."

"As you wish."

Thirty minutes. Before their time ran out, Connolly fancied that he would have a fair grasp of the neighborhood, approaches and escape routes.

Just in case.

You could not be too careful, dealing with the heathens.

It was all a part of making war, and Connolly left nothing to chance.

ABDUL HASSAN NAZEER had never cared for London. If he had to choose a European city in which to reside, he would opt for Rome or Athens, somewhere on the warm Mediterranean.

Somewhere closer to home.

Nazeer was Libyan, a businessman who prospered from his demonstrated skill at reading people, circumstances and events. He sometimes worked in concert with Khaddafi's Tripoli regime, as at present, and Nazeer felt that Libya's ruler was not an unreasonable man. He made allowance for profit, the incentive that would prompt Abdul Nazeer and others like him to assume the risks involved in spreading revolution far and wide, around the world.

Nazeer himself was not a revolutionary. He believed in the destruction of Israelis, to a point, but honest greed kept him in business, dealing arms and ammunition, sometimes drugs and other contraband, to Europe and a scattering of Third World clients farther south. Black-market guns had made him rich, but there was no such thing as being "rich enough."

No matter what a man collected or achieved in life, he always wanted more. It was the nature of humanity. Nazeer made no excuses for his avarice, preferring to devote his energies to more constructive causes.

Such as making money.

The hotel fronting Euston Square was not his usual. It lacked the flair and luxury Nazeer enjoyed, but these were special circumstances. Meeting with a brand-new customer on foreign soil was always hazardous. The guards who traveled with him on this trip to London were a small concession to security, as was the choice of meeting place.

Nazeer was sipping Irish coffee when the knock came. He nodded to the taller of his bodyguards and watched the young man move to answer, opening the door a crack, his partner moving up for cover. In another moment, two men were admitted to the room, both frisked and relieved of pistols carried in their belts.

"I see you take no chances, gentlemen."

The bearded one addressed Nazeer. "We can't afford to, friend. I understood we'd be discussing business privately."

"You are correct."

Nazeer received a nod from one of his companions, indicating that the men were clean. Their guns would be returned when he had finished talking business with them and they were prepared to leave. He nodded toward the door, his bodyguards departing on command and leaving him alone with his two customers.

"Be seated, please. Would either of you like a whiskey? Beer?"

"I'm fine," the Irishman replied. He did not have to introduce himself. Nazeer knew William Connolly by reptuation and sight.

"I wouldn't mind a beer," the Scotsman answered.

"Please, help yourself." Nazeer glanced toward the small minibar beneath the television set.

When they were seated, Nazeer regarded his two customers with an engaging smile. "To business, as they say. I have your shopping list. Two Steyr AUG assault rifles. Extra magazines and ammunition for both weapons. A dozen 40 mm rifle grenades, including six smoke and six high explosive. Serious merchandise, to be sure, but much smaller than my usual orders."

"We appreciate your patience and assistance," Connolly replied. "It's understood you'll have to charge an extra fee."

"Quite so, but we are reasonable men." The Arab almost laughed out loud at that, but years of dealing with fanatics had taught him to control his gut reactions in their presence. "I sympathize with your attempt to free your country, as I do with Mr. McEnroe."

"No names, for Christ's sake!" Connolly was livid. "Anybody could be listening to what you say."

"I'm not an amateur," Nazeer replied, offended by the Irishman's rebuke but clinging to his civilized facade. "The telephone and rooms have been examined—swept, as the Americans might say—for any listening devices. We are quite alone, I promise you."

"No names," the Irishman repeated. "I don't piss on you, and I won't have you piss on me."

"As you prefer."

"Three thousand pounds, or the American equivalent—five thousand dollars. I will leave the choice to you."

It was a minuscule transaction in the longer scheme of things, but this time he was acting under orders. Colonel Khaddafi had some knowledge of the Irishman's intentions, and he was determined that the effort should succeed.

Without apparent links to Libya, of course.

To that end, he had steered his buyers to the Austrian-made assault rifles, some of the finest in the world with their built-on launchers for grenades. Lightweight and compact, with a fearsome rate of fire, the Steyr AUGs would serve whatever purpose William Connolly had set.

"The money's not a problem," Connolly informed him, "but I didn't bring the whole lot with me."

"Very sensible," Nazeer replied. "The merchandise, of course, is not here either."

"But it is in London?"

"Ready for delivery, as soon as I am paid."

"Let's do it, then."

"How long will you require to fetch the money?" Nazeer asked.

"Not long."

The Arab checked his watch for the time. "King's Cross, not far from here. The railway station, yes?"

"I saw it," Connolly allowed.

"Be there at half-past ten," Nazeer instructed. "If you are not followed, one of my associates will meet you near the newsstand. Bring the money in a paper shopping bag. My colleague will exchange it for a locker key. The locker will contain your merchandise."

"I don't like dealing blind."

The Arab frowned. "I have my reputation to consider, sir. Aside from any risk you might pose to my person if I let you down, I have a business to conduct."

"If I were you," Connolly said, "I'd think a bit more on the risk and less about the cash."

"You have no cause to threaten me."

"Not yet." The Irishman appeared to feel his point was made. "Half-ten," he said. "King's Cross. I'll have another friend along for backup. We'll be watching for your man."

"Until tonight, then."

It was good to see the door swing shut and hear it latch behind them. As he poured himself another Irish coffee, heavy on the liquor now, Nazeer could not help wondering if he was getting in too deep. This Irishman had murder in his eyes while talking to a friend of sorts. What must he be like when his temper was aroused?

Nazeer did not intend to find out.

Their business would be done tonight. Tomorrow or the next day, he would catch a flight to Rome, and on from there to Tripoli.

It would be good to go home, Nazeer decided.

THE CROWD in King's Cross Station had begun to thin a bit by half-past ten, but there were still enough pedestrians around to cover Connolly and Breen when they arrived. They had their plan laid in advance and parted company before they left the underground, proceeding toward the railway station on opposite sides of Caledonia Street.

Inside the station, Connolly was casual as he approached the newsstand, walking with the folded paper bag tucked beneath an arm. Three thousand British pounds were in that bag, his muscle and the automatic pistol in his waistband all that Connolly required to keep the money safe for now.

Breen's job was observation and security. The Scotsman, McEnroe, had volunteered to tag along, but Connolly had put him off. Three men would only clutter up the set, and if the Arabs tried a fast one, if it came to killing, Connolly would need a trusted ally at his back.

He trusted Johnny Breen as much as any man alive.

And Breen knew what would happen if he let his leader down.

The Arab bodyguards were nowhere to be seen as Connolly apporoached the newsstand. It was almost time, perhaps five minutes left, and he remembered what the Scot had said about Nazeer's aversion to the early bird. There was a certain logic to it—punctuality was often critical in military operations—and he could respect the Libyan's approach to business.

Still, there was a chance Nazeer might let him down. In that event, vowed Connolly, the Sword of Erin would be dipped in Arab blood, as well. He had no sympathy for traitors, and they could expect no mercy if they fell into his hands.

He bought a tabloid paper, scanning the headlines for celebrity scandals before he turned to the naked young woman on page three. Such papers made their "news" up as they went along, mixing UFOs and "living dinosaurs" with fad diets and such, but at least they provided a visual distraction for your money.

Connolly glanced at the strangers passing by the newsstand. He drifted to one side and staked out a spot on a bench, pretending to read his paper. Every ten or fifteen seconds, he flicked his eyes toward the news-stand, waiting for his contact.

The Arab was two minutes late, and the bloody fool bypassed the kiosk entirely, moving straight toward the bench where Connolly sat. From Connolly's perspective, he did not appear to have a tail, but Breen would have to double-check.

Damned idiot!

There was no help for it as the Arab sat beside him, resting one hand on the brown paper bag placed between them.

"Slow down, son," the Irishman warned. "You owe me a key."

"It is here."

Just like that, holding out the damned key with its red plastic tag and the three digits printed in black. Connolly scanned the massive room again, knowing it was hopeless. Any one of three dozen persons might be surreptitiously watching the exchange. Suppose he sat there and refused the key, or dragged the Arab to the men's room for a bit of privacy?

Instead of making matters worse, he took the key and shoved it in his pocket, rising from the bench without a backward glance. He dawdled past the posted schedules, pretending to check out arrival and departure times while he waited to see if anyone would follow him or take unusual interest in his movements. Breen was drifting on his flank, eyes missing nothing as he covered Connolly from sixty feet away.

The Arab was gone when Connolly glanced back toward the bench. Good riddance to him. If the drop did not pan out, it would be no great task to track him down and punish him, together with the leech he worked for.

Bastards. All their righteous talk about heroic wars of liberation, and they cared only about the bloody payoff.

He drifted toward the lockers, still taking his time, watching to see if anyone "coincidentally" moved in the same direction. When no one did, he started checking locker numbers, moving down the line.

And there it was: 351.

A final check behind him revealed nothing obvious. He picked out Johnny Breen, roughly thirty feet away and on his left. If anybody tried to jump them, they could effect a telling cross fire and make a break for it in the confusion. Several exits were close at hand.

He tried the key, a final tinge of paranoia making Connolly expect that it would jam.

It turned, and the locker opened.

He was looking at a blue athletic bag, about two feet long and half that wide. Two rifles, disassembled, would be eighteen pounds, plus the grenades and loaded magazines. Say forty pounds or so. It felt right, dragging down his shoulder as he took the gym bag from the locker, left the key behind and turned away.

Now all he had to do was make it out of King's Cross Station, to his car and back to the small flat in Paddington. He carried the heavy bag in his left hand, leaving the right free for action if he had to use the pistol tucked inside his belt. He did not check on Breen now, trusting his lieutenant to maintain discreet surveillance and rejoin him at the car.

They reached the vehicle without a challenge, stowed the bag and motored west on Euston from the station, onto Marylebone. The flat was in a part of Paddington dubbed Little Venice, just off Edgeware Road. The neighbors would not give a second thought to two young men returning from an evening's workout at the gym.

Inside the flat, he placed the blue bag on the floor, knelt beside it and opened the zipper. Connolly extracted the component parts of two Steyr AUGs, assembling one in seconds flat while Breen took the other.

The Steyr measured thirty-one inches overall and weighed nine pounds with a 30-round magazine in place. It was constructed in the modern bullpup design, with a folding foregrip and the trigger group set forward of the magazine to reduce overall length. An optical sight was mounted over the receiver, and the AUG's muzzle was designed to accept the MECAR rifle grenade without a separate detachable launcher. Chambered in 5.56 mm, the compact rifle possessed selective-fire capability, with a cyclic rate of 650 rounds per minute in full-auto mode.

Connolly counted the grenades and extra magazines, making sure he had received his money's worth. There was an outside possibility that someone could have tampered with the weapons—snapped the firing pins, for instance—but even Connolly could not suggest a motive for such treachery. It would be nice if they could find a place and time to test the rifles, but a practice session multiplied their visibility and risks a hundredfold.

The guns would function on demand. He knew that in his heart.

The trick would be for Connolly and Breen to get in close enough and make their first shots count.

With Mr. Big, he knew, they would not have a second chance.

"I wish we had a few of these at home," Breen said.

"We might not need them, if we do our job."

"The Brits won't lay it down that easy," Breen replied. "You know that."

"Then, we'll do it all over again next year. And the year after. Sooner or later, the bastards have to learn."

"I'd like to have your confidence," Breen commented.

"Going soft?"

"You know damned well I'm not." There was a hint of irritation in Breen's tone. "I just don't think the bloody sods will fall apart because of one man going down."

"We won't know till we try. Just be there when I need you, Johnny boy. That's all I ask."

"I'll be there," Breen assured him, peering through the Steyr's sight as he began to sweep the room. "I want to see the bastard's face. Surprise, you bloody prick!"

"We'll start to check his schedule tomorrow. Maybe we can move things up a bit and see the job done early."

"Suits me. It can't be soon enough."

"Tomorrow, then. I've set it up with McEnroe to meet his source."

And that would be the next step in the dance, Connolly thought. He meant to see it through, no matter what the cost. He might not walk away from it, but he had tricks in store that his enemies hadn't seen yet.

Connolly looked forward to educating the bastards. School was in session, and it was Connolly's turn to drive the lesson home.

CHAPTER EIGHTEEN

For convenience and security, the Wednesday-morning rendezvous was fixed on Piccadilly Circus, in the heart of downtown London. Connolly rode the underground to Piccadilly Station, climbed the concrete steps and hit the street at 9:15 a.m. He fell in with a teeming crowd of tourists, shoppers, and locals on their way to work, drifting toward the statue of Eros perched outside the Regent Palace Hotel.

As always, he was early, checking out the field of play and watching for the opposition, any sign of an ambush. Connolly's disguise included horn-rimmed glasses and a paste-on beard that matched his own hair color well enough to pass for natural.

Somewhere behind him, in the crowd, he knew that Johnny Breen would be on watch, prepared to help. Of course, if anything went wrong, it could be over in a heartbeat, nothing Breen could do but save himself.

Should it come down to that, he trusted his lieutenant to carry on alone and do the job himself. One man could pull it off if he was brave and dedicated, not afraid to die in the attempt.

He spotted McEnroe approaching from the south with a young male companion, who wore a slightly rumpled gray suit. They made an odd couple, but there was nothing curious enough about them to rate a second glance from passersby in the heart of Piccadilly Circus.

Connolly stepped out to meet them, shaking hands with McEnroe and waiting while the Scotsman made the introductions.

"Mr. Smith, meet Mr. Jones."

No point in asking which was which. The youngster's hand was soft and damp, devoid of any strength at all. A pencil pusher, by the look of him, and happy with his civil servant's pension at the end of twenty wasted years.

"My pleasure," Connolly declared. He winked to put the younger man at ease, and got a kind of grimace in return. He turned to McEnroe. "I need to have a private word with Mr. Smith. Is that a problem?"

McEnroe did not appear to mind. If anything, the Scotsman seemed relieved that he was getting off the hook. "I'll just be going, then," he said. "You don't mind walking back alone?"

The young man frowned and shook his head. "Guess not. But I haven't got much time to spare."

"We don't need much time," Connolly said. "Let's take a stroll."

He found a theater at Coventry and Haymarket, a block away. It was a grind house, skin flicks around the clock to serve a clientele that never slept. He bought two tickets, smiling at the obvious discomfiture of "Mr. Smith," and led the way inside.

The place was nearly empty. One man was sitting in front, his head thrown back to ogle naked giants coupling on the screen. They sat in back, against the wall, with empty seats on three sides, no one close enough to overhear their conversation.

"So, let's have it."

"I was told there'd be some money."

"And there shall be," Connolly promised. "But first, I need to find out what you're selling."

"It's a copy of his confidential schedule, as requested. I should really ask for more, you know. It's not the kind of thing just anyone can lay their hands on."

"So, you want more money, then?" His tone of voice was harsh enough to give the young man pause.

"I didn't say that, did I? It was just an observation. We agreed on the price. Three hundred pounds."

"That's right." Connolly reached inside a pocket of his army-surplus jacket, then hesitated. "You've got the information with you, then?"

"Right here." The young man stroked a pallid hand across the left breast of his jacket, indicating treasures stashed inside.

"Well, that's all right, then."

Connolly had planned the move beforehand, running through it in his mind a dozen times. Coordination was the key, of course. He had to throw his left arm right around the young man's neck and clap one hand across his mouth to stifle any cries. The right hand held a stainless-steel ice pick, purchased at a London hardware store that very morning.

He punched the ice pick through his victim's jacket, through the shirt and flesh beneath. He found the gap between two ribs and put his weight behind the thrust, a six-inch spike unerringly directed to the heart.

There is a myth of instant death in stabbings, but in fact, a man can live for several seconds with a steel shaft in his ventricle. It sometimes takes a second, third or fourth thrust to complete the job. Meanwhile, the target's muscles are convulsed with pain and fear, his every instinct geared toward fight or flight.

Despite his slender build and general appearance of unfitness, "Mr. Smith" was nearly strong enough to wrestle free of Connolly's embrace. The Irishman had counted off eight seconds by the time his prey went limp and slumped back in his chair, a lifetime for the young man who would never see another birthday.

The inside pocket of the dead man's coat gave up a folded sheaf of papers. Connolly examined them as best he could in semidarkness, twisting to take advantage of the light reflected from the screen. It was a list of dates and times, with names of various connections, lifted straight from the official date book.

Perfect.

Connolly wiped the ice pick clean of fingerprints, then rose and left the theater. It would be hours, he supposed, before the staff thought twice about some lazy bastard dozing in his seat. If anyone remembered "Mr. Smith" arriving with a chum, they still had the disguise to cope with, nothing solid they could give to Scotland Yard.

The young man's death would cause a stir in his department, but the circumstances ought to sidetrack any hint of jeopardy to his superiors. The family would be embarrassed, but that could not be helped.

And McEnroe would keep his bloody mouth shut. That much was certain. Scot or no, he had as much to lose as Connolly if they were linked to the demise of "Mr. Smith."

Home free.

Emerging from the theater, he knew the best was yet to come.

ALAN KEEGAN CHECKED his watch, confirmed that he was late for work again and cursed his bloody luck.

The first time in a month that he had found a lass agreeable to sleeping over at his flat, and they had both drunk so much whiskey that he couldn't keep it up. Now, there were tiny demons hopping up and down inside his skull with hobnailed boots, and he was late again.

It was the second time this week, and he could hear his bloody foreman now. No lame excuses, damn it, Keegan! Get your ass to work on time, or find yourself another job to sleep through.

If he lost the job, there would be hell to pay with McEnroe. His steady job with the construction firm was part of Keegan's cover in the city, not to mention his connection to the sticks of gelignite that disappeared from time to time and wound up in the Tartan Army's stash. It wasn't all that much, a stick or two per day when there was blasting on the site, but every little bit helped.

He thought about the crowded subway as he pulled on his blue jeans and buttoned his shirt. The blonde was still asleep, snoring like a sailor. Keegan almost crossed the room to brush the hair back from her face and have a look, but he decided not to risk it. He would leave a note, inviting her to wait if she was so inclined. It was the best he could do.

He had no time for coffee, much less breakfast. Shaving was a waste of time he couldn't spare. His breath was something else—he reckoned it must smell like a distillery—and he rifled through the snoring woman's purse until he found a stick of gum.

So much for making himself presentable.

There was nothing around for the woman to steal, and Keegan left her to it, huddled in his bed. He locked the door behind him, pocketed his key and hit the stairs.

Two men were waiting for him on the landing, one flight down. It did not look that way at first, of course. They just stood there, the pair of them, like anybody would, two chaps with nothing else to do but stand around and chew the fat all morning, while the working class went off to worthless, dead-end jobs.

He had to pass between them, close enough to touch, avoiding them by turning sideways. Keegan didn't feel like offering apologies to such as these. Another time, he might have ordered them aside, but at the moment he couldn't be bothered.

He was almost past them when the taller one reached out and caught him by one arm. The hand felt like a vise where it was clamped around his biceps, fingers digging through the fabric of his denim sleeve.

"What's this, then?"

Number two stepped up behind him, Keegan picking up a whiff of shaving lotion. "We need a few words, Alan, if you wouldn't mind."

He smelled the stench of coppers then, and tried to wriggle free. The taller one held him fast, but that was only one arm. Keegan raised the other, aimed an elbow at the face behind him, striking hard enough to break the bastard's nose.

And striking empty air.

He did not see the stun gun coming, did not recognize it from the sudden pressure at his spine. It might have been a pistol or a fist, for all he knew.

All conscious thought was banished as a jolt of 50,000 volts surged through his body, turning muscle into rubber, bones to crumbling chalk. Before his mind went blank, he felt his legs begin to fold.

He hoped one of the bloody pigs would catch him before he smashed his face against the floor.

ON A WHIM, Connolly took a bus to Whitehall, checking out the heart of enemy territory. Here lay the seat of British government, but the Irishman felt right at home. It tickled him to stand outside the Northern Ireland Office, just below the cabinet war rooms, knowing that the bastards had a file on him upstairs. It would be interesting to read that lot, he knew, but there was not a chance in hell.

He dawdled past the Treasury, the Foreign and Commonwealth Office, making his way slowly toward Downing Street. He kept a guidebook in his hand, consulting it from time to time, the very picture of a tourist on holiday.

He drew the line at taking snapshots. They would be a waste of time, in any case. He did not need to memorize the layout of the Whitehall public buildings. Striking here would be the worst of all scenarios, a last resort.

This trip was simply for the atmosphere.

He wandered east on Downing Street, toward St. James's Park. There was a copper standing watch outside of number 10, but nothing ostentatious. If you did not know your way around the bloody government, it would never cross your mind that this was where the prime minister lived and did the best part of his business on behalf of queen and country. If you stood around all day, you might glimpse the man as he emerged and made a short walk to his waiting car, but that was all.

Still, there was something in the air on Downing Street. If power had a smell about it, something tangible, then Connolly believed that he could catch its scent along the sidewalk fronting number 10. He understood why men aspired to power, sought to dominate the lives of others. But he did not plan to spend the rest of his life as a sheep, led off to slaughter on the whim of some fat bastard sitting in the heart of London, light-years away from the soul of Connolly's own homeland.

Not that Mr. Big was really fat, per se. He came out looking fairly fit in front-page photographs, though you could never tell. It was the power craving that unhinged his kind and ultimately left them vulnerable to attack by those they feared.

If old John Bull was honest with himself and his benighted subjects, he would have thrown in the bloody towel years ago. The empire had been falling into ruin since the last world war—India, the colonies in Africa and all the rest of it—and still they clung to Northern Ireland like a souvenir of glory days gone by.

Some stupid bastards learned only when beaten on the head. It was a fact of life that Connolly had recognized back in Belfast, doing time in Long Kesh for his first offense. Unlike his enemies, he did not need a house to fall on him before he learned from his mistakes.

The yellow-livered Provies had been shying off from any bold assault for years, frightened of the repercussions. They seemed to think that England could be cowed by nibbling around the edges, knocking off a copper here, a minor politician there. It all reminded Connolly of that old Chinese myth, the Death of a Thousand Cuts...and it was taking just as bloody long to get results.

In vain, he had attempted to convince Mulavey and the others that his plan was feasible and necessary for the next phase of their liberating war. No matter how he tried, the message never got across.

So he was on his own, now, with the Sword of Erin—what was left of it—to see him through.

At least Mulavey would not be a problem anymore. Their parting gift had seen to that in grand old style, his death confirmed by wireless bulletins from Belfast.

He imagined how the other Provies had to be feeling now, confused and waiting for a strong man to appear and tell them what to think. Well, they could to without the help of William Connolly. His patience was exhausted when it came to armchair revolutionaries. Someday, when the victory had been secured, he might forgive the rank and file who only followed orders from above... but there was still a hard time coming for the leadership.

Oh, yes.

He had begun exacting his revenge already, and forgiveness for the bastards who had ordered his elimination was unthinkable. There was a payback coming, but he had to stage a breakthrough, make his move to seize the liberation movement first.

His master plan would do that... or at least place Connolly within reach of his goal. If he could pull it off and walk away, he would immediately stand preeminent among his fellows in the Irish nationalist movement. All he needed was intelligence, some patience, planning and a steady hand.

He visualized the headlines London's press would run the morning after. It made him smile to think of the metropolis convulsed by grief and panic, as his own home city had been racked by fear and violence for the best part of the century.

The Yanks would call it chickens coming home to roost.

For William Connolly, it was a simple case of justice long deferred.

He turned away from number 10 before the outer guard had any cause to notice him. He felt that he had seen enough, and it was time to scan the week's itinerary of his chosen target.

They would come together soon enough—within the next few days, if all went well. The Brits could weep and gnash their teeth when he was finished with them.

Perhaps then they would reconsider their position on the Belfast occupation.

THE FIRST THING Alan Keegan did, upon regaining consciousness, was vomit on himself.

"Right bloody mess you made of that," Darren Finch growled. "I hope you're not expecting me to clean it up."

The captive took another moment to discover that he was immobilized, bound upright in a straight-backed kitchen chair, hands cuffed behind his back, ankles secured to the chair's front legs by several twists of silver duct tape.

"Where?" he asked, still sounding groggy.

"Lord, they never taught him sentences," Finch said with a sneer. "This job could take all day."

Mack Bolan watched the SAS commando from the sidelines, sitting backward on a chair identical to Keegan's, arms folded over the back. He did not relish these interrogations, but he had a sense that they were running out of time, with Connolly prepared to stage his "something big" at any moment. Finch was something of a specialist at squeezing information from reluctant witnesses, and Bolan would not interfere.

The captive tried again. "Where am I? Who the hell are you?"

"Think of us as two concerned citizens, Alan. We hate to see a lot of lunatics run wild and damage innocent civilians with their little toys, all right? You're in a special hideaway." Finch smiled. "Feel free to scream."

"What do you want?" Keegan asked.

"Information, plain and simple. I ask questions, you supply the answers. If you play straight with us, I can guarantee you won't be harmed."

"By you, that is." The captive sounded sullen, apprehensive.

"Ah, you're thinking of your cronies in the Tartan Army, am I right?" Finch did not wait for Keegan to respond. "Of course you are. That's understandable. The thing is, Alan, that your mates don't have much future here in London—or anywhere else, for that matter. They're like the dinosaurs, about to be extinct. They just don't know it yet."

"How did I get here?"

"That? Oh, it was nothing."

Finch produced the stun gun from his pocket, held it several inches from the captive's nose and pressed the trigger. With a sudden crackling sound and a whiff of ozone, jagged bluish lightning closed the gap between electrodes, dancing like a slender wraith.

"Technology," the SAS commando said. "Super, don't you think?"

"Keep that away from me!"

"About those questions, Alan..."

Keegan scowled. "So, ask."

"Let's save some time. We know you're in the Tartan Army. That's a given. We're aware of your associates in London—some of them, at any rate. We also know they're dealing with a certain bloody Irishman to pull off something big within the next few days."

"If you know all that, you don't need me."

"That's where you're wrong," Finch said. "The broad strokes get us started, but we need the details. We can't be running off in all directions like a lot of twits and wasting precious time."

The captive shook his head. "I'm just a runner," he replied. "You think they sit me down and tell me everything? You're bloody daft."

"I think you know enough to get us started, Alan. You play straight with me, and we'll be friends. I might not have to fry your fucking eyes, all right?"

For emphasis, he held the stun gun close to Keegan's ear and gave a quick goose to the trigger.

Body memory took over, and the captive wet himself. A blush of shame suffused his cheeks, and Keegan sat with eyes downcast, his body trembling. Rage or shame, disgust or abject fear, it all came out the same.

"For Christ's sake, don't! I'll tell you what I know."

"Good lad. Let's start at the beginning, shall we? Who runs Tartan Army operations here in London?"

"Freddy McEnroe."

Finch glanced at Bolan, nodding to confirm a validation of the information in existing files.

"All right, let's have some other names, addresses, anything that comes to mind. We don't want any stray guns looking for you when we're finished, do we, son?"

"You're making me a bloody Judas!"

"A survivor," Finch corrected him. "It's not at all the same."

"You say."

"That's right, I say."

Reluctantly the Scotsman rattled off a list of names, many accompanied by home or business addresses. A small, voice-activated tape recorder caught it all.

"Okay," Finch said, "let's talk about the Irishman."

"I don't know much. McEnroe's a closedmouthed sort."

"He knows the mick, though?"

"I suppose." The captive shrugged. "I never heard a name. They talk about the Sword, but that's the lot."

"The Sword of Erin?"

"Right."

"You've heard a bit about his target, though, I'll wager."

"Well—"

"I didn't hear that, Alan. Are you running out of juice?"

The stun gun passed beneath his nose, and Keegan jerked away reflexively.

"All right! I had to put this lot together from the things I overheard in passing, right? It was supposed to be some kind of hit."

"Assassination?"

"Yeah."

"That's better, Alan. Now, we're almost finished. All I need from you is who the Irishman's gunning for."

The captive shook his head. "I thought it was crazy from the start, but no one asked me, right? I mean, you can't just reach him anytime you want."

"Reach who?"

"Who else?" The prisoner was smiling now. "Who would it be? The bloody-assed prime minister!"

CHAPTER NINETEEN

Bolan crossed the Lambeth Bridge at 10:15 a.m. and entered Southeast London in the two-door Chevrolet supplied by Darren Finch's contacts in the SAS. He had a list of targets memorized. A gym bag on the floor beside him was packed with the hardware he had chosen for the first phase of his London blitz.

The Southeast London neighborhood he entered was known as Elephant and Castle. Bolan did not have a clue as to the origins of that peculiar name, nor did he care. It was enough to know that one of his appointed targets occupied the suburb, giving him a place to start.

His first mark, off the starting block, was Phil Jaffray, tagged by Alan Keegan as an arms supplier for the Tartan Army. In the public eye, he was a sporting-goods supplier, licensed for the sale of certain long guns under British law. Behind the scenes, he stockpiled automatic weapons smuggled from the Middle East or pilfered out of military arsenals from Manchester to Wales. Thus far, investigators from the Special Branch of Scotland Yard had not been able to compile the evidence required for an indictment, but the Executioner was less concerned with legal proof than visible results.

At present, he was also driven by a newfound sense of urgency. The recognition of his adversary's target elevated his concern beyond a simple search of "something big." The SAS had passed word on to the prime minister's security detachment, but the threat would not be neutralized while William Connolly survived.

Before the Executioner could solve that problem, though, he had to track down his adversary.

The shop was situated on Fitzalan Road, near Lambeth Walk. The windows featured a display of fishing poles and tackle, nothing in the line of paramilitary hardware that was so familiar from American survival stores. He parked a half-block down and fed the meter, moving back along the sidewalk toward the shop.

It was tough, working in a public shopping district with civilians all around, and Bolan opted to rely on his side arm, a carbon copy of the Browning BDA-9S that he had left behind in Belfast. Fitted with a silencer, subsonic loads, it would allow the smallest possible disturbance to the neighborhood.

The rest of it was up to Bolan's enemy.

He stepped into the shop and let the door swing shut behind, setting off a chime that signaled his arrival to the staff. There were no customers in evidence. A short man in his thirties rose up from behind the counter, where he had been sorting merchandise and rearranging a display of knives.

"G'morning. Can I help you?"

"Phil Jaffray?"

The reaction was a frown that passed away almost before it had a chance to register. The warrior's quarry cast a furtive glance toward the street, to see if Bolan was on his own.

"Excuse me?"

Bolan had his answer then, but he decided to make sure.

"A friend of yours suggested that I get in touch."

"Which friend is that?" Jaffray asked.

"Alan Keegan."

Jaffray visibly relaxed. "That Alan. Is there something special that you wanted?"

"William Connolly."

The Scotsman stiffened, flinching from the name as if it were a physical assault. "I don't know what you mean," he answered, trying hard to keep the tremor from his voice.

"The Tartan Army throws in with a heavy hitter from the Sword of Erin, and they never get around to telling you? Get real."

The little man dropped behind the counter, coming up a heartbeat later with a double-barreled shotgun in his hands. Before he had a chance to fire, the Executioner lunged to his left, behind a rack of heavy rubber wading boots.

The first blast came in high and wide, a hasty shot that missed its target by a meter or more, boots flapping and disintegrating as a charge of buckshot whipped them off the rack.

Bolan palmed the Browning and came up firing for effect. His first round clipped the Scotsman's shoulder, spinning him, throwing off his aim. The second blast was wasted on a ceiling fixture, raining shattered glass on Jaffray's upturned face.

The shooter was recoiling, throwing up an arm to shield his eyes, when Bolan triggered two more silenced shots. They punched through Jaffray's armpit and slammed him over sideways, out of sight.

He did not have to check to know the wounds were fatal. There was no time to waste, when gunfire might have raised alarms.

Emerging from the shop, he turned over the Closed sign to deter potential customers. Two women passing by on his side of the street did not appear to give the Executioner a second glance as he retreated to his car.

Strike one.

He had been hoping to acquire more detailed information from his mark, but it was not an altogether wasted effort. Jaffray's death would start a shock wave spreading through the Tartan Army, even if its members did not know the source or cause. It was a start that he could build on, carrying the action to his enemies wherever they were found.

He put the car in motion, rolling toward the second target on his list.

THE WORST PART of guerrilla war, thought Gordon Fife, was waiting for the order to attack. He had been yearning for a chance to strike the enemy for months now, toiling on the night shift at an all-night gas station, smiling at the idiots who stopped to fill their tanks at 2:00 or 3:00 a.m.

He had not traveled all the way from Achnasheen to pump gas for the very bastards who had been his lifelong enemies, but Fife was wise enough to recognize that all good things took time.

And now, it seemed, he was about to be rewarded for his patience with a taste of action.

Ironically it took an Irishman to put the ball in play, but that meant less to Fife than ultimate results. The act of putting down the prime minister would be the signal for a general rising by the Tartan Army, both in England and at home. They might not win it all, but it had to start somewhere, sometime.

And best of all, it got him off the night shift.

He had called in sick on McEnroe's instructions, hung up on the station's supervisor when he started arguing and went directly to the rented loft on Chalton Street, in Somers Town, a half-block north of Euston Road. Four other men were there ahead of him, and two more followed after, each man bringing what he could in terms of weaponry.

In Fife's case, that consisted of a Polish PM-63 machine pistol and a stubby Colt Detective's Special .38. He kept the small revolver in a pocket of his slacks, the submachine gun with its several extra magazines inside a paper bag.

Fife did not have a clue on where he would be sent or who his target might be when the orders came from McEnroe. In truth, it hardly mattered. He had lived in constant readiness for three long years, with only two raids to his credit. It was time for him to make his mark and let the bloody fools of Scotland Yard know they had not suppressed the Tartan Army with a few arrests.

They seemed to think the group was dead, but they would soon be dealing with a very lively ghost.

His stomach growled, reminding Fife that he had left home without breakfast. They had sent Glen Herriot to fetch some takeout food, but he was slower than a tortoise in December. Fife considered several choice remarks for Glen when he returned, deciding it was best to wait and find out what the slow-coach brought.

As if on cue, there was a rapping at the door, the coded knock they had agreed on if one of them had to leave the loft. Craig Manson moved to answer it, a couple of others clearing places on the kitchen table, no one seeming bothered by the fact that Glen had taken so much time. Perhaps, Fife thought, he ought to let it go, not make a bloody scene.

He turned back toward the small-screen television, hearing Manson slip the bolt. What happened next was too confused for Fife to follow most of it, his senses overloading, numbed by shock.

The door burst open, he was clear on that, and it flattened Manson's nose, the explosive impact spinning him away. Fife turned as a stranger charged across the threshold, giving Manson a short burst from a submachine gun.

And that was all for Manson.

Everybody scrambled madly for their weapons. Fife snatched the bag that held his PM-63 and ripped it open, spilling surplus magazines across the carpet as he ducked behind the couch. He did not bother with the folding metal stock, but snapped down the foregrip and cocked the weapon, trying to maintain some trace of calm with thunder ringing in his ears.

To Fife's right, Angus Reid, Rob McQuarrie and Kyle Sutherland fired at the stranger with automatic pistols, getting off several rounds before a tight figure eight caught them in the chests and slammed them to the floor.

Charles Woolley rushed in from a bedroom as James Bannock started firing from the kitchen. They were trying for a cross fire, anything to pin the stranger down, and Fife knew he would never have a better chance.

He popped up from behind the couch, teeth clenched so hard it made his jaw ache, tracking with the little PM-63. The stranger was a blur of motion, moving left to right across his field of vision. Fife held down the submachine gun's trigger, fighting the dramatic recoil, cursing as his rounds went high and stitched an abstract pattern on the wall.

He was trying to control the Polish weapon when his target ducked and swiveled toward him, squeezing off a short burst toward the couch. Fife staggered, gasping at the impact of a giant fist against his ribs. He lost the PM-63 as he was falling, heard it hit the floor and spend its last rounds in a wild, erratic blast.

The rest was chaos, weapons hammering, the ugly sound of bullets striking flesh or plaster. Time had ceased to matter, lost in pain that radiated from his abdomen, a spread of liquid warmth along his belt line.

Days or seconds later, he was conscious of the stranger kneeling at his side. His eyes swam in and out of focus, finally capturing the gunman's face.

"Can you hear me?"

Fife replied—or did he? It appeared he had, because the stranger spoke again.

"I'm looking for the Irishman."

It started making sense, despite the crimson fog inside his head.

"Get stuffed," Fife muttered.

"One more chance."

"Too late." It felt good, making sure the bastard knew he couldn't win. "You'll never stop him now."

"I guess you're useless, then."

With that, Fife's young life ended.

"FOR GOD'S SAKE, not again!"

Before he reached the telephone receiver, Freddy McEnroe was sure that it would be bad news. There seemed to be no other kind available this morning. Just when McEnroe wanted some stability, a little peace and quiet, there was trouble all around.

"Hello?"

"It's me."

He recognized the gravel voice of Ian Gillies. From the background noise, he reckoned Gillies would be calling from his favorite pub, on Camden High Street.

"What's the chatter?"

"Have you seen the news on the telly?"

"If it's bad, I've seen it," McEnroe replied. In fact, he had the set turned off. A man had limits, after all. Nine soldiers dead, another missing, and McEnroe was frankly worried. Now, of all times, with the crucial action planned by Connolly, he did not need the kind of scrutiny that came with violence in the streets.

"You know about your little friend, then?"

"Friend?"

"The lad downtown."

It clicked, then, "Mr. Smith," his eyes inside the prime minister's office.

"What about him?"

"Seems he had a little accident this morning, in a porno house on Piccadilly Circus. It's funny, eh? You'd think a boy who carries ice picks would be careful not to stick one in his heart."

"He's had it, then?"

"Dead meat."

"That's it?"

"For now."

"I'll see you later."

McEnroe dropped the receiver back into its cradle. Jesus, this was all he needed. "Mr. Smith" stabbed dead in Piccadilly Circus meant that Connolly had either done the job himself or given orders for the hit. The bloody mick was burning bridges as he went...and what did that portend for Freddy and the Tartan Army?

McEnroe threw down a double shot of whiskey and listened to his own pulse throbbing for a moment. There was no point getting exercised about one civil servant, he decided. Connolly was simply being careful, making sure no spineless witnesses were left to point a finger after he was done with the prime minister. It did not follow that he would betray his revolutionary allies, after they had done so much to pave the way for his attack.

Not necessarily.

Still, there could be no harm in taking some precautions. He would have to call around and warn the boys he still had left. But what exactly should he tell them?

McEnroe did not believe that Connolly was killing off his soldiers. That would go beyond duplicity, verging on suicide. Whatever else he might have up his sleeve, the Irishman had no significant reserve of troops in England. If it came down to a shooting war, the Tartan Army held an edge that Connolly would find it difficult—if not impossible—to overcome.

But who, then, was responsible for the attacks on his men?

He felt the old, familiar paranoia kicking in. The government? A band of mercenaries hired specifically to punish freedom fighters when they felt victory was just within their grasp?

The best that McEnroe could do, just now, was to tell his people to be careful, watch their backs, shoot first and never mind the bloody questions.

THE BAR on Goulston Street, in Spitalfields, would not be open to the public for another hour and a half, but it was not unoccupied. From the car, the Executioner had watched his targets gather, straggling in by twos and threes, one man alone and carrying a heavy suitcase that was almost more than he could handle.

Ten minutes had passed since the loner had arrived, and it appeared that no one else was coming. Bolan made it seven, but his count was limited to faces he had seen. For all he knew, there could have been a dozen others waiting by the time he got there.

It was a gamble, but he did not let it slow him down. The Club Shilelagh was a favorite watering hole for members of the Tartan Army quartered in London. It was high on his list of potential targets, and while Bolan did not seriously expect to pick up any useful intelligence on Connolly's movements, he owed the effort to himself.

He reached inside the gym bag to extract the stubby H & K MP-5 K. A compact version of the standard MP-5, it had a cyclic rate of 800 rounds per minute on full-auto mode. He wore a leather swivel harness underneath his jacket, custom-tailored for the little submachine gun. Once he had the piece securely in its place, he slotted half a dozen extra mags into his outer pockets, locked the car behind him and struck off across the street.

The Club Shilelagh was a midsized tavern, for the neighborhood. A hundred years earlier, these streets had trembled at the name of Jack the Ripper, but the district had improved a bit since then. The prostitutes were still around, if you came looking after dark, but they were not the aging, unwashed legion of the nineteenth century.

He tried the club's back door and found it open. Careless, that, and Bolan's enemies would have no chance to learn form their mistake.

The tavern's storeroom was a crowded, quiet place, with crates of beer and liquor stacked haphazardly. A narrow aisle led toward the office, where a murmuring of voices drew him like a magnet, telling him exactly where his adversaries were.

He eased the MP-5 K out from under cover, thumbed the safety off and held the weapon ready as he moved across the cluttered storeroom, homing on the muffled sounds of conversation. Seven men, at least, but only two or three of them were speaking as he neared the open office door. It would require a moment to assess the field of fire, but time was tight.

Bolan stepped into the office doorway, sweeping left and right with cold blue eyes. There were six occupants, and that left one or more at large inside the club, to deal with later.

Right now, he had to deal with six men who were suddenly aware that Death had come to call.

Two Scotsmen facing the doorway spotted Bolan and bolted from their seats like the recipients of an electric shock. Both reached for weapons hidden under lightweight jackets, while the others took an extra heartbeat to determine what was happening.

He shot the two precocious gunners first, his subgun stuttering out three rounds apiece. The redhead on his left collapsed in his chair and went over backward with a crash. The second target, a sandy blonde with a peach fuzz mustache, was struck in the face by a pair of Parabellum manglers. The almost faceless corpse dropped out of sight behind the metal desk.

The rest of them went wild as they reached for weapons laid aside in the assumption of security. The nearest gunner on his right scooped up a Beretta AR-70 and spun toward the doorway. Bolan shot him in the chest, the impact punching him back against the wall. He was dead before his buttocks hit the floor.

Tracking across the cordite-reeking room, he caught another Scotsman with a shotgun swinging into target acquisition. He hit the shotgun artist with a rising burst that spun him like a top and dumped him like a flaccid sack of meal.

He took down the fifth, wedged into a corner, tugging at his holstered side arm. Bolan hosed him with a figure eight and dropped him where he stood.

And that left one that he could see.

The sole survivor of the six was huddled underneath the desk, an almost childlike figure, knees drawn up against his chest. He made a tiny mewling sound as Bolan aimed the MP-5 K at his ruddy face.

He heard the final shooter coming in a rush, shoes slapping concrete. He turned to meet his adversary, keeping one eye on the man beneath the desk, who seemed unarmed, with no great potential for resistance.

The odd man out came huffing into Bolan's line of sight, a shiny automatic in his fist. Before he had a chance to use it, Bolan put a short burst in the bull's-eye, crimson bursting from his chest where bullets opened flesh and fabric to the air.

"Come out from there," he told the sole survivor. "Make it quick."

The Scotsman wriggled from his hidey-hole but did not stand. He sat there with his back against the metal desk and waited for the other shoe to drop.

"I'm looking for the Irishman," Bolan said.

"He isn't here."

"I see that. My mistake." He paused a moment for effect. "I don't suppose you'd have a clue on where to find him?"

"No."

"It might be worth your life."

The trembling soldier thought about it. "There's a flat I heard about on Broadley Street, in Lisson Grove. Somebody special hiding out, was all they told us."

Bolan glanced around the small, blood-spattered room. "I'll catch you next time."

"No next time for me, mate. The first train out for Tayside, and I'm gone."

The Executioner was smiling as he backed off toward the office door.

"You know," he said, "that's not a bad idea."

CHAPTER TWENTY

"It's time to move," Connolly said. "There's too much bloody heat about."

"It feels a bit like Montreal to me," Breen said. "Or maybe Belfast."

"If you've got a point to make, let's hear it."

"Only this. We've had a bloody shadow on our heels from Canada, across the water to our own backyard. It's with us now. I don't know who's responsible, but they've been tracking us the whole damned way."

"Suppose you're right," Connolly said. "I'm not about to pass up everything we've worked so long and hard to organize."

"It might be wise to wait," Breen said.

"Like hell! We've waited long enough to teach these bastards that they've had their day."

"They haven't found us yet," Breen told him, "but they're bound to try again."

"That's why we're moving on. Before we went aboard Mulcahey's scow, I had another flat lined up. The Scotties don't know anything about it, John. There's no way they can fuck us, even if they try."

Breen hesitated for a moment, stubbing out his cigarette. "All right," he said at last, "I'll finish packing."

"Do that, John. And while you're at it, I'll just leave our friends a small surprise."

He had been back to see the Arab after Piccadilly Circus, taking out a measure of insurance for himself. Two pounds of plastique cost him extra, plus the tiny detonator, but the insulated wire dry cell battery was relatively cheap, available from any hardware store. The little trick he had in mind was nothing for a man of Connolly's experience with things that went *bang* in the night.

Breen was packing up their minimal belongings and the Steyr AUGs while Connolly prepared the booby trap. With plastique, you ensured a measure of stability, not like the problems seen with gelignite. It did not sweat or otherwise degenerate with age, a shift in temperature or climate, and a simple spark would never set it off. The only risk he faced would be a fumble with the detonator, as he slipped it in, and Connolly had built too many bombs to make that kind of lethal error.

As he worked, he thought about the recent rash of violence that had startled London. Tartan Army troops were dropping dead all over town, and spokesmen out of Scotland Yard professed themselves devoid of clues. As far as Connolly could tell, there seemed to be no evidence of government involvement in the killings, but it hardly mattered, either way. The Tartan crowd would tie up any hunters for another day or two, at least, and if his unknown adversaries happened on a lucky break...well, it would not be good enough or soon enough to foil his master plan.

For safety's sake and ease of exit, Connolly decided he would wire his special package to the window. Any raiders worth their salt would hit the door and window simultaneously, cutting off retreat, and with a two-pound charge he reckoned he could gut the flat.

Of course, it would be wasted if the bastards never tracked him down. In that case, Connolly supposed his little present would be waiting for the landlord when he came around, wondering what happened to his latest tenants.

The only good Brits Connolly had ever known were dead ones. Quite a few of those had died by Connolly's own hand, or on his orders. If he bagged the landlord, that would be fine. Whatever happened in the flat, it was a minor sideshow to the main event.

The prime minster had been on television earlier that morning, pouring out his hopes for an impending cease-fire in the Middle East. It was ironic that his death would be facilitated by an Arab, executed by a triggerman from much closer to home.

It was the same old story. Caring for the tattered remnants of a once-great empire made them careless, duped them into thinking that their tired, old island still had something to teach the world. As if a history of abject failure qualified one government to teach the rest how they should operate.

It was the arrogance his enemies displayed that made him love his work.

He finished wiring up the bomb, then checked the battery connections, smiling as he turned away.

"All ready here," Breen said.

"And me."

"Let's be away, then, shall we?"

"Coming."

With a final glance around the flat, he followed Johnny Breen outside and locked the door. He would drop the key in the first trash bin he found downstairs.

So, let the nameless bastards find him now.

He wished them luck.

All bad.

FOR ALL HE KNEW, the flat on Broadley Street was nothing, but he felt obliged to check it out. "Somebody special" could be William Connolly, and if it came down to a case of wishful thinking, then at least he would have tagged another Tartan Army hangout.

Darren Finch was interested enough to take a chance and tag along, once Bolan told him of the Scotsman's sketchy lead. "I know that neighborhood," he said. "It's just across the Edgeware Road from Paddington."

"You want to drive?"

"I thought you'd never ask."

"It might be nothing," Bolan told him.

"Nothing's what we have right now," the SAS commando said. "At least it shouldn't set us back."

That much was true, at least. The Executioner had felt a mounting sense of urgency the past few hours, since they learned the true identity of Connolly's intended target, but he also knew the risks involved in following up on slim leads.

On Broadley Street, Finch showed a set of bogus Scotland Yard credentials to the landlord and obtained a list of tenants for the middle-aged five-story building. Most of them had been in residence a year or more. The two exceptions were a newly-married couple from Jamaica, on the second floor, and a Scotsman who had signed a lease on number 403 the month before.

"We'll need to have a look around, upstairs," Finch said.

"I've got a pass key," the landlord replied.

The SAS commando smiled. "We'll borrow that, if you don't mind."

"I'll let you in myself."

"I'm sorry, sir. There could be risk involved, and, well, you being a civilian, there's the question of official negligence if we allow you to involve yourself."

"Oh, well, in that case, as you like." He fetched the key and saw them out, an old man trembling at the close proximity of death.

"Fourth floor," Bolan said. "That's a bonus. No escape hatch on the roof."

"There's still the fire escape," Finch pointed out.

"I'll flip you for it."

"Right." Finch dug inside his pocket and produced a shilling. "Heads I take the door, all right?"

"Suits me."

It came up tails.

"Right, then." If Finch was disappointed, he concealed it well. "The fire escape for me. Six minutes, shall we say?"

"I make that 12:05," Bolan said, glancing at his watch.

"Agreed."

Finch handed him the pass key and left without another word. Bolan started up the stairs alone. His jacket was unbuttoned, granting instant access to the MP-5 K submachine gun on its swivel rig, the Browning BDS-9S beneath his left arm in a fast-draw holster. He had left the frag grenades downstairs, but Finch was carrying a military stunner, just in case.

A slim black woman met him halfway to the second floor, and Bolan edged aside to let her pass. Jamaican newlyweds, he thought, and wondered if the couple would be looking for a new apartment in the morning, once the smoke had cleared.

There was a chance, of course, that he would not find anyone in number 403. In that case, it would be a wasted trip, and he would move on to the next spot on his hit list. If Finch was disappointed, it was something he could live with.

Bolan passed the second floor and kept on climbing, one hand tucked inside the pocket of his coat where he had slit the lining, fingers wrapped around the MP-5 K's pistol grip. He had memorized the faces of his major adversaries in the Sword of Erin, and if he met one of them on the stairs by chance, he would strike.

On three, he paused to listen, making sure that no one was behind him on the stairs. He did not make the landlord as a hero type, but you could never be completely sure. At the same time, he was concerned about the risk to other tenants if they stumbled into the midst of a firefight.

No footsteps below or above him, so far.

Bolan had a minute to spare as he reached the fourth floor, and took his time from there, moving along the hallway toward number 403. The walls were drab, doors nondescript except for pasted-on numbers. The warrior heard a television playing in the first apartment on his left, and someone on the floor was cooking cabbage, the aroma guaranteed to linger.

He stood and listened at the door of number 403, but no sounds issued from within. Did that prove anything? There was no law requiring that they play the radio or television set, and conversations would not carry through the door unless voices were raised.

On the other hand, if there was no one in the flat, that fact would soon become apparent.

With thirty seconds on his watch, Bolan braced himself, the MP-5 K out and ready, visible to anyone on four who chose that moment to emerge from an apartment. He stood there, waiting, counting off the seconds.

Twenty.

In his mind, he tried to chart the layout of the flat. The door would open on a living room of sorts—they always did, in small apartments—and the kitchen would be somewhere close at hand. Perhaps a corridor of sorts, to reach the bedroom and the bath. Based solely on the proximity of number 401, next door, he knew the sleeping rooms were on his left.

Ten seconds.

In the movies, this was where slow-motion might kick in, protracting every heartbeat, but in life, the time was gone before you knew it.

Time to move.

He stepped up to the door of number 403, the landlord's key in one hand, submachine gun in the other. Bolan had the pass key in the lock and was about to turn it, when the world exploded in his face.

THE FIRE ESCAPE had been maintained in good repair and the access ladder oiled and painted recently. It barely creaked at all when Darren Finch unfolded it. So far, so good.

The worst part of a fire-escape approach was passing windows where the other tenants might observe you and become alarmed, put through a call to Scotland Yard with a complaint of burglars on the prowl. If that occurred, the uniforms would not arrive in time to stop

Finch entering the target flat, but there would still be hell to pay in terms of explanations afterward.

It hardly mattered that his chief had given tentative approval to the action. Finch knew well enough that if the coppers nabbed him in the middle of a killing, he was on his own. The SAS was not about to claim an agent shooting people in the heart of London, not unless the operation was approved in triplicate from Downing Street and carried on the evening news.

So, he was on his own, except for Belasko. That was perfectly all right with Finch, at least for now. It might feel different if he landed in a prison cell, but he would cross that bridge in due time, if necessary.

He moved up the ladder, edging past a window here and there with curtains open, tenants—mostly housewives, at this hour—going on about their daily lives inside, behind a fragile pane of glass.

The MP-5 SD-3 submachine gun slapped lightly against Finch's hip as he climbed, two steps at a time. The stun grenade in his left-hand pocket helped balance the load. He hoped the "flash-bang" would not be required, but it was best to be prepared.

The curtains were closed on four. His watch showed forty-seven seconds as he huddled on the landing. Down below, the alley was deserted, no one to observe him as he drew the submachine gun from beneath his coat and flicked off the safety.

It would have helped to know how many men were in the flat, but he would have to handle this job cold, without advance intelligence. The risks were higher that way, but it would not be the first time he had gambled everything on unknown odds.

Initiative, they called it in the SAS. Without it, soldiers were reduced to robot status, fighting blindly under orders they could never truly understand.

Initiative, audacity and will. In proper hands, it was a winning combination.

Twenty seconds.

On a hunch, he tried the window. Locked. It would be straight in through the glass, then, and to hell with surreptitious entry. Sudden shock could have its uses, too.

Ten seconds.

Finch considered kicking in the glass, but then decided on a better way. The subgun's silencer made an effective bludgeon, if you kept your finger off the trigger and avoided any premature discharge. Once he had cleared the glass, it was a simple thing to follow through and put himself inside the flat. The noise would be enough to bring Belasko crashing through the door.

Five seconds.

Four.

Three.

Two.

Finch swung his weapon hard against the windowpane. He was prepared for anything—except the thunderclap that pitched his smoking body back and downward to the alley, forty feet below.

THE DOOR TO NUMBER 403 slammed into Bolan and propelled him backward, driving him against the wall. He landed in a heap, the door on top of him, and that was all that saved him from the storm of shrapnel whistling through the hall. The stench of smoke and high explosives filled his nostrils as he pushed the splintered door aside and struggled to his feet.

The small apartment lay in ruins, shattered from within by the blast. He stepped across the threshold, scanning for survivors, seeing nothing to suggest the room had been occupied.

A couch had overturned directly in his path, the scattered cushions smoldering, and Bolan stepped around it, calling out to Finch.

No answer.

Bolan shifted toward the tiny kitchen, hoping against hope for some sign of Finch, William Connolly, anyone at all. A few steps down the hall, a bedroom door stood open, showing the empty room beyond.

A wash-out.

He retreated to the living room and stood before a smoking hole twelve feet across. The blast had gone in both directions, part of its destructive force contained within the living room, the rest punched through the wall with enough force to twist the fire escape like tinfoil, straight out from the wall.

It was a sheer drop to the alley below, where Darren Finch lay on the pavement like a blackened, twisted mannequin. A pool of blood fanned out around him, simulating wings, but he was long past flying anywhere.

The Executioner retraced his steps and left the ruined flat. Outside, a clutch of frightened neighbors had collected in the corridor. They glimpsed his face, the submachine gun in his hand, and scattered for their own apartments on the double.

Jogging down the stairs, Bolan hid the MP-5 K underneath his jacket, unseen by the tenants who were rushing out in response to the blast and the spreading smoke. He moved among them, headed for the street, ignoring questions as he passed.

"What happened?"

"Is the house on fire?"

"Was it the gas main?"

Bolan met the landlord on the second-story landing, looking worse than ever, his face the color of modeling clay.

"What is it?" he demanded, spotting Bolan, still believing him to work for Scotland Yard. "What have you done?"

"If I were you," the Executioner replied, "I'd call the fire department."

"What? Oh, yes, I shall."

"Right now."

The small man turned and hustled back downstairs, with Bolan on his heels. A moment later, he was on the sidewalk, turning left and striding briskly toward his car.

He did not bother to check out the alley. Finch was dead, and there was nothing to be gained by lingering until police arrived.

He could not help the soldier now...but he could try to even up the score.

The bomb was all the evidence he needed that they had been close to William Connolly. Somehow, the Irishman had seen them coming—or, perhaps he made a habit of leaving booby traps behind him when he vacated lodgings on enemy soil.

Whatever, they had missed their prey this time, and Finch had paid the price.

As Bolan put the car in motion, he was thinking through the last few minutes, second-guessing every movement he and Finch had made since they ap-

proached the flat on Broadley Street. No matter how
he ran it down, no obvious mistakes revealed themselves. A simple coin toss put Finch on the fire escape;
it could as easily have been the Executioner whose
broken body lay behind the drab apartment house.

It was the luck of the draw, and nobody's fault except for the man who had wired up the bomb at the
window. Bolan pictured Finch, approaching cautiously. Perhaps the curtains were open, but it would
not matter if the bomb was down below the sill, beyond his line of sight. A trigger hooked up to the glass,
somehow, and that was all it took.

He had a list of targets yet to visit, but the Sword of
Erin's chief would not be found at any Tartan Army
hideout in the city. Bolan needed something more, a
different angle of attack.

He had a number memorized, a parting gift from
Darren Finch, for use in the event of an emergency. It
would connect him to the SAS—or someone with a line
on Finch's latest job, at any rate. They knew his code
name at the other end, and that was all.

But would it be enough?

A squad car passed him in the opposite direction,
headed toward the scene of the explosion. Bolan held
his speed down to the posted limit, taking no chances.

A few blocks farther on, he heard sirens blaring, and
a fire truck cleared the intersection, looking small in
Bolan's rearview mirror. It was followed by another
and another, responding to the reports of an explosion
and presumed fire in the old apartment house.

Despite this major setback, Bolan felt that he had a
job to do. As long as William Connolly was still alive
and the prime minister at risk, he could not walk away
from his assignment.

Bolan was not one to call Scotland Yard or Interpol and give them Connolly's agenda, let them handle the prime minister's security from this point on.

The Executioner had passed the point of no return.

CHAPTER TWENTY-ONE

The call paid off with greater dividends than Bolan had expected. There was minor difficulty getting through at first, before his code name clicked with the subordinate assigned to fielding calls and he was passed upstairs. The strong voice on the other end remained anonymous and interrupted only once as Bolan gave his terse account of what had happened in their raid on Lisson Grove.

"You're positive our man was done for?"

"Absolutely," Bolan said. "Police are on the scene by now."

"All right, then. Go ahead."

"I'm not about to let this slide," the Executioner informed his nameless contact, "but I need another angle if you've got one."

There was momentary silence. Next time the contact spoke, his voice was cautious. "As it happens, we've another name and address. I supposed our man would take it over, next time he checked in."

"I'm checking in. Let's have the name."

"Abdul Hassan Nazeer. A Libyan. Our information is that he supplies the Scots—or anybody else who has the price—with certain hardware not available through normal avenues."

"A mercenary dealer?"

"For the most part, but we have no doubt his orders come from Tripoli."

"He's in London?"

"As we speak. I have an address here."

He did not write it down, committing it to memory instead. "I'm sorry it turned out this way," Bolan said.

"No sorry to it," the solemn voice replied. "I take it you're proceeding with the mission?"

"Yes."

"Will there be any message for the folks at home?"

"Not yet."

"Good luck, then," the disembodied voice said. "I can't imagine we'll have cause to speak again."

"Not likely."

Bolan cradled the receiver of the public telephone and walked back to his waiting car.

The luxury hotel stood tall on Davies Street, in Mayfair, two blocks from the Roosevelt Memorial and the U.S. Embassy. It was the kind of place where sheikhs and presidents of global corporations stayed. One more wealthy Arab, more or less, would not be noticed in the crowd.

Nor, Bolan estimated, would another passing suit.

He dressed for the occasion, an expensive suit in charcoal gray, with wing tips and a red silk tie. He parked the car himself and breezed in past the doorman, no one looking at him twice. The busy registration clerks ignored him, bellboys stepped aside to let him pass. He shared the elevator with an anorexic-looking redhead and a couple in their early sixties. By the time he got to the eleventh floor, he was alone.

The Browning BDA-9S was fitted with a silencer that left it feeling bulky underneath his jacket. Still, it did not show unless an expert did the looking, and there was no hang up with the holster as he eased it free, flicked off the weapon's safety and thumbed the hammer back.

He stood outside the Arab's suite—1126—and listened to his own pulse drumming in his ears. Would this Nazeer have any information on his human prey? Whatever else went down, Bolan knew that he was about to close a pipeline bringing arms and ammunition to assorted terrorists on British soil.

He knocked and waited, was about to knock again when he heard muffled footsteps. In another moment, he was challenged from the far side of the door.

"Who is it?"

"Room service."

There was hesitation while the sentry thought about it, then he finally made up his mind. "We ordered nothing."

"Complimentary champagne and caviar."

It was a stretch, but worth a shot.

Another pause, then some whispered consultation. The watchdog sounded angry when he spoke again.

"We are not hungry. Go away."

Instead, he fired two shots directly through the door, chest-high and tracking on the sentry's voice. A swift kick punched the lock and slammed the door back. The warrior caught the falling man before he had a chance to drop and block the door with dead weight.

Number two already had his gun out, squeezing off his first round as the Executioner came through the doorway in a fighting crouch. The bullet sizzled over Bolan's head and drilled the wall behind him, across the corridor. The automatic's loud report was almost painful in his ears.

The Browning answered with a whisper, then again to make it stick. Two Parabellum manglers struck the

Arab's heart, and the man slumped backward, dead before the deep shag carpet tasted blood.

Abdul Hassan Nazeer was seated facing Bolan, rooted to his easy chair by shock and fear. His eyes were small and dark, clenched teeth as white as polished ivory against his dark complexion. Soft hands clutched the chair to keep from showing how they trembled.

"I don't have much time," the Executioner informed him, "so we'll have to dump the small talk."

"Who...who are you?"

"That's your first mistake. I'll ask the questions."

"Of course." A little of his nerve was coming back, but he did not relax his death grip on the soft arms of his chair.

"To start, I'll tell you what I know. Your name's Abdul Nazeer, you deal in weapons, and you aren't particular about your customers. You help supply the Tartan Army, and some others I could name. Oh, yeah—you've got about ten seconds left to live, unless I get straight answers off the top."

"I haven't heard the question yet," Nazeer replied.

"I'm looking for an Irishman named William Connolly. You recognize the name?"

"Perhaps."

A Parabellum round slugged home between the Arab's knees, its entry wound a dimple in the fabric covering his chair.

"I said straight answers. That's the last round that I'll waste on furniture."

"I know the man you seek."

"You sold him weapons?"

"Yesterday."

"Where is he now?"

The Arab frowned. "We made a bargain, as you have said. I did not take him for a wife."

"That's it? I don't hear much that's worth a life."

"Then you must kill me," Nazeer said, "for that is all I know."

"I don't suppose you'd lie to cover for a paying customer."

"He paid for merchandise, not loyalty."

"Right. One thing, before I go. That merchandise, did it include plastique, by any chance?"

The Arab swallowed hard. "He came to me a second time, for plastique and a detonator."

"I thought so. Here's a little something for your trouble."

Bolan's last shot struck Nazeer between the eyes and snapped his head back, crimson droplets speckling the wall behind his chair. The dealer's body sagged, arrested in its downward slide by cushions that absorbed his weight.

Bolan let himself out of the suite.

"...CANCELLING appointments here in London for the next few days, in preparation for a trip to the United States. A spokesman for the prime minister's office said this morning..."

William Connolly was crossing Southwark Bridge when the announcement struck him like a fist between the eyes. He almost swerved his compact to the curb, but caught himself in time to keep from blocking traffic.

"Shit! Damn it!"

Droning on, the bland voice of the radio announcer told him the prime minister would be embarking on his "urgent" trip to Washington that very afternoon. His topics of discussion with the U.S. President included trade restrictions in the Middle East, more aid to Russia and negotiations over human rights in Northern Ireland.

Connolly could only chuckle at the last bit, even as he watched his plans go up in smoke. The smarmy bastard he had knifed in Piccadilly Circus obviously did not have his finger on the pulse of British government activities as McEnroe had thought. A trip like this might come as a "surprise" to talking heads on television, but short of war, the prime minister did not drop what he was doing for an unplanned transatlantic flight.

He cursed again and slammed the dashboard with his fist. The bloody Brit's departure ruined everything. He had three choices now, and none of them appealed to Connolly. He could remain in London, never mind the heat, and take his chances waiting for the prime minister to return. He could declare the job a wash-out and return to Belfast with his tail between his legs. Or he could follow his intended target to the States and finish what he started.

So, there was really only one choice, after all.

Each day he spent in London multiplied his chances of arrest, with pressure mounting on his shaky allies in the Tartan Army from his unknown adversary. If he waited long enough, someone was bound to give him up, and it would all have been for nothing. They would link him to the latest bombing, to the Piccadilly stabbing, to events in Belfast... and he would not have to think about charges in New York for fifty years or so.

As for abandoning his plan, he could not face his brothers in the movement if he broke and ran without at least attempting to complete his mission. Failure in the heat of battle was acceptable, from time to time, but there was shame attached to giving up without so much as an attempt. If Connolly went home today, he would be finished in the Sword of Erin. Men who once had hailed him as their leader would dismiss him as a coward and a fool.

It was the States, then. There was no real choice at all.

He understood the cost, the risks involved in going back to the United States. The weapons purchased from Nazeer in London were a total write-off, but he still had travel documents and cash enough to make the trip. The Sword had contacts in America for arms and money, but he had to get there first, reach out to those he knew would help him if they had the chance.

The FBI and U.S. marshals would be waiting for him in the States, of course, but Connolly was fairly certain they did not expect him to return. From the perspective of a plodding copper, it was unadulterated madness—coming back to stage the ultimate assassination with a dozen murder charges waiting on the books and every lawman on the Eastern Seaboard studying his face on wanted posters.

Surprise could work to his advantage, giving him the edge he needed to achieve his goal. As for escaping once the job was done...well, that was something else again.

He meant to take it one step at a time.

Across the bridge, he motored north on Queen Street, turned onto Cannon, winding toward the backup flat where Johnny Breen was waiting for him. Breen would not be pleased about another trip to the United States, but Connolly would let him make the choice.

If necessary, Connolly would make the trip alone.

He parked outside the small apartment house on Norfolk Place, off Praed Street, locked the car and walked back to the flat. Breen saw him coming, and the door swung open before Connolly could reach for the knob. The Steyr AUG in Johnny's hand was loaded, pointed at the floor.

"You've heard the news?" Connolly asked.

Breen shook his head. "I've just been watching out for coppers since you left."

"We've missed him, John."

"Missed who?"

The bloody prime minister, who do you think?"

"Missed him how?"

Connolly stripped off his jacket and draped it across a chair. "He's flying to the States this afternoon or evening, canceling his schedule for the next few days."

"The airport?" Breen suggested.

"Not a chance. I'm all for martyrdom, you understand, but only when we've got a shot at picking off the target. He'll be covered seven ways from Sunday at the airport."

"Are we waiting for him, then?"

Connolly frowned, then shook his head. "Too much heat," he replied. "We'll get pinched or killed off while we're waiting around for the prick to come back."

Breen saw where it was going now. He sat down on the couch, the Steyr across his knees. "We're going back?"

"I'm going back," Connolly said. "I hope you'll join me, but it's up to you."

"So, what about the FBI and the state police? They'll be waiting for us."

"Nothing on the wireless indicates he's going to New York. As for the rest, we've got an edge. The last thing they'll expect is someone on their Ten Most Wanted list returning to the scene. We'll have to keep our heads down, granted, but we still have friends there."

"You make it sound a simple job," Breen said.

"Not simple, but it can be done."

"When do we leave?"

"It won't be long," Connolly replied. "But first, I want to leave a little farewell message for our British friends."

THE BOMB WAS SIMPLE to construct. Breen used the final quarter pound of plastique they had purchased from Nazeer the night before. He wired the detonator and a nine-volt battery to a kitchen timer, stuffed the parcel into an athletic bag and finished it with plastic gallon jugs of high-test gasoline.

It made a heavy load, but nothing Breen couldn't handle. Connolly was waiting for him when he took it to the car and set it on the floor behind his seat. The timer was not set, but it could wait.

They picked the target out at random from a London telephone directory, a fat department store in Mayfair, south of Oxford Street.

On their first pass, shoppers were bustling on the sidewalk, passing in and out of tall revolving doors. Connolly drove around the block and came up on a side street, double-parking long enough for Breen to reach around behind his seat, set the kitchen timer, zip the gym bag shut and take it as he exited the vehicle.

"I'll drive around the block," Connolly said. "You'll come back here?"

"As agreed," Breen replied.

"Good luck."

"Is that like 'break a leg'?"

"Be off with you."

He crossed the sidewalk, carrying the heavy bag, and walked around the corner to the entrance of the store. Most of the shoppers streaming in and out were laden with shopping bags, valises and packages. Breen's load was bulkier, perhaps, but no one seemed to spare a second glance as he maneuvered through the crowd, past bright cosmetics counters and racks of flimsy lingerie.

He made a beeline for the sign that offered Customer Assistance, well back from the revolving doors. There was a line of customers, all women, waiting to exchange some piece of merchandise or complain about a bill. He veered left toward a water cooler, drank his fill and left the heavy gym bag flush against the wall as he retraced his path toward the street.

With every step, Breen half expected someone to come running after him, a good Samaritan who saw this careless fool "forget" his bag and sought to help him by returning it. Each stride toward daylight helped reduce the crushing weight that pressed upon his shoulders, making Breen feel lighter and more liberated by the second.

It was strange, the way he felt sometimes, when he was in the middle of a misison and his life or liberty was riding on the line. He almost felt as if his mind and body were divided into two distinct and separate entities. The normal human feelings in a crisis situation—fear, anxiety, a lurking dread—were registered and noted, but he also operated on another plane.

The "other" side of Johnny Breen exulted in the preparation and execution of a strike against the common enemy. The very risk itself rejuvenated him, somehow. It was better than sex, as the Yanks liked to say—or different, at any rate.

He had set the timer for eleven minutes, to allow for strolling in and out, selecting where to leave the package once he got inside. He had consumed approximately half that time when he emerged onto the sidewalk. Ninety seconds more, and Connolly was pulling in to pick him up. Breen stepped off the curb and got in the car. They merged back into traffic.

"Done?" Connolly asked.

"Three minutes, forty-seven seconds."

"Right. We should be just in time."

He turned left at the intersection, sluggish traffic slowing their advance. Breen watched the mirror mounted on his door. He waited, ticking off the final seconds in his mind.

The blast was right on time, a crash of glass before he heard the detonation, jagged slivers blown out toward the street, and bodies reeling from the razor spray. The gas flames would be contained within the store, but smoke came next, the shock wave shattered windows, flattened bodies on the pavement. Thunder rumbled in the air.

Too bad about the women in the Customer Assistance line, but that was life. And death.

"We'll find a phone booth on the way to Heathrow," Connolly announced. "I want the bastards clear on who's responsible for this."

"It wouldn't do to waste it, eh?"

Breen's mind was elsewhere now, already drifting from the smoky scene behind them...circling, searching. There was still the matter of the raids in London, Belfast and Quebec. In Breen's opinion, there was no chance whatsoever that the strikes directed at the Sword of Erin and its allies were coincidental and unrelated. Logic told him there had to be a common hand behind the scenes, but whose?

His thoughts kept going back to the United States, the slaughter in New York, but could it be? The world knew that Americans were hamstrung by their own established rules and regulations, constitutional procedures and the like.

And yet...

It was poetic in a way, the more Breen thought about it, going back to the United States. The game had come full-circle by a twist of fate, although the goal had changed. His first time in the States, John Breen had gone to free his oldest living friend and bring him home. This day, he was embarking on a different sort of hunt, to find and kill the leader of his lifelong enemies.

One thing the never-ending war had taught Johnny Breen was that with planning and determination, any target could be taken out. Nobody was invincible. The trappings of exalted office did not make a politician bulletproof.

He was prepared to drive the lesson home again, as often as it took to change the great mass-mind in Britain and convince her leaders that the Ulster colony was too expensive to maintain.

The cause had been his life since Johnny Breen was old enough to toss a brick at soldiers in the street, and he was not deserting now. If it required another trip to the United States, perhaps his last trip anywhere, so be it.

War was all Breen knew, and killing was the one thing he did very well indeed.

CHAPTER TWENTY-TWO

The flight attendant glanced at Bolan's ticket and directed him toward business class, a short step up from coach, where he would have more leg room on the transatlantic flight. He pushed his carryon beneath the seat in front of him and settled in, the seat belt snug across his lap before the mandatory warning light came on.

It was the first flight from Heathrow to Washington, D.C., since he had tagged Abdul Nazeer. His nameless contact at the SAS had pulled a covert string or two to get him on the plane, and Bolan was relieved that he was heading back to the United States.

Not that his job was done, by any means. In fact, if his prediction was correct and Connolly was rash enough to try a hit on the prime minister in Washington, the worst was yet to come.

The Executioner was traveling unarmed again, his borrowed weapons locked up in the trunk of the compact loaner that had been left in Heathrow's overnight parking lot. In an hour or so, some nondescript soldier would turn up to claim the vehicle and that would be that.

Except for Darren Finch.

As they prepared for takeoff, flight attendants enacted the tedious routine of demonstrating seat belts and oxygen masks. Bolan sat back and closed his eyes, his thoughts focused on the taciturn SAS commando.

Did Finch leave anyone behind to mourn him? Parents? Siblings? Wife and children? Lovers? Would his passing be remarked by anyone other than the men he served with on a daily basis in the war against fanatic terrorists? Was he entitled to a brief obituary in the *Times,* or would that come too close to violating the Official Secrets Act?

Finch had known what he was doing all the way. He was a soldier, paid to risk his life if necessary in pursuit of a specific goal, and he had carried out his task as well as anyone could in the circumstances. But it would all have been for nothing if Bolan let his quarry slip away and score the winning point in Washington.

He put his thoughts of Darren Finch aside and concentrated on the task ahead. He had already contacted Hal Brognola in Justice to arrange for gear and transportation on the ground. A car with hardware in the trunk would be waiting at Dulles International when he arrived.

From that point on, his strategy was relatively simple. Flying blind, without a clue to Connolly's arrival time or whereabouts, the Executioner would have to find and tap a source of information that could put him on the gunner's track.

Once he had the information, it was easy. All he had to do was find his quarry, pick off any guards and execute the man responsible for so much death. Along the way, it would be nice if he could minimize civilian casualties and stay one jump ahead of the police and FBI.

Simple.

The flight attendant made a preflight pass with drinks, and he allowed himself a can of beer. No harm in letting down his guard a bit, when he would spend the next six hours cruising at an altitude of thirty thousand feet or better, hurtling like a speck across the gray Atlantic.

When he hit the ground, though, he would be prepared for anything.

"YOU STILL DON'T THINK we've seen the last of him?" Johnny Breen asked.

"The last of who?"

"The bastard who's been after us since Montreal."

A hurried glance behind him and across the aisle showed Connolly the nearest passengers were either dozing in their seats or concentrating on the in-flight movie, plastic headphones plugging up their ears. For all of that, he kept his voice pitched near a whisper as he answered Breen.

"You talk like it was just one man."

Breen shrugged. "One man or twenty, I don't give a damn. My point is that you still don't think we've lost him."

Connolly was silent for a moment. "We took one out in London, at the second flat," he said at last. "Maybe that's the end of it."

"You don't believe that," Breen replied. "I see it in your eyes."

"Suppose I don't? It's better being cautious. Trouble comes when you start taking things for granted."

"Trouble's all we've had since Canada. It seems like everything we touch falls into shit."

"Not this time," Connolly assured him. "It's a setback, but we haven't lost the big man yet. We'll find him waiting for us when we get to Washington."

"You called ahead?"

"It's all arranged. Our man at Noraid was surprised at first, but he'll come through. He knows the consequences, if he lets us down."

"We're using up a lot of favors, Billy."

"Never mind that, now. We have a job to do, by any means available. I offered you the chance to go back home, instead of coming with me. Don't forget that, John."

"I'm not forgetting anything."

A few rows forward, on the movie screen that hung down from the ceiling of the airplane's passenger compartment, cops and robbers were involved in a fantastic car chase through the heart of some American metropolis, guns blazing, vehicles exploding. It always puzzled Connolly, the kind of rubbish Yanks would watch when they were trying to relax.

"He'll have the Secret Service with him," Breen remarked. "It won't just be the standard bunch of boys from MI-6."

"No matter," Connolly replied. "I don't care if he's guarded by the frigging U.S. Army, Navy and Marines. We'll find a way."

"I've always envied you your confidence," Breen commented.

"Don't tell me you've been having second thoughts."

"Too late for that," his first lieutenant said. "It's just that sometimes I start wondering what happens afterward, you know."

The glue that held his stage mustache in place pulled tight as Connolly frowned. "After what?"

"Just after. When the job's done. When we die." Breen shrugged and forced a sheepish smile.

"You're getting morbid on me, Johnny. A man who thinks too much about his funeral in advance might just as well be in the ground."

"It's not like that," Breen protested. "Sometimes it's natural to wonder."

"Just concentrate on taking out the big man when we get the chance," Connolly said. "What happens after, happens. If the Brits are smart enough to learn their lesson, then we've won."

"They won't, though. That's not how it works."

"All right, then, we should be prepared to take advantage of their shock and gain as much ground as we can, before they sober up and start retaliating."

"You expect to survive the job?"

"I'm not a bloody martyr," Connolly snapped. "If I was looking for a kamikaze warrior, I'd have hired the Japanese to take it on."

"So, what's the plan?"

"I'll know more when we're on the ground. Right now, we're good for the equipment, vehicles, some extra cash. Our man with Noraid is supposed to have a schedule for us by the time we land. From there, we've got a day or so to choose the time and place."

"What kind of gear, exactly?"

"Anything we need. The States are still the biggest gun shop in the world. I phoned in a bloody shopping list ahead."

"That ought to please the FBI no end."

"Don't fret so, Johnny. We took precautions on both ends."

"Safe sex?" Breen tried another smile.

"The safest," Connolly replied. "If anyone gets screwed, it shan't be us."

Breen nodded, but he did not look convinced. "Our man at Noraid, is he still the same?"

"The very one. For all his cronies know, he's still a Provie through and through."

"I hope they're wrong."

"He's never failed us," Connolly said. "I hope you're not forgetting that he helped you in New York."

"I'm not. He'll have felt the heat since then, I shouldn't be surprised. Sometimes they melt."

"You think he'd grass?" The thought was more amusing than distressful, and he cracked a smile beneath the false mustache. "Not that one."

"Are you sure?"

"Let's put it this way," Connolly replied. "I wouldn't overestimate his loyalty in a pinch, but I'll bet everything I own that he fears you and me, the Sword, more than he does the bloody FBI."

"I hope you're right."

"Relax, old son. You ought to try and get some sleep. We don't want any jet lag bringing on fatigue at inconvenient moments, do we?"

"I'm not sleepy," Breen replied, but he leaned back and shut his eyes.

The movie had degenerated into nonstop chaos, and several members of the audience were chuckling as bodies vaulted through the air, propelled by Hollywood explosions. Connolly sat back to watch the climax, marveling as always at the gap between illusion and reality.

When they were finished filming this extravaganza, all the "dead" would rise, dust off their clothes and go to lunch at the buffet. Not so in his world, where the casualties were all too real.

Within a day, or two at the most, he meant to teach this lot another lesson in strategic savagery. If he was lucky, there might even be a televison camera rolling.

Guerrilla theater.

The Irishman was ready for his one-time-only starring role.

ACCESS TO BROGNOLA'S office in the Justice building was by appointment only, but the small man who faced him from across the desk was always welcome. They had known each other for a lifetime, or so it seemed. The two of them had done and witnessed things most men could not imagine...and would not dare sample, if they could.

"He's come back, then?" Leo Turrin asked.

"He's in the air," Brognola answered. He was chewing gum in lieu of the cigars his doctor had forbidden, working hard to ditch the craving. It would never be the same.

"They should have called the visit off."

Brognola frowned. "I ran that up the pole, but no one bought it. Anyhow, it might work out to our advantage."

"Oh?"

"Throw off their schedule," Brognola said. "Shake them up a little. If the target stayed in London, Connolly could take his own sweet time."

"Suppose he hangs around and waits for the return trip?" Turrin asked.

"It doesn't read that way. They're taking too much heat across the water, and he needs a score right now. On top of that, we caught a break at Noraid. Interpol and MI-6 think Connolly has allies there, won over from the Provos. Two or three specific suspects, as it happens. We've been watching all of them since the announcement. One got called away from home this afternoon. He drove two miles to use a pay phone, turned around and drove right back. Ma Bell confirms the call was international, a public booth in London.''

"So."

"He's on his way," Brognola said. "I feel it. Maybe more than one."

"Has anybody tipped the Man?"

"His flight is due in thirty-seven minutes. Maximum security is in effect until he leaves Monday night."

"For all the good that does."

Brognola shrugged and worked his gum. "We're doing what we can. It's Striker's job to deal with Connolly."

"Suppose he sends a stand-in? Just because the Noraid stooge phoned London," Turrin said, "it doesn't mean the first string's coming out to play. I mean, he has to know the States are hot as hell right now."

"He'll take it as a challenge," Brognola said.

"Maybe."

"Care to place a bet?"

"Not this time. Who's coordinating Striker's action?"

"I am. Secret Service wanted part of it, but I persuaded them to take a hike."

"That leaves the Bureau," Turrin said.

"They're out of it. I made some calls and got the AG on their case. They're handling the fugitive investigation, just like always, but they won't get anywhere, unless we mess things up so bad it all hangs out."

"That's reassuring."

"Striker's got wheels waiting for him out at Dulles, plenty of equipment in the trunk and some spending money in the glove compartment."

"We'll be lucky if it doesn't get ripped off."

"Relax, it's covered." Brognola was frowning. "You know, I ought to be the one with butterflies. It all comes down to me, if anything goes sour."

"Maybe it's contagious," Turrin said. "Besides, if Connolly gets lucky, we've still got our desk jobs and our pensions. Striker gets a cold hole in the ground."

"Don't sell him short. He's handled worse than this and walked away."

"Granted, but the timing on this is as tight as I've seen. The shooter's losing half a day on lag time, just for openers. We don't know where he's coming in, so maybe there's some travel time on top of that. He'll know the target's schedule, more or less, which means he'll have to push it to the wire. That could mean more aggression, less precision on the firing line. Civilian casualties, bystanders . . . Hell, I don't like this at all."

"We don't get paid to like it," Brognola replied, "just to clean it up. I'll put my trust in Striker every time."

"What happens if we blow it?" Turrin asked. "I mean, beyond the obvious."

"I'm not a diplomat. Use your imagination. Turn the thing around. Suppose the President got hit in London?"

"Shit."

"And then some. Shit for us, and shit back home. Above all, shit for every mother's son in Northern Ireland, you can bet on that."

"I guess we'd better get it right the first time," Turrin muttered.

"That's the plan."

"Sometimes I wish I was a praying man."

"It's just like falling off a bike," Brognola told him with a smile. "You never quite forget."

"I get a busy signal every time I try."

"He's got 'call waiting,' what I understand."

"You ought to do a stand-up gig on HBO."

Brognola spat his gum into the trash can and popped another stick into his mouth.

"How long till Striker lands?" Turrin asked.

"Four hours and eleven minutes, if they make it in on time."

The men were silent, aware of the drama that would unfold in the coming hours, hoping that Bolan would come out on top.

HALFWAY ACROSS the dark Atlantic, Bolan slept...and sleeping, dreamed. The images were vague at first, as if he viewed an alien, surrealistic world through drifting veils of smoke, but in another moment he could pick out human figures moving through the haze. Some shied away at his approach, while others stood their ground and waited silently for him to draw near.

It was, he realized subconsciously, the persistent dream that came to him no less than half a dozen times each year, more often in the spring and summer, for unknown reasons. Some of the casualties of Bolan's war turned out to greet him, and he reviewed their ranks in silence, making eye contact with those who faced him squarely, passing over those who flinched or turned away.

These days, it sometimes took an effort to remember all of them. They never aged, but years had passed since he had seen the first of them, in Vietnam or in the fierce campaigns for Pittsfield and Los Angeles, when he was driven by the recent slaughter of his family to wipe out blood with blood.

Some of the faces had no names, and never would. They had been glimpsed by Bolan for only a heartbeat, caught in a sniper's scope or lying prostrate on the field of battle, frozen in his memory forever. Conversely there were many well-known faces that eluded him in dreams, no matter how he tried to win them back for one more look, a parting word.

Every time he had the dream, there were a few new faces added to the ranks. A few were friendly, others frankly hostile, but they never spoke or tried to interfere with him in any way. A rule of deathly silence governed all who entered there, and Bolan knew instinctively that he would not be able to respond if one of them had somehow found his voice.

It came as no surprise, tonight, when Darren Finch stepped forward from the mist, a half-smile twisting up one corner of his mouth. He was in uniform, complete with spit-shined boots, and while the Executioner had never seen him dressed in military garb, the outfit seemed completely natural.

Behind Finch, barely visible, were several younger men whom Bolan recognized as members of the Belfast IRA. Their chief, Mulavey, was not with them, but he might turn up the next time, in another dream.

The dead were like that, sometimes. Headstrong and perverse. You never knew where they would show up next, or what their attitude would be.

He paused in front of Finch and wished that there was something he could say to make it right. The guilt was not on Bolan's head, but they were both aware that Finch would still be living if he had not been assigned to play a role in Bolan's war. Bad luck or destiny, it all came out the same.

The soldier's smile had faded now, and he was staring into Bolan's eyes as if to pass a message on by force of will alone. It was not working, though, and something like frustration pinched the corners of his mouth.

Finch tried to speak. His lips were parted, moving. In another moment, Bolan thought, the deathly silence would be broken. He would hear—

The dream evaporated in a heartbeat and his eyes snapped open, focused on the glowing seat belt warning sign. The plane was trembling, and he listened to the pilot's rote apology for unexpected turbulence. A combination of warning chimes, the aircraft's pitch and the announcement had cut through his troubled sleep.

And none too soon.

The Executioner was not a superstitious man. He did not share the popular belief that walking underneath a ladder brought bad luck or falling dreams were harbingers of death. Still, it was for the best, he told himself, if he and Darren Finch did not have words.

Not now.

He checked his watch, subtracted the departure time and reckoned he had two more hours in the air before the Boeing 747 started its approach to Dulles International. Brognola and his team would be collecting information, anything at all to help him trace his quarry stateside, but it might not be enough.

When it was time to move, the Executioner would have to trust himself above all others, falling back on his experience and instinct. The night and day ahead would likely add more faces to the ranks of silent dead, and he would get to know them all in time. Whatever else transpired, he knew they would be waiting for him in the mist.

CHAPTER TWENTY-THREE

Silver Spring, Maryland

The rented cottage stood within an easy three-block stroll from the campus of Columbia Union College, roughly one mile from the northeast city limits of Washington, D.C. The nearest major road was Sligo Creek Parkway—a good Irish name—connecting with New Hampshire Avenue for a straight run into the heart of the nation's capital.

The cottage would not have been John Breen's first choice, but then, no one had asked his opinion. Strategically he would have preferred an apartment complex, with plenty of neighbors to get in the way if a firefight erupted. Even the FBI's bloody great SWAT team thought twice about shooting up little old ladies or children at play, and the attempt to clear a block of flats would give their target ample warning if he stayed on the alert.

The cottage was a different thing entirely. Separated from its neighbors by a wooden fence and grassy walk on either side, a spacious yard in back, it could be cut off and surrounded with a minimum of risk to innocent bystanders. Telephone calls could empty the nearest homes without fuss or furor, if the tenants kept their wits about them and remembered not to panic, leaving Breen and Connolly isolated without a single human shield to call their own.

But it was done, and there was no point in complaining once the dice were tossed. Defensibility was one thing, but he had no reason to believe the FBI would find them here. It was absurd to think that Connolly would risk another trip to the United States, much less stop off to rest within spitting distance of the White House.

He had the blinds drawn, sitting on the bedroom floor with yesterday's newspaper spread out around him, fieldstripping the second Uzi to check for hidden defects. When he was finished there, Breen would start on the rifles—an Armalite AR-18 with a pistol grip and folding stock for rapid fire, the bolt-action Iver Johnson Model 300 with its telescopic sight for distance work. After that would come the pistols, twin Berettas fresh out of the box. When he was finished with the guns themselves, he would proceed to strip the several magazines, reloading them with special care, so there was nothing left to chance.

Their man at Noraid had surprised him with the Iver Johnson. The sniper's weapon was chambered in 7.62 mm, feeding its rounds from a detachable box magazine. It weighed in close to thirteen pounds and featured a twenty-four-inch free-floating barrel, fluted longitudinally to reduce vibration and whip when the rifle was fired. The nine-power Leupold scope was accurate to 1,500 meters—almost a full mile.

Whatever happened with their target, whether they were forced to come at him from near or far, Breen reckoned they were ready for the job. Of course, they had to find him first, and it was no good simply knowing that he had a supper meeting with the bloody President that night.

Specifics were what counted, and the bastard's movements when he was not locked up in the Oval Office or some bloody formal dining room, with Secret Service agents pouring tea and kissing ass. Regardless of the range involved, they had to catch him on the street somewhere in the open, where they had a chance to take him down.

A radio was playing in the bedroom, at his back. He heard the target's name, pricked up his ears, but there was nothing new. It was a repetition of the same old garbage Breen had listened to since this time yesterday, about the prime minister's visit, bonds of friendship with the new administration, this and that. Sometimes the talking heads would mention Belfast and the Troubles, but they kept it brief and moved along to "more important" topics with alacrity.

Billy switched off the radio and joined him in the living room, circling the makeshift carpet of papers to reach a nearby easy chair. "How long before you're finished with the lot?" he asked.

Four weapons yet to go, thought Breen, without the clips. "Three-quarters of an hour, if I do it right."

"Here, let me help you."

Connolly got down on the floor and started with the Armalite. It was the favored weapon of their snipers back in Belfast. He could strip the rifle with his eyes closed and reassemble it with one hand tied behind his back.

"I need to go out in a bit and meet our friend," he said.

"I'll keep you company."

"Not this time," Connolly replied. "I'm going into Washington. The chances are that no one's even looking for us, but the two of us together make it twice as risky, right?"

"I hate just sitting here," Breen stated.

"Have patience. When the time comes, you'll be right there at my side."

"Be careful with our friend, all right?"

"You still don't trust him, do you? Even after he supplied us with this hardware and a roof above our heads."

"Mistakes can happen, Billy, even to an honest man."

"I'll look both ways before I cross the street."

"You do that."

"And I'll telephone before I double back, if he's got anything to say of special interest."

"Telephone regardless."

Connolly smiled. "Why, John, I didn't know you cared."

"Don't be a bloody sod."

"All right, never fear. I'll be in touch."

Breen finished with the Uzi and reached for the Iver Johnson sniper's rifle. It would be a treat, he thought, to frame the bloody prime minister in its telescopic sight and blow his head to tatters while the television cameras caught it all.

He took his time dismantling the unfamiliar rifle.

All things come to those who wait.

THE MAGIC OF GEOGRAPHY and time zones made it possible for Bolan to arrive in Washington, D.C., five minutes after he had lifted off from Heathrow, on the far side of the ocean. Even so, despite the relatively spacious seats in business class, he still felt stiff and awkward as he grabbed his carryon, rose and started down the aisle to exit from the plane. A smiling flight attendant thanked him for his patronage, and Bolan wished her well.

He moved along the jetway to the terminal and past the gate, following posted signs to the nearest ground-floor exit. From there, it was a brisk three-minute walk to the parking garage, where a silver-gray Chrysler stood beside a numbered pillar, seven spaces north of Elevator B. The keys were in their place, tucked underneath the bumper, and he checked the trunk before he slid into the driver's seat.

An OD blanket formed the cushion for his latest stock of hardware, with another draped across the several canvas cases for a bit of privacy. The cases held an M-16 A-1 with an M-203 40 mm grenade launcher mounted below the muzzle; an Uzi submachine gun; a Desert Eagle semiautomatic pistol chambered in .44 Magnum and a Beretta 93-R autoloader with selective-fire capability, mounting a custom-made silencer. Holsters, slings and combat webbing finished off the stash, with an assortment of spare magazines for the various guns.

He glanced around the airport garage, saw no one close enough to trouble him and shed his jacket. Seconds later, he had slipped on the fast-draw shoulder holster, secured the sleek Beretta and a brace of extra magazines in their respective places, covering the whole rig with his coat.

The Executioner felt better now. At least he was not naked and defenseless in the world.

He thought about the relatively short drive west and south, to Stony Man, but such a detour was not in the cards. Not this time. He was on his own, except for contact with Brognola's office to obtain directions.

Coming back to U.S. soil was an advantage, in a way, but he would still need targets to continue with his blitz.

He chose a service station totally at random and parked beside the phone booth. He dropped a coin and tapped the private number out from memory, smiling as Brognola answered on the second ring.

"Hello?"

"Are we secure?"

There was a measure of relief in the big Fed's voice as he answered. "Swept this morning, but I'll keep it brief. Safe crossing?"

"Uneventful."

"That's the only kind to have. You ready?"

"As I'll ever be."

"The pigeon's name is Tom O'Herlihy. He works for Noraid, lives in Arlington. I've got a home address and office. Take the office first."

"Go on."

Brognola rattled off the number of an office block on L Street, Washington. The target's home lay south of Wilson Boulevard, next door in Arlington.

"All clear on that?" Brognola asked when he was done.

"Got it."

"Right. We know he took a call from London at his home, went out and used a public booth in Arlington. The callback linked him to another London pay phone. Nowhere else to go from there, but it was in the neighborhood of where your last play came apart."

"That's good enough for me." The warrior's voice had taken on an icy edge.

"Me, too. He must know something, but I wouldn't want to speculate on his desire to share."

"He's covered?"

"Cautiously and from a distance. He's been sitting home alone since he went out to make the call."

"No family?"

"They're visiting a cousin in New York, or some damned thing. You've got him to yourself."

"Call off the eyes."

"No sooner said than done."

"I'll keep in touch."

"Good luck."

The Executioner severed the connection, walked back to his car and slid behind the wheel. He put the car in motion and eased back into traffic.

At least he had a place to start. If he began to question Brognola's connections, there could be at least a dozen explanations for the calls between O'Herlihy and London. Noraid had been working with the IRA from its inception, covering shipments of weapons and cash in the guise of "humanitarian aid," and transatlantic calls were commonplace. He had no proof that William Connolly was on the London end of either call, but that was where experience and intuition leant a hand.

The London phone booth had been near the flat where Darren Finch was killed. The conversations with O'Herlihy, from all appearances, had taken place a short time prior to Connolly's evacuation of the flat. By then, the Sword of Erin's leader would have known his target's plans for visiting the States.

Coincidence?

Not likely.

Bolan was prepared to gamble, for the very reason that he held no other cards. If Tom O'Herlihy was not his mark, then it would be a waste of time, but he had no other prospect at the moment.

He was about to drop in on a total stranger for a chat. The stakes were life or death, and one of them would never be the same again.

IT TOOK HIM all of forty minutes, driving into Washington and west on Constitution Avenue to Henry Bacon Drive. Connolly found a space between a sports car and a station wagon, in the parking lot reserved for visitors to the Lincoln Memorial. Instead of visiting that landmark, though, the Irishman struck off to the southwest, passing the Vietnam Memorial, moving with determined strides toward the Reflecting Pool. The floodlights made it easy, showing him the way.

As always, Connolly was early for the meet. Not so much that he would be endangered, singled out as loitering, but just enough to scan the field, make sure that no trap had been laid to snare him.

They would have to recognize him first, and he had taken pains to rule that out. His hair was streaked with gray now, adding decades to his age, and he had glued a different mustache to his upper lip—a bushy gray one this time, sagging at the corners. The horn-rimmed glasses finished his disguise. The only vestige of his former self was a tiny plastic shamrock pinned to his lapel—that, and the Beretta automatic tucked inside his waistband at the back.

He dawdled by the water, killing time. Two minutes remained, and no one gave him so much as a second glance. A group of veterans passed him, some in wheelchairs, others pushing, headed toward the memorial to America's famous defeat in Southeast Asia.

Someday, Connolly believed, the bloody Brits would build a monument like that in London, to the soldiers she had thrown away in Belfast, trying to suppress the people's will. Perhaps his mission here would speed that day along.

O'Herlihy could not afford to come himself. It had been risky, even talking on the telephone, and Connolly did not expect the man to keep a rendezvous when he was very probably the target of surveillance. Personal considerations aside, it would have jeopardized Connolly's mission, and that he would never allow.

O'Herlihy's appointed stand-in was a young, redheaded man with freckles, carrying a copy of the *Washington Post* folded under his arm. On his lapel, he wore a plastic shamrock just like Connolly's, the recognition signal that O'Herlihy suggested in their final conversation on the telephone.

They came together casually, all smiles and handshakes, like a pair of mismatched friends out for an evening on the green. No one was near enough to eavesdrop as they walked and talked together, but they kept their voices low-pitched all the same.

"You're taking on a lot," the redhead told him, sounding half admiring, half incredulous.

"No risk, no gain," Connolly said. "You've got the information I require?"

"Right here." The young man switched his folded paper from one hand to the other, bringing it closer to Connolly's hand. "I was told to explain this is all we can do. Too much heat, otherwise."

"It's enough, if you got the right goods."

"Scheduled movements from now till he flies. You'll not see him tonight, I can promise you. Feds have him locked up as tight as Fort Knox for the evening. You might catch a glimpse as he goes on his rounds after that, but I don't fancy anyone getting a shot."

"That's my problem."

"You're right. And we can't help you out if you blow it, all right?" The young redhead was solemn, his voice going stern. "Not with lawyers, and not with a lift out like last time. I'm ordered to tell you that this lot pays all."

"So, you've told me."

"No hard feelings, eh? Myself, I wish you all the best of luck."

"I'm sure."

"The thing is, even if you pull it off, O'Herlihy believes the Brits will just crack down the harder, not to mention the Americans, it happening right here and all. We'll have more work to do than ever, and we can't spend everything on one or two men, when we've got an army to support."

"Waste everything on one or two, you mean."

"That's not my word."

"Don't let it worry you. I'm used to doubting Thomases, in my line. Find yourself a hole to hide in when the shit comes down, but don't get lost in there. We've got a new world coming, son. A brand-new day of freedom."

"I hope you're right."

"You'll see."

"Good luck, then."

As he turned to leave, the redhead handed Connolly his folded paper. Tucked inside its pages, he would find the target's personal itinerary in Washington—an itemized list of meetings and events the prime minister would be attending in the next three days.

There was time enough to pick the place and moment that would best serve their cause. If three days couldn't do it, then he might as well give up and catch the next plane back to Belfast.

Three days was ample, if he kept his wits about him and did not allow himself to falter.

Up ahead, he found a bench beneath a pole light, and he sat to read the paper. Flipping through its pages, Connolly found his target's schedule in the entertainment section.

He started to read, but stopped a few lines down the page and smiled.

That simple. Could it really be?

It meant a restless night, but he would still check in with Breen to let him know the plan. He knew that Johnny would be pissed at getting left out of the final act, but there was nothing Connolly could do now. He had to get himself in place without delay, or it would never work.

And first, he had to find a public telephone.

THE EXECUTIONER TOOK Highway 50 through the heart of Arlington to pick up Wilson Boulevard. He had been killing time, to let Brognola call his watchdogs off, but he could spare only so much. O'Herlihy was sitting on the information he required to finish off his strike against the Sword of Erin, and a sense of urgency compelled him to proceed.

He understood that Noraid had been organized by zealots of a sort, Americans of Irish background who were raised with a disdain for British policy in Ireland dating from the days of the potato famine, when their ancestors had fled starvation, looking for new hope in the United States. Some of them still had family on the Emerald Isle, and all could be depended on to turn out wearing green for a St. Patrick's Day parade, but they were sadly out of touch with the realities of civil war at home.

They did not seem to understand that times had changed since 1922, when heroes of the IRA stood tall against oppression by the brutal Black and Tan militia. Even the upheaval sparked by Catholic civil rights demands in Northern Ireland during 1969 had been forgotten in a quarter century of violence.

Along the way, the Provos had adopted Marxist dogma as their own and gone with hats in hand to seek assistance from the Kremlin. Once the KGB went out of business, they were drawn to Middle Eastern despots like Khaddafi and Saddam Hussein, fanatics rich and powerful enough to spread their hatred of the West abroad at any cost to human life and suffering.

In the United States, though, from New York and Boston to Chicago, San Francisco and Los Angeles, transplanted Irishmen and women still imagined their donations, cash and arms alike, were being used to wage a war against the British over issues that had been obscured, perhaps obliterated, by a generation of chaotic violence. They could not seem to grasp the fact that the exalted "good old days" had passed them by forever, lost in the obscuring mists of history.

O'Herlihy, the Executioner suspected, would be something else again. He knew what he was doing when he veered off from the Provos, cut a bargain with the Sword of Erin, and the chances were that he had made a profit for himself along the way. In fact, his motives were irrelevant to Bolan at the moment just as long as he gave up the necessary information on demand.

The house was dark and still at half-past ten o'clock. He drove past, looking for the sort of "unmarked" cars that always gave themselves away, and found no signs of a surveillance team in place.

If Brognola had done his job, it should be fine. If not, the watchdogs were about to witness something they would not soon manage to forget.

He found a place to park, protected from the nearest streetlight by an overhanging elm, and stripped his jacket off. Another moment freed him of his slacks, the blacksuit underneath designed to fit him like a second skin. He wore the sleek Beretta 93-R in its armpit holster, with the custom silencer attached, stilettos and garrotes concealed in pockets of the blacksuit.

Bolan thought about the Uzi, tucked beneath the driver's seat, and left it where it was. There might be lookouts, but O'Herlihy would not have called out an army to watch his house, assuming he had one at his disposal. Silent penetration was the way to go, and Bolan hoped to manage his objective with a minimum of fuss.

He cut through four backyards to reach his destination, pausing at the final redwood fence to stand and listen. In the yard beyond, there was a swimming pool, the underwater lights extinguished. Despite the darkness, he could still make out a figure seated on a folding deck chair near the pool, a riot shotgun braced across his kness. The sentry smoked and shifted in his seat from time to time, but made no move to stand up and patrol the yard.

Bolan scaled the fence without a sound and landed in a crouch on new-mown grass. He drew his side arm and advanced silently until he stood behind the sentry. He gave no warning before rapping the butt of his weapon hard against the man's skull. His victim pitched forward onto his knees before dropping to the ground.

The sliding doors were easy, even though O'Herlihy had locked them with a stick wedged in the runners. Bolan pressed and lifted, freed the right-hand panel from its track and set it to the side. Another moment put him in the house, and he proceeded to the master bedroom, following the sound track of a television comedy.

The door was open, and he stepped inside without an invitation, clearing his throat to catch O'Herlihy's attention. The Irishman was sitting up in bed, sheets pooled around his waist, a half-filled glass of amber whiskey in his hand. At sight of Bolan and the pistol, he forgot his drink and lost it, soaking himself.

"Aw, Jesus."

"Keep a grip," the Executioner advised. "A few straight answers and I'm out of here. You change your sheets and get a good night's rest."

"I'm sure."

"You never know unless you try."

"What do you want?"

"You're working for the Sword of Erin. I suspect the Provos wouldn't like that any more than I do. If you help me out, they never have to know."

"And if I don't?"

"Well, it's a toss-up. But the bad news is that either way, you lose."

"That sounds familiar."

"William Connolly. You're helping him, I want him. Tell me where he is and make it easy on yourself."

O'Herlihy was thinking fast, eyes darting here and there around the room. "I'm not alone," he said.

"The guy out back? He's out of the picture for the moment."

"Who are you?"

"Someone with a loaded weapon and a minimum of patience. One more time—where's Connolly?"

"How do I know you'll let me live?"

"You don't," he said. "But what choice do you have?"

"I guess that's right." Reluctantly the captive rattled off a street address in Silver Spring, Maryland, a dozen miles from their present location as the buzzard flies.

"I hope you're smart enough to tell the truth," Bolan said. "If I have to ask again, you won't like how it goes."

"I haven't liked it much this time," O'Herlihy replied.

Bolan was backing toward the door, half turning, when the Noraid leader made his move. It was expected, planned for, though he had not decided where the gun would be concealed.

It was the nightstand on the left. O'Herlihy was quick, you had to give him that, with one hand in the drawer and coming out again as Bolan crossed the bedroom's threshold. There would still have been a chance for him to make the shot, but Bolan saw it coming, pumped two bullets through his face from twenty feet away, and left him sprawled across the king-size bed.

He had the address now, and it would have to do, because his source was gone forever. If O'Herlihy had conned him, he would be out of luck.

But luck was what you made it.

The Executioner was pressing on.

CHAPTER TWENTY-FOUR

It is no accident that warriors often choose the pre-dawn hours for surprise attacks against their enemies. In fact, psychology and physiology combine at such a time to lower the defenses of a human being. Eyelids droop, anxiety recedes, the brain and muscles cry out with fatigue. In early-morning darkness, even predators are sometimes taken unaware and trapped or slain before they can defend themselves.

The Executioner had first discovered that phenomenon while he was training as a member of the Special Forces at Fort Benning, Georgia. His instructors warned against the dangers of relaxing in the hours prior to daybreak, and he learned to launch attacks, whenever feasible, within that peculiar window of vulnerability. At first, he simply took the sage advice of veteran soldiers that a given tactic worked, but later he began to seek explanations for himself.

As far as he could tell, it seemed to be a kind of universal human trait, perhaps a racial memory. Primeval man relaxed with dawn's approach because he had survived another night of watching out for larger carnivores, stoking a fire at the mouth of his cave and clutching a spear in self-defense against predators bolder and stronger than he. The night watch brought fatigue, but there was also sweet relief in knowing that the killing hours had passed.

Ridiculous? Perhaps. He knew only that several hundred thousand years beyond those early ancestors in Africa and Asia, sentries still dozed off more frequently near dawn, and many of the deaths in hospitals or rest homes fell around that time, as well. In parts of Europe, 4:00 a.m. was dubbed the "hour of the wolf," in recognition of the increased danger to a shepherd's flock.

The wolf drove into Silver Spring at half-past three on Thursday morning, pausing at a lighted intersection long enough to get his bearings from a street map, rolling on from there to find his target in a quiet residential suburb.

Tom O'Herlihy had given him the address, cringing in the face of death, but there was still a chance he might have lied. Without clear evidence of hostile occupation, Bolan would be forced to use the soft approach—no HE charges through the windows, raking silent beds with automatic fire, or burning down the house before he satisfied himself that there were enemies inside.

There might, in fact, be no one home. The house might not exist, for all he knew, but there had been no opportunity to put O'Herlihy on hold for later grilling. If Bolan missed connections with his quarry here...

He found the cottage, verified the address painted on the curb in black and white and motored past to circle the block. The houses here were back-to-back, with no alley in the rear to make things easy for a prowler. Bolan pulled into the driveway of a darkened house downrange, with a For Sale sign in the yard.

Nobody home.

The dome light in his car was disconnected, no light to betray him once he finished stripping to his black-suit, slipped on the military webbing and left the car. He took the Uzi submachine gun, crossed the first yard at a trot and slowed on the next two, watching for dogs and late-night strollers. A car rolled past, and Bolan flattened in some bushes while the headlights swept above him, but it was not a police car and the driver went about his early-morning business, never looking back.

The cottage was dark and silent, nothing to suggest that it was occupied by anyone, much less a gang of terrorists. Another weakness of his plan, he realized, was total ignorance of the enemy's strength in numbers. He did not believe that Connolly would come alone, but logic told him that his quarry would not have the time or inclination to import an army from Belfast to America.

Still, there were local zealots on the team, as proved by O'Herlihy, and he would have to watch his step.

He passed the front porch and moved along a grassy strip beside the house. He paused to look and listen at the windows, alert for any sight or sound that would betray an enemy. There were no lights within, no television sounds or voices. All was deathly dark and still.

He had to get inside, and quietly.

The back door had a simple lock, no strain to pick it with the tools he carried in a pocket of his blacksuit. He felt around the doorjamb for the wires or tape of a burglar alarm and came up empty. Still, an alarm might be wired on the inside.

Another moment, and the knob turned in his hand. The door eased open one inch, two...and stopped. The chain was fastened, bolted to the door and jamb at eyeball height.

It would be easy, Bolan thought, to kick the door in and rip the chain from its moorings. Unfortunately it would warn the occupants—and possibly the next-door neighbors—of his entry, put them on alert and thus increase his danger.

Instead, he took a pair of compact, heavy-duty cutters from another pocket and clipped the chain in two. It made a single snapping sound, then rattled loosely for a heartbeat as the two halves dangled free.

He waited, finger on the Uzi's trigger, half expecting some alarm. He was prepared to fight or flee, whichever seemed more reasonable. But the house stayed dark and silent, ignorant of the intruder on the doorstep. In another moment, Bolan slipped inside.

The kitchen smelled of chili and some kind of meat. He waited for the inner darkness and his eyes to reach a point of mutual accommodation, moving only when he felt that he could navigate the rooms without banging into walls and furniture.

Adjacent to the kitchen was a smallish dining area, the empty living room beyond. A hallway on his right led to the bedrooms and the bath. He had to check them each in turn, to either find his enemy or satisfy himself that he had come out on a wild-goose chase.

The hallway was a pit, defying Bolan's night eyes, but he reckoned he could feel his way along the wall if necessary, watching out for photographs or paintings that would scrape against the plaster if he touched them.

He was halfway to the entrance of the corridor, advancing with determination, when a submachine gun opened up and sent him diving for the deck.

BREEN NEVER KNEW what had wakened him. It was a snapping sound of some kind, sharp, metallic, that had pierced the haze of fitful sleep. His eyes snapped open, focusing on the ceiling overhead. There was no light from the window, with the curtains closed, but the bedroom door was open, and he caught the barest trace of light from that direction, coming from another room.

The streetlight, he decided, shining through an unprotected window.

Possibly the moon.

Breen lay atop the sheets and bedspread, fully dressed except for shoes, which he had left beside the bed. His right hand rested on the Uzi submachine gun, and he let the fingers curl around its pistol grip. A simple movement of his thumb released the safety with a sound that barely reached his ears.

All was quiet now. Perhaps the sound had issued from his own imagination, or the street outside.

Breen raised his left arm, held the watch six inches from his eyes and read the luminous dial. It was 4:27 a.m., and he was wide awake.

The next sound did not come from his imagination or the street. It emanated from the kitchen, so he thought, the barest protest of a floorboard under human weight...or was the cottage simply settling?

Breen sat up and placed the Uzi in his lap. He did not hold his breath, because it always made the pulse throb in his ears and made it difficult for him to hear. Instead, he took silent, shallow breaths, leaning forward and straining to pick up any sound from the house at large.

He picked out muffled footsteps in the living room.

Or had he? Could it be his imagination? Had he risen from a fitful sleep to search for nonexistent demons in the unfamiliar house?

No, there it was again.

He almost called aloud to Connolly, remembering in time that Billy was not coming back. His phone call had explained the plan and warned Breen against helping him in any way. Breen was supposed to wait until he called again, or news of his demise was broadcast by the media. If Connolly was killed, Breen would make his own way back to Belfast when he could.

Now there was someone in the house, and it could not be Connolly. He ran the other options in his mind, dismissing each in turn. Police would come with lights and bullhorns, crashing through the doors and windows in a rush. A simple burglary was possible, considering the rate of crime in the United States, but Breen dismissed it as a wild coincidence.

The sound of slinking footsteps in the living room meant danger.

Breen slid off the bed and reached the open doorway in three swift strides. Kneeling, he leaned out into the hallway, the Uzi braced against his hip.

Faint light spilled from the bathroom doorway, on his left, and made it difficult for him to pick out details in the darker living room beyond. He waited in the shadows, listening, prepared to fire at any target that appeared.

His mind flashed back to Montreal, and from there to Belfast, London, their departure from the British capital for a return to the United States. Someone—some group, perhaps—had stalked them all the way... but could the hunters have discovered them in Maryland, so soon?

He broke off speculating as a shadow moved across his field of vision, in the living room. At first, Breen thought it might be cast by passing headlights, but he heard no sound of cars outside.

If they had tracked him here, at least he might buy time for Connolly to finish off the work they had agreed on. Breen had never planned on living to a ripe old age. It did not suit a revolutionary warrior, somehow, when he thought about it.

There! The moving shadow!

Instantly, instinctively, his finger tightened on the Uzi's trigger, and he leaned into the compact weapon, squinting at the muzzle-flash to save at least some vestige of his eyesight in the dark. Breen heard his bullets slapping into plaster, striking furniture, and then a heavy, solid object hit the floor with the resounding impact of a body going down.

Was that a kill? Could it be done that easily?

Experience told Breen that death was sometimes quick and sometimes slow. He hesitated, crouching in the bedroom doorway, loathe to fire again without a better target. Given his surroundings and the hour, there was still an outside chance the neighbors might have missed that first, short burst, but they would certainly be shaken from their beds by long, protracted firing.

He waited and listened, then shifted his position, edging farther through the doorway. A muzzle-flash erupted from the darkened living room and submachine gun bullets cut a ragged pattern on the wall immediately to his left. He fell back, cursing as a cloud of plaster dust began to filter down around him.

No mistake, then, and it had not been a simple kill. At least one hunter was inside the house, there could be more outside, and he was definitely cut off from the car. At that, retreat was not the last thing on his mind.

It all came down to buying time for Connolly. Not quite the role Breen fancied for himself, but he would do what had to be done.

It took one problem off his mind, at least—he did not have to fret about the neighbors now. In fact, if his attackers were affiliated with some dark, clandestine agency, publicity would be the last thing they desired.

With that in mind, Breen fired a long burst from his Uzi toward the bedroom window, bullets ripping through the draperies and smashing glass. They wouldn't take a first lieutenant in the Sword of Erin quietly, without a struggle.

Half a magazine expended, and he still had no idea how many guns were ranged against him. There had been no firing from the parlor since that first, reflexive burst, but Breen was not naive enough to think that he had finished the intruder, wounding him so badly that he managed one last burst before he died.

The bastard would be waiting for him, crouching in the dark—perhaps with infrared equipment—looking for a target he could hammer to the floor. If Breen grew careless now, the game would soon be over, and his stab at buying extra time for Connolly would be a bust.

It had to be hours yet until breakfast time. How long could he hold out? They had not pitched in tear gas yet, but any kind of chemicals would flush him in short order. If it came to that, his choice would be to go down fighting, let the bastards do their damnedest to interrogate a corpse.

There was a chance that Connolly had gotten clean away, his plan unknown to anyone but Johnny Breen. In that case, Breen decided, death was not so much a proposition to be feared, as an escape hatch to be cherished as a last resort.

But he would take as many of the bastards with him as he could, before they cut him down.

He scrambled to the bed and found the spare clips for his submachine gun, took them with him as he raced back to the bedroom doorway.

"Come on, you bastards!" With a grin, he poked his weapon through the doorway, squeezing off another burst. "You want me, you can bloody well come in and get me."

He was ready for them now.

HE HAD BEEN LUCKY, Bolan finally decided when his ears quit ringing, that his enemy was firing high. If he had any doubts about who occupied the cottage, they were wiped out in that first, short burst of submachine gun fire.

Most citizens of Maryland, excluding mental patients and convicted felons, had the right to keep a firearm in their homes and use it in defense of lives and property. Machine guns were a different matter, though, restricted to the likes of registered collectors, law-enforcement officers and military personnel. The odds of Tom O'Herlihy directing him to any one of the above were nil, and Bolan knew that he had found his quarry.

So far, it seemed to be a single gunner, and he did not know if that was good or bad. He hoped that it was Connolly, of course. But what if the Irishman had come with reinforcements?

Bolan answered the initial fire, a quick burst of his own to keep the shooter's head down while he shifted to his left. With any luck, it just might spoil his adversary's aim enough to give the Executioner an edge. He needed time to spot the muzzle-flash, allow for obstacles, and hose the shooter with Parabellum rounds before he could withdraw. A seesaw battle in the dark meant wasted time, patrol cars rolling in with lights and sirens—everything, in short, that Bolan wanted to avoid.

And yet the next burst, when it came, was not directed toward the living room at all. He heard a crash of glass and braced himself. A window! Was the shooter bailing out?

Bolan heard a scuffling sound of footsteps from the bedroom. Running? Should he charge and risk it all to trap his quarry while he had the chance?

"Come on, you bastards!" came the shout. "You want me, you can bloody well come in and get me!"

And with that, another burst of automatic fire exploded from the shadows, several bullets snapping over Bolan's head, most of them striking somewhere to his right. A floor lamp was hit and shattered. One round punched out a window in the kitchen.

He sighted on the muzzle-flash and squeezed off half a magazine in answer, rolling farther to his left as soon as he released the Uzi's trigger. It was cheap insurance, just in case he missed his target altogether and the shooter used his own trick, guiding on the muzzle flare.

He had his answer soon enough, as a long burst ripped up tattered strips of carpet on the spot where he had lain a moment earlier. It was impressive shooting, with the gunner there and gone, retreating from the line of fire before he found himself pinned down.

His sole advantage seemed to be that he was squared off with a solitary gunner, penned up in the farthest bedroom down the hall, but even that could change if

Bolan let him shift positions, slip from one room to another in the dark.

Or if he got away.

Bolan pictured one man holding down the fort while others scrambled clear and made their getaway. The image galvanized him, drove him forward, wriggling on his belly to the hallway's very mouth. Next time his adversary fired, the bullets rained down plaster dust on top of Bolan's head.

He palmed a frag grenade and pulled the safety pin, his fingers clamped to keep the spoon in place. It would require deft handling and precision timing, but it seemed to be his only hope of breaking through the standoff, finding out how many enemies he faced and whether some of them had slipped away.

He came up firing with the Uzi in his left hand, emptied out the magazine to keep his target guessing, while he lobbed the grenade with his right. It struck the doorjamb, ricocheted, dropped out of sight and detonated with the sound of pent-up thunder in the small suburban house. A shock wave rippled through the walls, clearing windowframes of jagged flying glass.

He rushed the bedroom, firing on the run, a long burst high and low to cover any stragglers. Crouching just outside the open door, he waited for the smoke to clear, then poked his head inside the room.

The solitary occupant was lying stretched out on his back, feet toward the doorway, quivering with pain. His right arm had been nearly severed by the blast or bits of shrapnel, but his left was straining toward the Uzi he had dropped just out of reach. Beneath the soot and bloodstains, Bolan recognized the face of Johnny Breen.

He kicked the submachine gun farther out of reach and crouched beside the dying gunner, leaving footprints in the spreading pool of blood. Breen saw him now and squinted through the haze of smoke and agony.

"One man?" he asked.

"Sometimes that's all it takes."

The Irish rebel tried to laugh and wound up with a hacking cough.

"You missed him, didn't you?" Despite his pain, Breen seemed immensely pleased. "That's it for you, then."

"Missed him where?"

"You lot are all alike. You want it on a silver platter, save yourself some work and cash in on the glory afterward."

"You know you're dying, Breen."

"Since I was born," the Irishman replied. "You reckon I should sell my brothers out for peace of mind before I go?"

"It wouldn't hurt to put things right," Bolan said, knowing it was wasted effort.

"They'll be right enough when Britain finds out how we deal with tyrants. See what good it does you, killing me. The big man still had lead for breakfast, didn't he?"

The last defiant outburst seemed to drain his energy, as the horrific shoulder wound was draining off his life. The light went out behind Breen's eyes, and he relaxed in death, the spastic trembling in his limbs subsiding by degrees as muscles slowly got the message from his brain.

He had been dazed and suffering from shock, no doubt, but there was something in his final words that rang a bell with Bolan. Lead for breakfast. It could be a simple reference to violent death, or else . . .

At least one neighbor would have telephoned the police by now. His time was up, and William Connolly was definitely not at home. Wherever he had gone, pure logic told the Executioner that he had mayhem on his mind.

He had to get in touch with Brognola as soon as possible, to check the target's Thursday-morning schedule. Maybe it was nothing, but he could not take that chance.

If he was right, three total strangers had a breakfast date with death.

CHAPTER TWENTY-FIVE

Alexandria, Virginia

The early-morning dew had soaked his clothing and the undergrowth surrounding him, but William Connolly was not especially uncomfortable. It was warm out, once the sun rose and began to burn a layer of creeping ground fog off the land. The latest weather broadcast spoke of seventy degrees or better for the daily high, but Connolly did not expect to be around that long.

Whatever happened, he expected to be finished with his business shortly after nine o'clock.

His target's schedule dictated Connolly's plan. From the moment he began to read the prime minister's new itinerary it was obvious that he would never find a better time or place to make his strike. The breakfast meeting was a wild departure from the normal round of conferences and photo opportunities in Washington, a little something extra in the grand Virginia countryside.

Presumably the prime minister and his host were hoping for some time alone, in which to hammer out the rudiments of their discussion prior to going public with the press. It was a sensible arrangement, with security in place, but they had not allowed for a determined adversary operating alone.

The great estate was situated west of Appomattox Court House, where the epic War Between the States had ended in Confederate surrender, back in 1865. By that time, Connolly's ancestors had been battling the British for a hundred years or more, but he was still impressed by sacrifice in the defense of what appeared to be a hopeless cause.

Invading the estate had been no problem. Connolly had placed the call to Johnny Breen, rejecting his lieutenant's bid to come along, which would have merely slowed him down. From there, he hit an all-night market, stocking up on nourishment—beef jerky, candy bars, two quarts of bottled juice. He wrapped up the bottles in paper hand towels from a public rest room, to prevent their clanking when he walked, and used the plastic bag they came in as a carryall.

The drive from Washington to Alexandria was quick and uneventful in the dead of night. He found his destination, drove a full mile past and hid his car in shaggy undergrowth beside a narrow access road. It was secure enough for now, and if he did not make it back alive, it would not matter when or how the vehicle was found.

Alone, he walked back through the woods, keeping the road on his right to avoid getting lost, until he reached an eight-foot chain-link fence topped with tangled coils of razor wire. The fence was not electrified, but Connolly refrained from touching it in case it had been fitted with some kind of unseen sensors or alarms. Instead of cutting through or looking for a tree to climb, he walked along the fence for two hundred meters, through ferns and bushes bristling with thorns, until he found the weak point he was looking for.

At some point in the recent past, a stream had undercut the fence and gouged a channel roughly three feet wide and two feet deep. The cut was clogged with weeds and creepers now, some of them tangled in the chain-link fence so that the gap was barely visible. Connolly discovered it and set about removing the obstruction with his bare hands and a three-inch pocket knife.

From that point on, he took his time to find the central compound, moving cautiously from tree to tree, alert to any sign of dogs or foot patrols. If there were motion sensors on the grounds or cameras hidden in the trees, it was beyond his power to avoid them. He would have to take the chance and see what happened.

At last, with ninety minutes left before the sunrise, Connolly stood looking at the buildings where his target would be feted in a few short hours. The prime minister would be flying in from Washington by helicopter, and the wisest course of action seemed to be for Connolly to locate the helipad and find a sniper's nest where he could track his target from the landing to the buildings clustered thirty meters distant.

Lying in the tall grass with ferns for extra camouflage, he broke his fast with spicy beef and chocolate bars, washed down with tepid orange juice. When the sun came up, he watched the compound rouse itself from sleep, the staffers rushing here and there to make things ready for their guests.

He feared a final sweep of the surrounding grounds, perhaps with dogs, but no one seemed to give security a second thought. The President would have his team in place, of course, and that was fine. His execution was not on the Irish rebel's list of things to do this day.

And so he waited, shifting once to urinate downhill, then returning to his post. The Armalite was cocked and ready, lying at his side, the muzzle aimed downrange.

THE ALEXANDRIA RETREAT was not on any list of recognized vacation spots or sanctuaries for the President of the United States. Camp David was the best known of a tiny handful, but the Man required a place from time to time where only the most intimate of family and aides could track him down. In Alexandria, he had a place at once removed from public view and yet convenient to the White House if a sudden need arose for consultation with his cabinet.

And it was good for some selective entertaining, on the side.

The place was news to Bolan when he called Brognola in the hour of the wolf and woke his old friend from a restless sleep. He told the big Fed what the dying Irishman had said and confided his suspicion. Brognola left him waiting at the phone booth in an all-night filling station while he woke another government employee, pulled the necessary strings and called back moments later with directions to the meeting site.

In theory, Brognola could probably have spoken to the Secret Service and arranged for Bolan to be placed on the approved list for the breakfast gathering, but the warrior had not asked, and the Justice man was not inclined to put his warriors in the public eye. Without discussing it, they both knew Bolan's best chance of defeating William Connolly—assuming his suspicions were correct, and Connolly showed up—would be for him to move in quietly and use his well-honed hunting skills.

The fence would need some work—a mental note to speak with Brognola about security, if feasible—but that was good for Bolan as he scaled a sturdy oak, climbed out along one solid limb that overhung the razor wire and dropped on the other side. The Alexandria retreat was two square miles in area, and Bolan had no doubt that there would be at least a dozen places for his enemy to breach the fence, if he was so inclined.

It would be hopeless, searching for a set of recent footprints in the woods, and the warrior made a beeline for the central complex, knowing it would beckon irresistibly to Connolly if he came this far in the game. The biggest gamble, Bolan knew, was picking out a spot from which to wait and seek his human prey.

The blind had to offer both concealment and a panoramic field of vision. Altitude was preferable, if he had the choice, but not so much that he was trapped above the earth while Connolly was free to dodge and run at will below him, staking out his VIP.

Make the Very Important Prey, Bolan thought, selecting a shade tree that stood on the edge of the woods, thirty yards from the helipad, fifty yards or so from the buildings. His tiger-striped camouflage blended quite well with the foliage, and Bolan selected a fork fifteen feet off the ground for his perch. The M-16 A-1/M-203 lay horizontally across his lap as the warrior scanned the compound with a pair of small binoculars, dismissing staffers with a glance and concentrating on the crowded forestland.

There were a million places for a rifleman to hide within an easy killing radius. He might go high or low, depending on his preference, and there was no law that required him to stake out the helipad. If Connolly had other plans—or if he thought the target would be driving in from Washington—he might be on the far side of the complex, absolutely safe from Bolan in his sniper's nest.

Assuming he was right, though, and the gunner was in place, prepared to drop his target on the short walk from the helipad to cover in the nearest building, Bolan faced a major disadvantage. Barring pure dumb luck, he would be forced to wait for Connolly to fire the first shot, thus reveal himself, and make it possible for Bolan to retaliate.

By then, he knew, it might be too late.

The Secret Service was another problem, swinging into action in the face of any danger to the President. At best, there was a possibility that they would get in Bolan's way. Worse yet, when he returned fire, they were certain to suspect a cross fire and attempt to deal with him as one more terrorist.

It would have been so simple, Bolan thought, to stand back, let the Secret Service agents do their job and mop up afterward. It was the easy way to go—but it would not have suited Bolan in the least.

He made another sweep with the binoculars, perked up his ears at the approaching sound of helicopter rotors somewhere in the sky behind him, to the north...and froze.

Was that a subtle movement in the weeds directly opposite the helipad, some ninety yards away?

He leaned into the glasses, one hand dropping to his M-16 A-1 and resting there, as the report of chopping rotors filled his ears.

IT HAD BEEN TRICKY, getting on the presidential chopper, but Hal Brognola managed. He was barely off the telephone with Bolan, in the early-morning hours, when he placed a second call, made contact with the White House. U.S. presidents are used to being wakened in the middle of the night, but few have been disturbed by such a strange and urgent message bearing on their own security and that of an important guest.

The Man had listened, asking brief, insightful questions here and there, considering his options. Calling off the meet had been one way to go, but Brognola had counseled otherwise. Their adversary could be dodged, delayed, but he would keep on coming back for more until somebody stopped him cold—and that meant face-to-face confrontation.

A second possibility was using stand-ins, the political equivalent of body doubles, but again Brognola managed to dissuade the Man. Their shooter might be fooled by hasty profile glimpses of a bogus U.S. President, but he would know the British prime minister at any distance. A telescopic sight would show the ruse for what it was, prevent the triggerman from giving himself away.

Redoubling security around the Alexandria estate could be accomplished with a presidential phone call, but Brognola was afraid the extra guards might keep their man away. Bizarre as it might sound to a civilian's ears, postponing contact with a killer might, in fact, be detrimental to the target, giving his assailant more time to prepare, select a time and place where he could strike with total confidence.

Brognola's plan was simpler, more direct.

The President knew all about Brognola's secret teams, of course. It was a secret handed down from one chief executive to the next, no leaks so far, and while each President in turn seemed startled—even shocked—at first exposure to the workings of Stony Man Farm, none had failed to call upon its teams for special help when he was in a special bind.

Which brought Brognola to the helicopter, speeding south-southwest from Washington to Alexandria. He sat directly opposite the British guest, the Man a few feet to his right. Eight Secret Service agents packing military hardware finished off the chopper's human cargo, giving Brognola the feeling that he was about to touch down in a combat zone.

And if his man was right, Brognola thought, it might turn out to be an apt analogy.

His cover for the morning was a Secret Service pin in his lapel. It did not fool the veteran agents, eyeing him askance, but they were under orders to cooperate at all costs short of jeopardizing presidential life and limb. The British guest knew nothing of Brognola's ruse, but he had been informed—directly by the Man, Hal understood—of the suspected danger to himself.

It was a credit to the prime minister that he insisted on proceeding with the breakfast conference, as planned, and he was smiling now, conversing with the President in friendly tones, as if he did not have a problem in the world.

Brognola thought of Striker as the helicopter hovered into its descent.

"I hope you're down there, guy," he muttered to himself. "I really do."

THE PRESIDENTIAL helicopter, large, unwieldy looking, seemed to settle lightly, almost gracefully, upon the concrete helipad. From his concealed position, William Connolly was watching as the large side door rolled open and the first of several Secret Service agents exited beneath the slowing rotor blades.

He waited, staring down the barrel of the Armalite from forty meters away. The guards were young, clean-cut, professional. They fanned out on the helipad, establishing a rough defensive perimeter, the last man out communicating with the passengers who still remained inside.

The sniper held his breath as three more figures stepped out into daylight. First, there came a tall, broad-shouldered man with salt-and-pepper hair, his craggy face unknown to Connolly, who stood beside the airship waiting for the others to emerge. Next up was the chosen target, looking perfectly at ease, pausing on the folding steps to turn and pass a brief remark across his shoulder.

Connolly was lining up his shot, simplicity itself, when the prime minister stepped down and shifted to his right, obscured behind the body of the tall, broad-shouldered stranger. Both of them were waiting as the President appeared, lips curving in the famous campaign smile. He wore a nylon jacket and a sport shirt open at the collar, denim jeans, and loafers on his feet.

A man of the people, Connolly thought, sneering against the fiberglass stock of his rifle.

The party was moving now, proceeding at a steady but relaxed pace toward the nearest building, thirty meters due south of the helipad. The Secret Service agents formed a loose protective circle, but they clearly saw no reason for a human shield of bodies to protect their charge in this, his private sanctuary.

Connolly pursued them with his gunsights, tracking, waiting for the prime minister to emerge from the coincidental cover of the tall man on his right. How did the hulking bastard manage to remain in step so perfectly, as if he had it planned?

A few more paces, and he knew that he would lose them. Passing up the shot would mean another wait of indeterminate duration, lying in the grass while sweat ran down his face and chiggers feasted on his flesh. His target would eventually return, but it would be a desperation shot by that time, Connolly compelled to blast away at anything that moved or lose his chance entirely.

There was killing pressure either way, but he was ready now.

The tall, broad-shouldered man would have to die, his price for rubbing shoulders with the rich and famous at the wrong place and time. As for the President, well, Connolly would have to wait and see how things went down.

He took another breath, released half of it, swallowed hard to lock the rest inside. Connolly's pulse was hammering inside his ears as he began the final countdown, index finger taking up the trigger's slack.

He barely heard the first shot, soaking up the weapon's minor recoil as a 5.56 mm bullet sped downrange.

EMERGING FROM the helicopter, Hal Brognola bet his life on the topography of his surroundings. On his left or east, the chopper blocked a sniper's view of the emerging passengers for several paces, and a broad expanse of open lawn beyond meant any sniper would be pushed back to a range of roughly two hundred yards, with buildings angled to obstruct the best part of their walk between the helicopter and the lodge.

By contrast, on his right or west, the trees were almost kissing close, perhaps one hundred fifty feet away. It was the obvious approach, though he could not rule out the trees behind them, on his north. A gambler from the old days, he decided that the major risk lay westward and responded accordingly, placing himself between the prime minister and the hypothetical sniper's nest on his right.

It seemed a long walk to the buildings, though he knew the distance measured less than forty yards. The Secret Service agents had their parts down to perfection, several of them looking barely old enough to shave. They gave the shooter room, no wall of flesh to warn a would-be killer that his move had been anticipated. If they lost him here, without a shot, they might not have another chance to pin him down.

Brognola had begun to worry by the time they reached the halfway point. He did not relish acting as a human shield, but it would be worse in the long run if his warning to the President turned out to be an empty threat.

When it came, the blow struck high and hard, an inch back from the shoulder joint. With better aim, it would have missed the Kevlar vest entirely, drilling through his armpit, lungs and heart. Instead, it pitched Brognola to his left with stunning force, the chain reaction of his fall immediately toppling the prime minister and the President like dominoes.

The next two rounds went sizzling overhead, a member of the Secret Service team collapsing on the pavement with a bullet in his chest. The other guards were brandishing their weapons now, returning fire in the direction of the tree line, when a muffled *pop* resounded from the north, immediately followed by the crash of a grenade exploding to the west.

A flying squad of Secret Service men were turning to confront the secondary target when Brognola staggered to his feet. He palmed his badge and lurched in front of them, their weapons jutting in his face.

"Back off!" he warned. "The second guy's with me."

It took another heartbeat for the President to chime in with a confirmation from the knot of scowling men who had him covered and surrounded on the deck.

"Do what he says," the Man instructed, "and for God's sake let's all get inside!"

THE SNIPER'S FIRST three shots snapped off in rapid fire, grass flinching from the muzzle blast, and Bolan answered with a 40 mm HE round. He followed with a short burst from the M-16 A-1 to pin his target down, then leaped from his perch in the tree to the grass below.

There was a sputtering of fire from someone in the Secret Service ranks before Brognola interposed himself and somehow calmed them down. The presidential entourage was moving toward the safety of the nearest building at a run as Bolan broke across the open grass and charged the point where he had last glimpsed William Connolly among the trees and ferns.

His 40 mm round had gone off in the trees, sheared through the lower branches of an elm and detonated in an airburst, scorching leaves and grass. Unfortunately Bolan saw that another tree had shielded Connolly from shrapnel and the worst of the concussion, giving him a brief head start before the Executioner was on his trail.

That trail was clear enough to follow, though, as Bolan reached the tree line, found his mark and plunged into the woods. The Irishman was running for his life and making no effort to cover his tracks. Where he had passed, the undergrowth was beaten down, small branches dangled from their broken ends and sliding footprints had been gouged into the loam. From up ahead, just out of sight, the Executioner heard telltale sounds of thrashing in the brush.

He put on speed, alerted when the sounds in front of him abruptly ceased. A lifetime of engagements in the jungle killing grounds tipped Bolan off that it was time to hit the deck, a twisting dive that took him to the left of his selected track and put him facedown in the shadow of a bristling fir.

The burst of automatic fire that would have gutted him came a heartbeat later, clipping ferns and branches, gouging bark in divots from the trunk above his head. He rolled a few yards farther to his left and came up firing, homing in on the echo of his adversary's weapon, hoping more to startle Connolly and spoil his aim than bring him down.

It seemed to work, the Irishman retreating in a headlong flight to nowhere, making for the fence. He had to know that the police and Secret Service were on full alert by now, converging on the Alexandria retreat from every nearby jurisdiction, but it made no difference. Connolly had missed his shot, and he was bound to run or die in the attempt to get away.

A seasoned jungle fighter might have gone to ground and trusted silence as his friend, but Connolly was city born and raised, an urban warrior more at home with asphalt and concrete than trees and creeping vines. He kept on running, and the noise he made not only gave

he Executioner a point of reference for the chase, but
t also covered sounds of Bolan's progress, coming up
behind his prey.

They reached the fence fifteen seconds apart, Connolly's sense of direction solid enough that it brought
him back to his point of original entry. He was kneeling in the mud and ripping loose weeds from the gully
cut beneath the fence when Bolan got there, coming up
behind him through the trees.

"That's all," Bolan said, and his words froze Connolly in place.

The Irishman turned slowly, one hand clutching
some uprooted grass, the other empty, hovering a foot
or so beside the rifle at his knee. "Who are you, then?"

"Your judgment."

"It's like that, is it? What about your precious Bill
of Rights?"

"I'm not a lawyer."

"No, you haven't got the look. You're not half soft
enough."

"Let's get this over with."

"My pleasure," Connolly replied. "Would you prefer I turn around?"

"Your choice. It all comes out the same."

"I guess that's right." He hesitated, frowning. Then
he said, "I'm glad it was a soldier, anyway, and not a
bloody pig."

The move was swift and sure, but Bolan saw it coming from a mile away. He let his adversary reach the
Armalite before he stroked the trigger of his M-16 A-1
and emptied half a magazine at nearly point-blank
range. The 5.56 mm manglers ripped through Connolly as if he were made of cardboard, a convincing
silhouette on some elaborate shooting range. The im-

pact pitched him backward, bounced him off the chain-link fence and dropped him lifeless on his face.

There was no need to check his pulse or verify the kill. The only thing that mattered now was time, and bailing out before the cavalry arrived and Brognola ran out of stories to elicit their cooperation.

It was finished, after all the miles and wasted lives . . . and it was time to go.

He wriggled underneath the fence as Connolly had meant to do, and put the Alexandria retreat behind him. Half an hour later, driving along the highway toward the nation's capital, he had a chance to wonder what had been achieved.

It was another holding action in his never-ending war against the savages, and that was all the Executioner could hope for in a world where human nature generated more brand-new opponents in a day than any soldier could eliminate in twenty years of front-line duty.

In the hellgrounds, there was no such thing as final victory, but he could stall the predators, prevent their seizing new ground and corrupting more lives when he saw the chance.

Today, it was enough.

Tomorrow, Bolan thought, would take care of itself.

In the Deathlands, the past and future
clash with frightening force....

JAMES AXLER
DEATH LANDS®

Trader Redux

Years of struggle in the lawless remnants of humanity have made
Ryan Cawdor a bold and undisputed leader. Yet now, he may have
to contend with his former mentor, the enigmatic Trader, as their
survival skills are tested on a perilous journey down the mighty
Colorado and into the Grand Canyon's mile-deep crags.

Imagine your worst nightmare. It's called Deathlands.

In February, look for a new piece of action
from Gold Eagle...

D.A. HODGMAN

STAKEOUT SQUAD

LINE OF FIRE

A skyrocketing crime rate forces Miami Chief of Police
John Kearn to create a special police unit. STAKEOUT SQUAD's
objective is to ambush violent criminals at the scene,
sending an unmistakable message to would-be perps.

Don't miss LINE OF FIRE, the first installment of Gold Eagle's
newest action-packed series, STAKEOUT SQUAD!

Look for it in February, wherever Gold Eagle books are sold.

Or order your copy now by sending your name, address, zip or postal code, along
with a check or money order (please do not send cash) for $4.99 for each book
ordered ($5.50 in Canada), plus 75¢ postage and handling ($1.00 in Canada), payable
to Gold Eagle Books, to:

In the U.S.	In Canada
Gold Eagle Books	Gold Eagle Books
3010 Walden Ave.	P. O. Box 636
P. O. Box 9077	Fort Erie, Ontario
Buffalo, NY 14269-9077	L2A 5X3

Please specify book title with order.
Canadian residents add applicable federal and provincial taxes.

SS1

America is the prime target in a global holocaust

STONY MAN™ 14

DEADLY AGENT

Joseph Ryba is the man who would be king—of a new
Bohemian empire. The Czech official is poised to unleash
a plague that would put Europe at his mercy. Germ warfare
missiles hidden stateside would render the world's watchdog
powerless. Mack Bolan, Able Team and Phoenix Force race
along a tightrope to find and dismantle the deadly arsenal
without forcing Ryba's hand—a situation that would result
in nothing short of global holocaust.

**Don't miss out on the action in these titles featuring
THE EXECUTIONER®, ABLE TEAM® and PHOENIX FORCE®!**

The Terror Trilogy

Features Mack Bolan, along with ABLE TEAM and PHOENIX FORCE, as they
battle neo-Nazis and Arab terrorists to prevent war in the Middle East.